LEST THE DEW RUST THEM

By

Michael Drakich

Traanu Enterprises
Amazon Edition

First Edition Traanu Enterprises, February 2013

Cover Mary Drakich
Editor Kate Richards

Dedication

To all of my friends in the Bruce Road Cigar Club
who have urged me on in my writing career

Chapter One

Robert Grimmson paced the hallway, waiting for the forensics officer to complete his task. From inside the apartment, the camera flashed again and again in an attempt to retain the ghoulish expression for posterity. Unsatisfied, the photographer clicked away six more times from various angles, trying to best capture his subject. But there would be no helping the expression upon the face of the severed head on the floor. Having examined all facets of the victim and its surrounding environs, the crime scene expert waved the coroner's agents toward the body.

As the two men knelt to lift the corpse onto the stretcher, the lead detective put a staying hand on one attendant's shoulder. "Wait. There's still one more examination before I can allow the body to be moved."

From his kneeling position, the coroner's man stared up at the detective. "Who we waiting for?"

The second detective neared, gesticulating for the body to remain down. "Homeland Security. It's our job to notify them whenever we suspect terrorism. And a severed head always fits that definition. I don't want to hang around here any more than you do, but it's my ass on the line if I don't follow procedure, not yours, so just cool your jets. Besides, their man is here now."

Robert stepped into the room and after the perfunctory handshakes, placed his fists on his hips and surveyed the area. After he remained still for several moments, one of the detectives whispered to the other "Mr. Teapot" as they waited by the door. Robert ignored the snide remark. *Playful banter between two policemen who want to go home.*

At five-foot-eight, he did not strike the most impressive pose. A tad overweight and in his forties, his midlife bulge was there to stay. There never seemed to be time to get to the gym anymore, and sitting behind a desk didn't help.

A simple room, Spartan in its furnishings, the main living area of a small bachelor apartment, with a kitchenette in one corner, a bed tucked in the other. The furniture consisted of one loveseat, a dining table with two chairs, and a dresser with a Hindu shrine set upon it. The single picture hung on the dingy wall showed an Indo-Asian family looking very somber. Robert picked out the victim in the scene, so surmised it was his family.

On the table, the remains of an unfinished dinner sat with a portion still on the fork. No sign of forced entry. The victim had let his murderers in. Either he knew them as friends or some other reason persuaded him to open the door.

The victim lay sprawled on the floor, directly in front of one of the kitchen chairs where he must have been seated when the deed occurred. Dressed in simple clothes—blue jeans, a simple cotton t-shirt, bare feet. What must be a dime store watch on his left wrist and a braided hair wristlet on the right. From a spouse? A sweetheart? Or a relative? The questions would need to be answered.

His hair cut short, face clean shaven. The head had rolled a few feet past the rest of the corpse. It appeared the severing had been done in a single stroke—either a very sharp blade or a very strong stroke, or some combination thereof.

Finally, having etched the scene in his memory, he signaled the men from the coroner's office to proceed. With deep sighs, the fellows hoisted the body onto their stretcher and whisked it out the door. As the room cleared, Robert delved into his pocket, producing a card for the detectives.

"Keep me informed of your progress, gentlemen. I'll need to know all the particulars of the case, as you discover them. Likewise, I'll keep you up to date on my own investigation. Wise of you to call us, as this is indeed something which has terrorist implications."

The two men glanced at each other. Their job had become more complicated. The closest one turned to Grimmson. "How do you figure?"

Returning to his previous position, Robert knelt and waved them closer then pointed out what caught his eye. "Even with the scuff marks from the shoes of everyone who has contaminated the crime scene, the indications are still slightly visible."

They hunched at his side, scratching their heads and muttering to one another. After a moment of intense staring, one shrugged. "I give. I don't see anything."

Robert took a deep breath in through his nostrils to control his disappointment in the policemen. He swirled his index finger toward three identical spots on the floor in a perfect triangle pattern. "There, there and there—the toe signatures of a tripod. The beheading appears to have been captured on video. It looks like you fellas are going to be reporting to me on this one."

Chapter Two

Mohamed El-Barai enjoyed his job at John F. Kennedy airport where he'd been a baggage handler since his immigration from Egypt over twelve years before. His duties never varied, except those days following the September 11th disaster. It had been a disappointing time. His supervisor had requested he stay home for thirty days. When he returned to work, he'd been assigned janitorial duties in the public washrooms for the next few months.

But that was long in the past. As a skilled jitney operator, he performed his tasks without complaint and thanked Allah every day for his work, his family, and his American way of life.

Pulling the second load from the transport plane, he was maneuvering the forklift neatly to bring it toward the waiting truck, when Tim, the new inspector, stepped in front of him. Pulling off his ear guards, he powered down the forklift and leaned out. "What's up?"

"I want to check that load."

"Sure, fine with me, but did you clear it with the dock manager?"

"I'm not interested in what the dock manager has to say. My authority supersedes his."

"Okay, okay. It's just he wants this docking bay cleared, and the truck I'm off-loading to is parked there."

"Then the sooner you get down and open that shipment, the sooner we can get this over with."

"No problem, I'm just surprised you want to check this one, that's all. According to the manifest, it's a load of personal items." Mohamed glanced at his clipboard. "From Bolivia."

Carlos Jose Santiago worried when he saw his pickup singled out. From the safety of his delivery truck he watched the handler unbundle the load and the inspector heft one of the cases. It wasn't the concern of being late with the delivery as what the company he worked for promised to all its customers. The fact of his illegal immigrant status is what weighed heavily with him and he felt afraid they would pull him in for questioning. As he watched, he pondered the question of what he should do next - stay or go.

***

Timothy Jones was thrilled with his new job as an inspector at JFK. The pay was good and the work never boring.

For the first two weeks, he had been accompanied by a senior inspector to make sure he learned the ropes and understood the work. Today, for the first time, his senior partner took a break and left Tim alone on the job. So when the shipment in question arrived by air freight, he took it upon himself to verify what was arriving. The fact the manifest read personal belongings of an Alexander Suten-Mdjai gave him pause. Faced with a large number of identical cases, he wondered if it might be, rather, smuggled goods to be sold in the United States, or something even worse.

Tim checked out the name badge of the baggage worker. "Okay, Mohamed, lets open this up shall we?"

Mohamed produced a pair of metal clips and undid the binders

5

holding the cases together. "All set, let me know when you're done, and I'll come clean up later."

Before the handler could climb back into his jitney, Tim grabbed him by the elbow. "No, no, no, no, no. You're going to stay with me. I need a witness for the records."

Mohamed stuck his hands into his overalls and leaned against the forklift while Tim grabbed one of the cases. Oblong, he noted, perhaps three feet in length, a foot wide and about six inches deep, made of stainless steel with a single handle midway down one side, three hinges, and two locking clasps. "You certainly couldn't pack much into one of these." He stepped back to better take in the view, scanning from left to right. "How many of these things are there?"

Mohamed grabbed the manifest. "It says.... Fourteen hundred and thirty-two."

"Fourteen hundred?"

He put the manifest away. "And thirty-two."

Tim tried to open the one in his hand. After several unsuccessful tries he gave Mohamed a head shake in the direction to his right. "Screw this. Follow me."

With Mohamed in tow, he headed back to his office to chase down his partner and put the item through an X-ray machine.

***

James Munroe stretched out in his chair, feet up on his desk, eyes closed, arms folded across his large belly. As an inspector for almost twenty years, for Jim, prior to 9-11, the job had been an easy one. But with all the new rules from Homeland Security, things were a real pain in the ass.

6

With a new guy on the job, he figured he could relax a bit and let the kid handle the bulk of the workload. So when Tim came traipsing in with one of the baggage workers in tow and a long metal box under his arm, he felt less than pleased at having to rouse himself from his prone position. "What the hell are you up to? Can't you see I'm on my break?"

Tim paused where he was for a moment, gawked at him, then proceeded toward the X-ray machine. "I'm sorry, but I wanted to check out a sample from this cargo load. It seems awfully suspicious to me. It'll only take a second."

Jim glowered at him. It was bad enough for the new guy to interrupt his nap, but worse, to bring the foreign baggage handler with him. He should know better than to bring anyone without clearance into the office. And he didn't trust anyone who didn't fit into his idea of an honest, hard-working American, which nowadays, was just about everybody.

Tim placed the case on the conveyor belt and moved to watch the screen as the container passed through the machine. Jim plopped back into his chair to wait out the whole scene. He figured it would be over soon enough and he could get back to his nap.

Tim's eyes widened as he took in the image. "You'd better come take a look."

"What now?" Jim made a great show of getting out of his chair and ambling around the machine. The image on the screen held no doubt. Inside the container, some two feet in length, lay the metal outlay of what could only be surmised to be one thing, a sword. "How many of these did you say were out there?"

"Fourteen hundred."

Mohamed chirped. "And thirty-two."

He spun toward the baggage handler. "Shut up, Mohamed. I know it." He reached for the phone. "We need to call Homeland Security."

Jim knew the protocol as well. But he wanted to be certain, before he opened a can of worms. "First, go get another couple of cases, just to be sure. I'll check the manifest on this stuff."

***

Tim, with the baggage handler in tow, went back out to retrieve two more of the boxes. "Mohamed, move the rest of these into loading dock six, then come and get the stuff already on the truck."

He motioned to the truck driver. "Kill your engine and come on in."

When the man blinked a few times but didn't move, Tim reached for the door handle to pull it open, but the driver put the vehicle in gear and pulled away.

He took a couple of quick steps toward the moving truck then stopped in his tracks. He grabbed the radio strapped to his shoulder. "Give me security."

"Officer Ballard."

"Listen, I'm Inspector Timothy Jones at receiving. A transport van just flew out of here with half a load we want impounded. Santiago Moving, box truck, deep green. Intercept it before it leaves the grounds."

"Roger, we'll look out for it."

He glanced over at Mohamed, sitting in the jitney. Conspiracy theories ran rampant through his mind. "You better get down from that thing and come into the office. Security is on the way and they're gonna want to talk to everybody."

Tim grabbed two of the cases and went in to inform his supervisor of what happened.

Jim listened to the story and broke into a sweat. A quick examination showed two more swords, though each different in style. He grabbed the telephone and made the call to Homeland Security.

Chapter Three

He found the flight tiresome, the food barely palatable, the service deplorable, and despite first class, the space uncomfortable. Alexander Suten-Mdjai chuckled to himself. *I'm spoiled.* He did not think he led an opulent life style. He felt the countless hours he spent training were enough to offset the finer things in life he treated himself to.

At last, the seat belt sign turned off and he could rise. He hadn't sat so long in one place since he was a child and his father moved the family to Bolivia from Argentina. Alexander stretched his six-foot-two frame out and pressed his hand against the ceiling of the airplane as he waited for the door to open so he could depart. Lucia, his wife tsked. "Alex, sit down. You're making a scene. You can wait just one moment more before going through your gyrations in a crowded airplane. Honestly, you don't need to be showing off all the time."

He plopped back into his chair and reached down to tickle her in the ribs. "When we get to the hotel, I'll take you through a few gyrations."

Lucia squealed as she tried to avoid his tickle. Grabbing his hand, she leaned in close. "Idle threats. Let's see if you follow through."

He stole a quick kiss, as the flight attendant invited people to leave the plane. The door opened, but before anyone could exit, two airport security men entered and spoke with the flight attendant. Alexander, retrieving his carry-on luggage from the overhead rack, kept a close eye on the two men. Although he could not make out their words, his stomach sank when the woman pointed to him and his wife. *What's going on?*

The uniformed men edged through the crowded aisle to his side.

10

"Mr. Alexander Stan Madgi?"

He winced at the mispronunciation. "It's sue-tan-madge-eye."

The man rolled his eyes. "Whatever. Would you and your wife please come with us."

The second guard stood back one step, his hand resting on his sidearm. *This is serious.*

Lucia rose from her seat. "What's going on, honey? Why do these men want us?"

He held out a hand to her. "Come, darling. I'm quite sure there is some simple misunderstanding here. Let's go clear the matter up and be on our way."

Before he could shoulder his carry-on, the first guard took both bags and started for the front of the plane. As their fellow passengers watched, he and Lucia followed the men into the airport. In the hallway, two more were waiting. "Four guards? To what do I owe the honor?"

"Just walk this way, please."

Alexander expected they would be brought to some type of briefing room, but instead they were taken to a holding cell. He and Lucia were stripped of their shoes, belts, and identification. The security men refused to answer their startled questions, instead locked them in the cell then left the room. *In hindsight, maybe the airplane comforts weren't really so bad.*

***

Robert Grimmson sat in his office reviewing reports from both the police and his own staff in regards to the beheading. The victim had arrived as a refugee from Malaysia a number of years ago and worked

11

at a janitorial service where many of his countrymen were employed. He had been of Tamil heritage and Hindu religion.

The possible motives for the crime were multitudinous. Had his murder been a religious thing? Malaysian? Tamil? Or Al-Qaeda? No family in America and no past history of any problems. The Malaysian authorities were slow in providing any details, which made tracking the man's activities prior to his arrival in the United States impossible. As a result, they were attempting to track down all Malaysian immigrants in the general area.

Why had the man been killed?

As he tried to postulate an answer to the question, a rap came on his door frame. "Hey, Bob, I don't know if this has anything to do with that case of yours, but they caught some guy down at JFK trying to import hundreds of swords. It takes a sword to chop a man's head off. Maybe there's a connection. Do you want check it out?"

"Sounds like something worth looking into. Grab a couple of the guys. We'll zip over there."

Robert grabbed his coat and jumped into the car. Turning on the Bluetooth, he contacted the Homeland Security office at the airport. "Director Grimmson calling, what's the status on those swords?"

"Hi, Bob. We're holding the guy right now. The number of weapons he's trying to bring in is staggering. We've transferred them to a safe location."

"Good job. I'll be there shortly."

Swords. What would strike more fear in people than a rash of beheadings? A cold chill came over him as he contemplated the implications. Since 9-11 there had been no major acts of terrorism on American soil. Such a thing would bring countrywide panic.

His resolve hardened. This thing needed to be stopped, and

quickly. He stepped harder on the accelerator.

Chapter Four

David Crombie still felt the exaltation. Never having witnessed a man killed before, he experienced a certain euphoria, a tingling down the spine, when reliving the event in his mind.

The telephone rang and he checked the display. He paused, his hand hovering above the receiver, then sighed and picked it up. "Hello, Lakshanthan."

"Did you do it yet?"

"Not yet. I'm working on it now."

"Com'on, David, you're our tech. Everyone's counting on you."

"I know, I know. I have to be sure there're no identifying marks and the dialogue is masked."

"Okay, do what you have to. Just make sure it's up today."

"It will be. Out of curiosity, how did we choose our target? He's not even American."

For a moment, on the other end, silence. Finally, Lakshanthan relented. "When I was a teenage soldier for the Liberation Tigers of Tamil Eelam, I went with my father to Malaysia to solicit money from the Tamil population. My job included trying to induct other teenagers to the cause. Some were willing, many were not, and when the police came and forced us to board a plane and leave the country, I ingrained in my mind the face of the young man who stood with the police, the one who turned us in.

My father brought me to the United States where he felt the pockets would be deeper and I could grow up as an American. Now, all these years later, who in all the world would have thought this same fellow would be working maintenance in the very apartment building where I lived. Passing him in the hallway, there was no mistaking the

14

recognition in his eyes."

This is crap. He's using us for his personal vendetta.

"I wondered why we deviated so quickly from the plan. Our intention is to target Americans, to make *them* understand the daily terror, the constant threat to life most of the world lives with."

"We needed to start somewhere."

"Yeah, but I'm not convinced. Everybody in the group is different, and probably have their own agendas, too. Saleem hates Americans, Miguel is a follower, and I think Ivan's in it for the kicks."

"What about you. David? What's your agenda?"

"I want to make them pay. Regardless, with this first decapitation done, I'll use the Internet to spread fear. I'm not the top computer geek at my firm for nothing. I can obtain the video and post it without getting traced or caught. You disappoint me, however. My preference would have been we started with something a little more *American*."

"Don't worry, there will be others. We've only just begun."

"Alright, alright. I'm about ready to download it. I'll talk to you later." David hung up the phone.

He found himself on a crusade. He detested the use of the word *jihad*, not being Muslim, but just like the saying "Six of one, a half dozen of the other," one would identify little difference. He did not fit the profile of a terrorist. At five-feet, eleven inches tall, one hundred and seventy-five pounds, with dark blond hair, he showed none of the outward appearances of a hard life. Well educated, good job, and from a solid family, life was good.

With skiing, skydiving, motocross, and a variety of other extreme sports, he tested his limits. When he vacationed, he went to war-torn countries, only to be near the action. The thrill of it attracted David. His crusade involved taking his life to an extreme edge. And this new crusade was as exciting as it could get.

Getting down to business, his loading of the video to the Net would hold no difficulty making his cyberspace trail undetectable, a touch more challenging. He considered the video and the details he was supposed to load with it. Saleem had done the talking and called their group "The American Jihad" at the beginning and end of the piece. David opposed the Muslim moniker and so, with the video in his sole possession before posting, completed some careful editing then loaded

Now, instead of "The American Jihad," his computer altered voice introduced the group as "The Sword Masters," a name he'd picked up online that struck a resonant chord with him, though he couldn't quite put his finger on why.

He delighted in bypassing security and posting their message on a high profile site.

Smiling to himself at the job well done, he signed off and prepared to head out on his date for the night with an attractive young thing he'd met at the nearby coffee house. Nothing would be better than to cap off a good day with a good night of hard sex.

Chapter Five

"I *am* the Sword Master."

Flabbergasted, Robert Grimmson found the response incredulous and stared at the man who smiled back at him. *Is he being smug?* No, more self-assured, confident. Robert took pride in his ability to determine whether someone was lying. He faced a sincere challenge to the skill. Alexander portrayed a coolness under questioning Robert had not encountered before. In addition to his controlled composure, the fellow appeared in extreme good condition. His every simple movement, even reaching for the coffee before him, evidenced a litheness that made Robert wonder whether he would be able to react fast enough should the man decide action was better than words.

He took one step back to give himself more reaction time if necessary. But then his heart skipped a beat as the suspect narrowed his eyes and nodded before once again breaking into a warm smile. For a second, he fought fear of someone who politely discoursed with the others in the room. He suspected very little got past him. Robert glanced around the room, disconcerted to discover to the officers' focus on the wife, Lucia. Even in her seated position, he could tell the Latin bombshell was a voluptuous woman of five-ten or eleven. Her long brown hair with a hint of a curl framed a face more than just attractive, with full lips and deep hazel-green eyes. Full-breasted, he guessed a C cup at least, if not a D, and a figure which would put almost any other woman to shame. With a start, he realized he'd seen her gracing the covers of magazines, when he was standing in line at checkout counters.

He forced his attention back to suspect took a seat across from this enigmatic individual. "So you are a sword master you say. Am I to infer you mean ... you are skilled in swords, or you deal in them?"

***

Alexander Suten-Mdjai smiled at the middle aged man addressing him. He had taken the measure of everyone in the room, starting with the airport inspectors, Tim and Jim. He allowed himself an inward chuckle at how their names rhymed. One young and inexperienced, the other old, fat and tired. The three other Homeland Security people were standard police doctrine; authoritative, presumptuous in their title, and looking for an opportunity to exert it.

But the man in front of him was another story. Exuding intelligence, but humble, no bravado. Alexander decided he liked him and would show him the respect an equal deserved. "Skilled. My swords are not for sale. They are the tools of my trade and many are antiques, a collection of my heritage, each with its own story to tell."

***

Robert instructed one of the others to take notes. Although the interview was being video recorded, he preferred to focus on what was being said, and wanted the notes to refer to as they went along. "Alright, let's take what you are telling me at face value. So what brings you and all these swords to America? Not a vacation, surely. Have you been hired to come here and train someone in particular?"

Alexander sighed. "It looks like this might take a long time. Actually I am here on an invitation from your government for

18

a…favor… I performed for them. I have, as you say, vacationed here before, and thought this might be a good place to live someday. Set up shop, so to say. If you would permit me my travel bag, I would like to show you something."

Knowing it had already been searched and held no weapons, Robert snapped his fingers. "Please give our guest his bag."

Mr. Suten-Mdjai took it from the guard, rooted through for a moment, and produced an envelope. "Ah, this is the one."

Robert received the document from the man and retrieved the letter contained within. The letterhead was from the office of the secretary of state, though not signed by the secretary himself, but by some other individual. The letter confirmed what Mr. Suten-Mdjai claimed, a thank you for services rendered and an invitation to consider relocating to the United States where his skills might be more readily available.

When he finished, he found Alexander waiting with a bemused smile. "As one of my stipulations, I requested American citizenship." He produced from his valet newly minted American passports for him and his wife.

Robert wanted time to think. There were too many variables to take into account. He needed to verify the documents were legit. "So what service *did* you provide my, I guess I mean, our government?"

Alexander waved a hand in dismissal. "Unfortunately, I am not at liberty to reveal the details to you. You will have to take it up with your superiors."

A myriad of possibilities raced through his mind, as he instructed one of the men to go and verify the passports. "Well, Mr. Suten-Mdjai, while we wait for a chance to confirm your story, perhaps you can tell me a little bit about these swords of yours." Robert placed one of the cases on the table. The craftsmanship was exquisite. He examined the emblem embossed on both sides. "Do I have your permission to open your property?"

A small chuckle escaped from Alexander. "I'm afraid you will not be able to do so without destroying the case."

Robert focused on the two clasps. There were no keyholes, just large black pads "Alright then, how does this contraption work?"

Alexander have rose from his seat and held out an open hand. "If I may?"

He hesitated, but in the end consented. "Just unlock it. I will open it."

Smiling, Alexander took the case and faced the clasps toward him. "As you please." He placed his thumbs, both facing inwards toward the handle, and pressed down on the two black squares. With a distinct click, the case unlocked and the lid, with the pressure released, popped upwards a quarter of an inch. He swung the case around, and then leaned back in his chair.

Robert rose and lifted the lid to expose the blade inside. It didn't take an archeologist to recognize the weapon was ancient. A blade twenty-one or two inches long bore numerous scars and nicks, indicating heavy usage. And the carved wooden handle, black from age and oiling, showed many cracks. The leather bindings, though old, were hard and strong. They gleamed with oil. The lining of the case consisted of stiff foam rubber shaped to hold the exact weapon in a snug manner. No amount of jostling would have moved the sword even the slightest fraction of an inch during travel. He swung the case so Alexander could see it from where he was sitting. "What is this? It looks like it could be a thousand years old!"

***

Alexander focused on the face of the man. From the case, he knew which blade was inside. "Try two thousand. My ancestor Tiberius carried that weapon."

The surprise was evident on Robert Grimmson. "So…what, he fought for the Roman army?"

Alexander gazed at the ancient sword. He resisted a strong urge to heft the weapon. Such an action would frighten the Homeland Security people and he wanted to avoid a confrontation. After a heavy sigh, he slouched in his seat. "Is there any more coffee? Each sword has a tale, and I prefer to recite them as they were taught to me."

The Tale of Tiberius Suten-Mdjai.

Decimus strode across the practice yard toward the stables. *Now where did that lad get to? There are duties to attend to and the newest arrivals to the Suten-Mdjai school of swordsmanship require looking after.* "Tiberius, lad! Where are you?"

The tall strapping youth leapt down from the second floor of the stable, bounded once, and in a perfectly executed maneuver, swept past Decimus in a handspring to land feet planted in front of the sword master, hands on hips. "Here I am, Father."

Decimus swayed between complimenting the boy on the acrobatics and chastising him for showing off. "Never mind the theatrics. We have a new group from Rome to train. Stable their horses and stow their belongings in the guest house."

***

Tiberius peered over his father's shoulder to see four men getting off their horses by the gate. Military all, they wore the uniform of the Roman legions and insignia showing them to be men of rank. He loped over and gathered the tethers to the horses. "Greetings gentlemen, welcome to my father's school. My name is Tiberius, and I hope I can be of assistance when you need it."

The four men shared a glance and deferred to the one closest to Tiberius. That man reached out to clasp him on the shoulder. "Thank you. My name is Arminius. My friends and I look forward to your father's hospitality, but more importantly, his teachings. They say he is one of the best in all of Rome."

Tiberius led the men toward the guest house. "Whoever says that is a liar and deserves to be punished. My father is the best in *all the world*!"

The three other men chuckled. Arminius though, stopped in his tracks. "Be careful when you boast, lad. Such bravado should not be espoused so lightly. You would do well to show some humility, lest your father not live up to expectations."

Tiberius reddened at the insult but controlled his anger. These men were paying guests, and there would be plenty of time in the practice yard for them to learn the truth. "My apologies, sir. Excuse me for my exuberance. It's the pride of a son in his father. Though only fifteen, I have been a student of his since I was five and have not met a serious challenge since I turned twelve."

The laughter changed to a series of "Oh hos" just as his father joined the group.

"Good sirs, please excuse my son's boasting. I have been trying to teach him to be humble, but apparently I have failed miserably." Decimus produced a small switch from his belt and in a flash, hit his son across the ass. Tiberius yelped but then before a second hit could be levied, he moved out of reach.

Arminius moved between Tiberius and his father. "Perhaps a little sport might be in order. Why not let the lad face one of us, so we can see how much a boy could have learned. It will undoubtedly give us a measure as to what we can expect to learn from you, Master Decimus."

His father glared at Tiberius then faced the guests once more. "I am sorry, good sirs. I would not wish it to appear I am shirking my duties as your instructor. As per our contract, your lessons begin at daylight tomorrow."

His father strode away.

Arminius glanced around again at his comrades and Tiberius. "Tomorrow at sunrise. We still have the balance of today. What say you, boy?"

Tiberius weighed his options. If he refused, his father would be happy, but his own pride sullied. "I will meet you in the sand court behind the stables in a few moments. Give me a chance to chase down some practice swords."

The four men emerged from the back into a circular fenced area with a sand floor some fifty paces wide. Tiberius met them with an armful of wooden swords cut and weighted to appear as the gladius each carried. Tiberius took center court and awaited the first of the men. The smallest fellow hefted his practice sword and gave a short laugh then charged, with a roar.

***

It took all his concentration for Arminius to follow the speed with which the lad countered, slashed his comrade across the belly and stepped away with ease.

Tiberius twirled the wooden sword. "You're dead. Who's next?"

The next man, a brawny type, stepped forward in more cautious manner and held his weapon lower in a protective stance as he advanced on the boy. A couple of very fast feints by the lad threw the poor fellow off balance. In an instant, Tiberius tapped him across the back of the neck. "Two down. Let's make this sporting, shall we? I'll take the last of you at once."

Arminius shrugged and he and the remaining man as his partner in this match proceeded onto the sand court. They spread themselves so they might be able to pincer the boy between them. As they tried a simultaneous attack, the lad rolled through them, tapped the one fellow in the back of the calf, sprang up and knocked the blade away from Arminius, and then laid the tip of the blade on his chest.

I'll be damned. Bested by a scrawny youth, a good hand shorter than me.

"Gentlemen, four of Rome's finest; I expected better. Time to even the odds. All four at once, shall we?" The lad waved his sword in a circle toward the four of them.

Arminius retrieved his weapon from the sand, and the group fanned out to encircle the boy. They were hesitant as to who would attempt to strike first, but Tiberius resolved the problem. After quick hits on the swords of two of them, he reversed his attack and caught the men behind him by surprise. The sound of the wood sword banging against the shoulders and upper torsos of the four men was background noise to the blur flashing in and out among them. Wild swings and curses filled the air as the men ignored their supposed injuries and

24

chased after the lad. Tiberius continued to hit them at will, until finally, bruised and battered, the quartet conceded the match and two of them collapsed into the sand.

Arminius rubbed at several sore spots. "Wood or not, the thing hurts when it hits, and no doubt there will be a few new bruises in the morning. Enough already. You've proven your point, young Tiberius. I, for one, am not prepared to suffer any more punishment. Give us respite so we can lick our wounds and be rested for the morrow when our lessons begin with your father"

He and his men trundled off toward the guest house, leaving the victor the task of cleaning up and putting away the swords. Movement drew Arminius's attention to the barn loft where Decimus stood. A faint smile crossed the father's countenance, and then he disappeared into the shadows.

***

The days of training were arduous to say the least. Tiberius' father was unhappy with the men's conditioning and put them through rigorous workouts between sessions. Other trainees came and went, and at times the yard rang with the shouts of would be swordsmen.

At night, Tiberius would steal off to the trainees' campfire to listen as they talked about life in the Roman legion.

One night, Arminius sat next to him. "What's on your mind, lad?"

"Tell me, Arminius. You command a Roman legion, yet you aren't Roman, you're Germanic. How is that so?"

He chuckled. "None of the men in the Cheruscan detachment who serve under me are Roman. The Romans are currently at peace with the Germanic tribes, and we, in turn, offer our services as soldiers. We owe our allegiance to them. They are, after all, masters of the world. It would be foolhardy to challenge that. But deep down, we all still honor our heritage."

"If you are at peace with Rome, then why does it need so many men fighting for them?"

"Not all are at peace. When we leave here, we must head north to Pannonia where rebels are threatening. War still exists."

"Why are they fighting? Is not Pannonia part of the empire?"

"It is now, but it wasn't always. I suppose they would rather fight and die than serve Rome."

A man threw some logs onto the fire and a shower of sparks broke Tiberius's attention for the moment. As they descended and faded, he looked to Arminius once more. "What if Rome wanted to expand the empire to include the tribes, and they didn't want to be part of the empire? What would you do?"

Arminius pulled at his chin, then reached out and tousled Tiberius' hair. "Enough talk for tonight. Don't muddle your young head with what ifs."

"My father says it is better to ask the questions than not know the answer when you need it."

"Your father said that, did he? Well then, I would say he is a wise man."

"So what would you do?"

Arminius scratched his head then sighed. "I don't know."

***

The time arrived for Arminius and all the men assigned to him to leave the training of Decimus Suten-Mdjai. Over the weeks, their numbers had swelled significantly and the surrounding grounds were filled with tents. As he spoke his goodbyes with Decimus, Tiberius approached. "Father, I've decided to go and join the legion. You will accept me, won't you Arminius?"

Arminius waited for Decimus to deny the lad's wishes, but the father seemed lost in thought. It was the first time Arminius had seen the master swordsman stumped. *I guess this is a question not previously asked.*

He decided to take charge of the situation and help the poor fellow out. "I am honored at your request, young Tiberius, but at fifteen, you are still too young to join our…"

"No, it's alright. Let him go."

He gaped open mouthed at Decimus. The young man, face set in dogged determination, also froze. Decimus reached out and placed both hands on the shoulders of his erstwhile young son. "You have my blessing. Go, and make me proud. That is, if Arminius will take you."

Decimus faced Arminius. "He will be sixteen in a fortnight. It will take you that long on your march north to reach where you are going. He will serve you well."

Arminius sighed. "I…I suppose so."

Tiberius leapt into the arms of Decimus to give a large hug. "Thank you, Father."

After a moment, the older man pushed his son back. "You best go tell your mother. I'll be sleeping in the stables for the next little while for letting you go."

Tiberius ran off to say his goodbyes, Decimus headed toward his armory. Both father and son reappeared at the same time. The boy, who must have packed in advance, pulled on the reins of a horse Arminius knew him to favor. Decimus unrolled an oil soaked cloth to show a leather sword belt complete with scabbard and protruding weapon. "I made this as a gift for your sixteenth birthday, but as you will not be here, it is best I give it to you now."

Tiberius pulled the blade clear of the scabbard. It was exquisite. Arminius leaned in for a better look. Without a doubt, the lad held the finest gladius he had ever seen. He caught the eye of the lad. "No more wooden swords for you."

Tiberius whooped and took the sword through a number of gyrations. The boy remarked how the balance felt perfect, the weight exact. He stopped to stare down at it one more time and then re-sheathed it in the scabbard. Once more he gave his father a tight hug. "Thank you again. When I return I will tell you of the tales of the sword; it will become legend."

***

Arminius mounted up and the troop headed out the gate with Tiberius looking back at Decimus to wave several times.

When at last they were out of sight, he sighed. "I have no doubt, son, that it will." Decimus reached up to wipe the tears from his face. They would serve him no good when he went in to face his wife.

***

Tiberius and the other lieutenants arrived at the tent of Arminius together. Waiting for admission, he nudged the man to his left. "What's going on? I was told to hurry here immediately."

"I know not. The only thing I can tell you is the Emperor's envoy was just here."

28

"It must be new orders from Rome then. We've been sitting around doing nothing for three years since we smashed the Pannonia revolt."

The flap flew back and Arminius beckoned them in. "News it is, but not what I expected. Come in, everyone. Sit down, we have much to discuss."

The tent, about fifteen paces across, featured a large fire pit surrounded by benches. Once the lieutenants sat down, Arminius paced between the benches and the fire. "Rome, it seems, is no longer satisfied with its borders. My orders are to take the legion and march east, expanding the empire as I go."

Tiberius felt the shock of the statement. "But that would take you right through the Germanic tribes!"

"Exactly, my homeland."

A round of grumbling went through the men. Arminius held up his hand for silence. "I know you are all faithful to me, as are the troops. But it is one thing for faith when I lead men into battle. It is entirely another thing when I ask what I must ask next."

Tiberius broke the silence. "Go against Rome?"

Arminius chuckled and clapped him on the shoulder. "Yes, go against Rome. Only the innocence of youth like yours allows you to speak what so many others think."

Arminius spun to take in the whole group. "Emperor August has sent three legions to assist us, and we are to be led by none other than Publius Quinctilius Varus himself."

One of the others stood up. "We're with you, Arminius, all of us. So what's the plan?"

Arminius stepped between two benches, wrapped his arms over the shoulders of two of his lieutenants and leaned forward. "Okay, gentlemen, we are to lead the legions of Varus through the Teutoburg Forest. Here's what we're going to do…"

***

Tiberius rode with Arminius and the other lieutenants into Germanic territory. Nearing the Teutoburg Forest, Varus called Arminius near. "Send out a reconnaissance. I don't want to enter these woods without a vanguard."

An unexpected wrinkle in the plans. "I shall go and gather the troops from my legion to take the lead."

"Never mind that. I have enough here already to do the job. I don't want to wait for you to call up your men. You need to bring your men under my banner."

"As I told you before, Imperator, my troops await us on the far side of the forest. These woods hold no enemy."

"Still, they may have scouts of their own. I won't chance being caught by surprise. Go, bring your legion in line. We have passed our secured borders."

"Yes, Imperator."

Varus motioned to one of his lieutenants to order the scouts forward and Arminius urged his horse into a trot.

Tiberius spurred his own mount. "Wait, Arminius, I will go with you for a ways and perhaps ride with the vanguard for a time."

Arminius frowned at him. Tiberius nodded and spurred his horse ahead.

He passed the lead column as he set off to catch the scouts. The group spread out through the trees, some on foot, and some on horseback.

30

Tiberius rode into the clearing where the advance guard lieutenant stood with three of his riders, stood and unleashed his sword. He dispatched two before the others could react. The next two fell almost as quickly. Tiberius grabbed the tethers of all four horses. Pulling them aside, he gave thanks not to be seen.

The reconnaissance teams would be stretched out over several miles in pairs, a lead lookout and a runner. With a few leagues until the ambush point, none of the runners should be returning yet. He needed to track down the teams in haste, but he could not ride his horse crashing through the underbrush or the men would hide on his approach. Speed and stealth were required, and considering the distances, stamina.

With no time to waste, Tiberius set off to the far side of what he estimated to be the reconnaissance envelope. He planned to work from the outside in across the umbrella. With the men required to stay within eyesight of each other as they progressed through the forest, they would be no more than a few hundred yards apart. They would not always be checking, but he didn't want to chance being seen from two different sides.

Running behind them he counted the teams until he spotted what should be the last of them. Drawing his sword, Tiberius raced in and caught the first man from behind. The second had barely turned when Tiberius ran him through. To his left, a second pair advanced. So far, his actions were unnoticed.

Hiding the bodies first, he circled back behind to repeat the same encounter. He found it amazing how scouts looked only in front of them, never checking their tracks behind. Checking left again after striking the last ones down, Tiberius saw two men were charging toward him He would not have to chase these men down in a foot race.

31

Ducking the front man's swing he stepped through to catch the next fellow in the throat. Dancing around the falling body, it gave him a temporary shield to prepare for the second attack of the first fellow. The man hadn't even moved—a mistake. Tiberius made him pay.

Through the balance of the morning, he raced through the entire twenty man vanguard of the Roman force. Exhausted, Tiberius retrieved his horse just before the main column came into view. He stood between two large forces about to go to war. If he remained, both sides would think him the enemy. *I think it best I move under cover.*

***

By midafternoon, when the front of the Roman column marched a couple of leagues past the ambush line inside the Teutoberg Forest, Arminius gave the order to attack. His forces struck with ruthless savagery, hacking and hewing their way through the caught-off-guard Romans until the last man lay bleeding out from his wounds.

Varus stood with his honor guard of ten when Tiberius rode in. "What happened? Why didn't the reconnaissance scouts report the enemy?"

He dismounted. "Because I killed them all."

The eyes of the Imperator went wide. Varus motioned to his guards. "Kill him!"

Only four men drew their swords and rushed at Tiberius. The first mistake. The second occurred when the others stayed where they were, instead of backing up their comrades. In a few moments Tiberius dispatched the four, and turned his attention to the remaining men. Two ran and two died where they stood. Varus, flanked on either side by the two remaining guards, drew his own sword.

He walked forward to look Varus in the eyes. "For Arminius."

In lightning strokes he killed both guards and Varus screamed, dropped his sword, and fell to his knees. "Mercy!"

In one powerful stroke, Tiberius swung his sword and cut off the head of Publius Quinctilius Varus.

With the battle turned into a route, Arminius arrived. "Where is Varus?"

Tiberius reached down and picked up the head of the Imperator. "A present for Rome. So they can know the terror facing them should they desire to return to Germania."

Chapter Six

The undisturbed advance of his hand on the girl's thigh got David thinking it was about time to take his date home when he felt a tap on his shoulder. Saleem, one of the guys from his group. "Hey, David, the guys want to see you."

"Now? Can't this wait? Can't you tell I'm busy?"

Saleem scowled at the girl. "You can wait. I need David for a while."

The man has no graces. David made a few polite excuses to his date and followed Saleem out of the bar and into the waiting car out front.

Ivan Gregorski put the car in gear and pulled into traffic. "Hi, David."

He stretched out in the backseat. "What's going on?"

Ivan watched him from the rear view mirror. "The guys are pissed you edited the video and changed the name of the group."

Saleem turned, leaning his chin on the passenger seat, his eyes darting between him and Ivan. "You had no right, David. This is a jihad against the American oppressors."

David waved his hand in dismissal. "Cut the crap. Most of us aren't even Muslim. I decided to change it so people would think we are Americans with an issue, not foreign radicals."

The balance of the ride continued in stony silence. The farther they drove, the more he began to wonder where they were headed. In time, they arrived in a lower end neighborhood full of small, two-story frame houses. They pulled into a dark alley, got out of the car, and worked their way across a few backyards and entered the back door of a run-down old home. He was somewhat surprised to find the balance of the group awaiting them inside. A trembling Hispanic woman was tied to a chair. David guessed her to be at least sixty, if not older. She was sobbing through the gag tied across her face. "Who's this?"

Miguel, the Venezuelan member, pointed at the woman. "Our next victim."

David froze. All the others were turned to at him. "What?"

Saleem held forth a sword, different than the one Lakshanthan had used. "We want you to do the honors. Since you've decided to take charge of things, you shouldn't go un-bloodied."

David placed his hands in his pockets. Not about to be bullied by the others, he went on the offensive. "So let me guess what's going on here. You pick an old lady. None of you want to kill an old woman, so you find a reason to pass the buck to me. Who is she? How did she get picked? Why do my suspicions fall to you, Miguel?"

Miguel stepped back, but it was too late. David had guessed right on. Everyone faced Miguel. Was it possible they didn't know his motives either? His eyes darted back and forth, and then his face purpled and he exploded. "We agreed he should do it. Not me, David. It was agreed!"

Lakshanthan took the sword from Saleem, walked over to Miguel, lifted the Venezuelan's hand, and place the hilt into it. "David is right. *You* picked the woman. It's your duty, just like the first victim was mine."

Miguel whimpered. "But, but …we agreed."

Lakshanthan stepped back a pace. "Yes, we did because we were angry, but anger clouds judgment and mine is now clear. You picked this woman because she is Columbian and she was at the rally last week in front of the Venezuelan embassy protesting, and threw the egg

35

that hit the Venezuelan ambassador. You told me so yourself. So now you need to be the one."

Miguel's hand shook, the blade wavering in his grip. He took two very small steps toward the woman and froze. Though bound, her struggles increased as he neared.

David raised his hand. "Wait, where's the camera? We need to record it."

Ivan handed him his phone. "Use this? Okay, but it will be bit shaky." Crouching to get a good angle, he began recording. The others all donned masks of one sort or another. Saleem started talking again about the evil American empire while Miguel edged closer to the old woman.

When came the time to strike, Miguel hesitated. *What a big talker. It's one thing to talk of murder and beheading people, it is quite another thing to actually do it. He is about to piss his pants.*

Miguel closed his eyes and swung. He wobbled and the blade went low to clip her shoulder. Blood streamed out of the cut. At her muffled scream, he stumbled back and opened his eyes. He swung again, in a wild stroke. Closer to the mark, but he caught the back of her skull and though blood spurted, she still lived. Miguel screamed in Spanish and shortened his strokes even more into a short chopping pattern. It took him seven more strokes before he succeeded in severing the woman's head. Blood was everywhere and the top of the woman's torso a hacked up mess as he continued his attack.

Ivan put a hand on his shoulder and he spun, sword in hand. Everyone was yelling for him to stop, and Ivan fell over as he dodged the dripping blade. Only then did Miguel regain control and stop. He dropped the sword and slumped to his knees, crying. Ivan stood up and helped him up from his knees. "I'll take him home."

Very somber, the rests of the group headed for the exit. David pocketed the phone. "I'll edit out the` last part."

Lakshanthan gave him a very hard stare. "Make sure you do, and his screaming, too. Shiva knows what the hell he was saying." Then he took a step closer and lowered his voice. "And don't think we have forgotten about the other stuff. Do it right this time. There's too much at stake here. This isn't one of your x-games, this is for real."

On the ride home, while Saleem relived the entire thing out loud and poked fun at Miguel, David sat quietly with his own thoughts. Miguel had appeared a mess, no doubt about it. He resolved, when his time came, he would be ready.

Chapter Seven

A knock broke Robert Grimmson from his reverie. The door opened to admit the agent sent to verify the passports. "They check out, Mr. Grimmson."

Robert scratched his chin. "Well, Mr. Suten-Mdjai, I don't believe I'm going to hold you at this time. One of my men will take you to your hotel. I'll be holding on to your inventory for the moment until I can catalogue it. I would appreciate it if you would return in the morning to assist me with the opening of the cases."

Alexander smiled and stood, Lucia as well. "I would be glad to, Mr. Grimmson. I can fully understand your concern and confusion. It's not every day someone like me arrives on your doorstep with a truckload of weapons. Some red flags are bound to go up. I should have anticipated that. My apologies.

Robert rose as well and accepted Alexander's outstretched hand. "I'm glad there's no misunderstanding. Would it be too much to ask you to be here by eight? I would like to get things done early."

Alexander draped an arm around his wife and hoisted his in-flight bags. "No problem. Eight will be fine. A pleasure to meet you, Mr. Grimmson."

Robert interrupted his exit. "Just one last question, how much of that story you were telling us is true?"

Alexander Suten-Mdjai smiled over his shoulder as he ushered Lucia out. "Why, all of it, Mr. Grimmson. All of it, and more."

The door closed behind the couple, and one of the agents snorted in derision. "What a load of crap!"

"Now let's not be so hasty. There's no doubt the sword in the case

38

is ancient. Based on those papers he produced and those passports we verified, they are officially American citizens, so holding them would be a political nightmare. Before you go espousing the terrorist legislation laws, understand this, there's a lot of pressure for those laws to be revoked and I for one am not going to give anyone any ammunition to do so by holding an innocent man. So let's get going. Someone take this sword and find a metallurgist to verify its age. While you're at it, find an archeologist who can recognize this and give us an insight to it. And get me an historian to check this story of his."

A couple of the agents packed up the sword, making sure not to lock the case, and headed for the door. He watched it go, then he headed off for his car.

A fine piece of luggage.

The custom fingerprint ID to open it must have cost a pretty penny. And the sword looked as real as they came. If it was a fake, it sure could have fooled a lot of people. As to the story, the whole thing could have been a fabrication.

What bothered him the most was the ending with the beheading. And the head count being the same. Just a tad too damned much coincidence for his liking. No, despite the letter and those passports, he wasn't going to let this fellow go without turning him inside out.

What in heaven's name was the State Department thinking when they gave him citizenship?

This was definitely something he needed to get to the bottom of.

Robert was just about to get in his car when his cell rang. "Bob? You'd better stop in the office before calling it a night. That video you were worrying about showed up on the web tonight. We didn't catch it until after it had been up for an hour. Staff here figures it might have had a couple hundred hits in that time. We managed to shut it down but the calls are coming in."

Cursing, he climbed in his car and sped off for headquarters. Turning on his Bluetooth, he pumped his aide for more details. "What site did it show up on? Holy shit, how'd they get it on there? You don't know? Did you track it? What do you mean you can't...? What about the IPO, have you contacted them? You did? And what did they say? They don't know either? They had to shut down the entire site to fix it? Uh huh... Okay, obviously we are dealing with a high level of computer savvy here. Pull the list of all the hackers we think could do this. Put on a pot of coffee, it might be a long night. I'll be there soon."

***

After adding cream and sugar to his coffee, Robert Grimmson plopped down in a chair in the tech center. "Okay, show me what you got."

The techie played the video recovered from online. Four men in masks surrounded the victim in the chair, so counting one more holding the camera, it added up to at least five. Robert congratulated himself for recognizing the position of the camera exactly where he found the tripod marks. Using benchmarks in the room, they calculated the approximate height and weight of each of the men.

One of guys in the video read a script decrying the evil American empire and its destruction of other countries, other peoples, other religions, its responsibility for world pollution, global warming, and on and on. Unfortunately, his team could not do any kind of voice recognition, as the sounds were modulated. The techies were still working on it, but without knowing what to reverse, it would take a while on a hit and miss basis.

40

The speaker paused, and then one of the men produced a large sword and with a single stroke, beheaded the man in the chair. The head and the torso fell forward and landed where they were found, verifying the body had not been moved. The type of weapon remained unidentified.

The techie paused the replay. "Watch this part, Bob. Whoever did this altered it. The words don't match the lip movements, and it's a different modulation." He hit the play button again.

This is a warning to the United States of America. You must change your ways now or suffer more deaths at the hands of the Sword Masters.

Robert straightened in his chair and blinked twice. "Get me the tape of the fellow we held at the airport." One of his men produced the recording and he played back from the start until he heard, Alexander Suten-Mdjai speaking the words, *I am the Sword Master.* "Sonofabitch! I knew I'd heard that expression before!" How many coincidences were there going to be with this fellow? His men were to drop the Suten-Mdjais at their hotel with instructions to return Alexander in the morning.

"I want to go over everything we've put together on this character again. And I want to personally re-interrogate everyone in connection with this. And I want to speak to whoever at the State Department made this guy a citizen first thing tomorrow."

As his staff hustled off to get things started and Robert glanced at the time.

It's late, best get home and get some rest. Tomorrow's going to be a one hell of a day.

Chapter Eight

When Alexander got up at five in the morning to go down to the hotel pool and exercise area, he discovered the Homeland Security agent who'd escorted him from the airport parked outside his door. "I thought I wasn't needed until eight o'clock?"

The agent looked somewhat surprised by his early activity. As he stood he stumbled and sent his chair sprawling. "Sor...sorry, sir, orders. I'm to accompany you when you are ready. Eight o'clock is still the time, just didn't expect you to be up and about by now."

Had the poor fellow been there all night? "Come on then, they have some nice deck chairs down by the pool. You can relax in one of those until I finish."

The two men headed down to the exercise area. For two hours Alexander worked on various machines and capped off his exercise with a one mile swim. While the Homeland Security agent relaxed in a deck chair, Alexander put himself through some difficult paces to keep his conditioning still remained at a top level.

At eight o'clock sharp they arrived at the warehouse where Alexander's inventory was being held to find a small army of people assembled.

Robert Grimmson extended a warm handshake "Thank you for coming, Alexander."

"Did I have a choice? Your man was waiting at my door."

Robert smiled, and then waved at the stacked cases. "If you wouldn't mind?"

He sat at a table and men brought the cases to him one at a time. As he opened each one, it was swept off the counter to be replaced immediately by another.

The container would first go to a table where it was scanned with ultra-violet lights. Now and then, a technician would take a swab to the sword. At another table, a photographer would shoot a barrage of photos, capturing the weapon from all angles.

During all of this, an old portly fellow flitted from one to another as they were examined. "Amazing!" "Astounding!" "Unbelievable!" When the last was unlocked, the man approached Alexander as he sat to the side sipping a morning coffee. "You must excuse me, but I have to know, where did you get this collection? This is the finest in the world. In fact, this is finer than all the other collections in the world combined. And all authentic. I'm beside myself. I must have this collection to display. Would you lend them to me for a month or two?"

Robert chuckled. "Mr. Suten-Mdjai, allow me to introduce you to one of the curators at the Metropolitan Museum of Art. Mr. Bartholomew Higginbottom, isn't it?"

Bartholomew grabbed Alexander's hand with both of his and shook it hard. "Yes, yes, Higginbottom, that's me. Your collection is simply priceless. When I saw the photo of the gladius sent to me last night, I simply knew I had to be here personally. How did you come in possession of such wonders, and in such amazing condition?"

Alexander stood up in an effort to extricate his hand from the swarming grip. "The older ones are all family heirlooms, passed down from generation to generation. The newer ones are my personal collection that I use to apply my trade."

Bartholomew Higginbottom would not be so easily dissuaded. Grabbing Alexander by the wrist he ushered him to the swords arrayed around the room. "You must come with me and tell me more. I need to know the history of each and every one of these treasures."

43

***

Robert failed to hold back a small smirk at the demise of Alexander. "You go ahead, Mr. Suten-Mdjai. I have some other business to attend to this morning anyway. I'll catch up with you later."

He headed out the door, preoccupied with his pending appointment with the two airport inspectors and the baggage handler. He wanted to review the facts of the swords and their interception. He already knew the report detailing their discovery, but there were times when Robert trusted his own job as to whether all the bases were covered.

When he arrived at the office, the three men were all waiting. Robert wondered about the coincidence of Mohamed, another Muslim, having been the one responsible for transferring the cargo at the time of its arrival. Could there be such detailed planning, even to who the baggage handler would be. Could such things be arranged? *Another coincidence.*

He interviewed the men and satisfied his investigation was complete, he was prepared to go, when James Munroe decided to inflame things. "Well, what did you expect? Stan Majay or Alexander Majay or whatever his name was? Just another Muslim Arab terrorist getting into the country too easily. If you ask me, all these people should be put in jail. Or even better yet, thrown out of the country."

Mohamed El-Barai, who until now had sat quietly, leapt up. "You are the problem—you! Why do you hate us so? It is you who should be in jail with all your bigotry."

James stumbled back and tripped over his chair, crashing to the floor. Before Mohamed could advance any farther, Robert rested a hand on his shoulder. "Easy now, let's not do anything stupid."

44

Timothy helped James struggle to his feet, who was spluttering in rage. "See? Violence. It's in their nature. You gotta do something about those people!"

Robert, on the verge of losing his patience, waved his hand from Munroe toward the door. "Get him out of here!"

Timothy half led, half pulled James from the office. Once the door closed, Mohamed sat down again. "It's not even a Muslim name."

Robert spun to face the baggage handler. "What was that?"

"Suten-Mdjai, it's not even a Muslim name, at least not one I've ever heard of. It is the ignorance of men like him that causes all the problems in the world. I want to go now. I don't want to talk no more."

Damn, the idiot, Munroe. Now Mohamed's defenses are up. He resigned himself to wrapping things up. "Thank you, you can return to work. If I need to talk to you again, I'll bring you to a more hospitable location."

He headed for the door. The baggage handler would already be uncomfortable and distrustful of authority. His service record showed he'd been sent home for a month after 9-11 without pay. Munroe's bigotry wasn't limited to him. No wonder so many Muslims in America were disenfranchised.

He checked his watch. Time to head over to the police station. A certain truck driver was still being held there at his request.

Chapter Nine

David Crombie sat at home finishing the editing of the previous night's video. Since it was Saturday, he felt lazy and yet to shower or dress even though it was well into the day. He still dwelled on the events of the previous evening and the situation he'd almost been thrust into. Did he have what it took to cut a man's head off? Though Miguel managed to complete the task, he ended up a mental shambles by the time he finished. Would he show such weakness as well? He hoped not.

The Adventures of Robin Hood with Errol Flynn in the title role played on the television. He watched mesmerized as the great actor cut a candle, and it stayed in place.

Getting up from his chair, he walked over to the wall where the sword from his great-grandfather, the U.S. Cavalry hero Percival Crombie hung. Lifting it from its place, he unsheathed the weapon and gave it an experimental swish through the air. The weight caught him a little by surprise. In the movie, they swung the swords with relative ease. Perhaps the props were lighter.

David moved into the center of the room and tried a few more jabs and thrusts. He began to get a feel for the sword and the weight in his hand.

In a corner of his living room, there stood a candelabra. In a rush, he descended upon the stand and swung hard at the candles in an effort to reproduce the effect of Robin Hood. Chunks of wax flew everywhere, but more disastrous, the metal stand careened across the room and smashed into the flat screen television. With a loud *whumpf,* the screen shattered and fell to the floor.

At first, he felt pissed at having broken the TV but then, he shook his head and chuckled. "That would have made for a hilarious video for YouTube."

He replaced the sword in its sheath and remounted it on the wall.

"So much for seeing the end of the movie."

Still laughing at himself for his own stupidity, David stomped off to get a garbage can and vacuum.

Once things were tidied, he returned to his computer. His mind wandered as he surfed the web for a new television. Stupid of him to think he could do the stunt from the movie. The whole thing was not possible, just a visual effect for the viewers.

His idiocy had, however, confirmed his skills with a sword were non-existent. He needed some hands-on training to complete the task that lay ahead. He switched his Google search to sword training.

His first attempt produced a whole bunch of Samurai sword and fencing lessons, but nothing in the use of a good, old-fashioned American saber. After refining his criteria, he came across an advertisement for a new school for swordsmanship of all types opening in his area. The site showed a large variety of weapons. Although none were exact matches for the sword on his wall, there were some were of the same type. According to the posting, the classes would open in a few days. He pulled his credit card from his wallet and registered online for the first available weekend lesson.

Just the ticket. Hopefully, I won't show the ineptitude Miguel did when my turn comes. As long as this sword master is as half as good as he claims in his promo, everything should work out all right.

And there was something familiar about this fellow he just couldn't put a finger on. If he didn't think about it, it would come to him sooner or later. Things like that always did.

The video from the night before, still waited for him to deal with.

David sighed. *Time to head out and get it sent off.*

Chapter Ten

At police headquarters, Robert checked in with the station chief. "Seamus! How've you been, you old dog? Still pushing that desk around? I hope they've been treating you well."

Seamus stood to greet him from his seat at the front desk, revealing a rounded belly. He rose with a groan, the junior years of his life as a beat officer having worn on his body.

"Bobby, you mistake for a horse's arse, still wasting billions of tax dollars chasing crazies, I gander."

The two men exchanged hugs and handshakes and Seamus waved him into his private office and settled behind his desk. "So what can I be doing for yer?"

Robert stretched and put his feet up on the empty chair next to him. "I've come to see the fellow you're holding for me, the one from the moving company. Did my office send anything over? I asked them to forward the file here, since I'd be stopping by."

Seamus grabbed a print out in front of him and handed it over. "Came through this morn. I put our notes in there as well so's you'd have a complete record."

The Irish cop continued with idle banter about old times while Robert scanned the report in front of him.

It seemed the driver they apprehended was not only an illegal alien, but had ties to a suspected drug cartel in Brazil. The man's cousin was a successful businessman in Rio de Janeiro with business holdings around the world, including the trucking firm in New York. Strong suspicion existed; he was also the head man for drug trafficking through Rio's port. Locally, his firm was under surveillance by the vice squad.

49

The cousin also had holdings and a personal residential estate in Bolivia. What was the connection to Alexander Suten-Mdjai? The trucking company records had revealed the order to pick up the swords at the airport came from the head man himself in Rio and stated in bold letters, *at no charge.*

"Can you bring the detainee to an interview room? I'd like to ask him a few questions."

Seamus reached for a phone. "Sure thing, Bobby... Hello... Yeah, it's me. Bring the fellow from the trucking firm up to interview room one" He stood. "Right this way. I'll show you to the room."

Robert followed Seamus to where he could observe Carlos Jose through the one-way window. The man fidgeted as if the seat had nails sticking through it. When he stepped through the door and seated himself across from the driver, Carlos tensed, his eyes flicking toward the door, but there was nowhere to go.

Robert turned on the tape recorder and adjusted his seat. Watching Carlos from the corner of his eye, he took his time opening a package of chewing gum, crinkling the paper as he went. If he yelled "Boo," the man would jump through the ceiling. Once he felt the gum chewed enough so he could guide it easily to the side of his mouth with his tongue, he squared himself on the prisoner. "Okay, now's your chance to come clean. Tell us why you bolted yesterday and we'll send you home."

Carlos stilled, and a quizzical look came across his face. "Home?"

Robert leaned back and put his feet on the table. "Yes, home. But not where you currently reside. You're here illegally, so you'll have to return to Brazil. Unless, of course, there is something we need to worry about with you. And staying means, not in your home, but in one of ours, meaning jail."

50

The fidgeting returned. "Please, good police man, I just doing my job, driving truck. I know I am an illegal, and so when I saw airport police coming my window, I got scared. I don't want get deported. I want stay here, in America. I want become an American."

A window of opportunity. "If you want to stay and become an American, you need to act like one and answer my questions truthfully, without sidestepping them. Let's start with your cousin back in Rio and this Alexander Suten-Mdjai you were transporting for."

Carlos averted his eyes and gripped his hands together in front of him. "You must understand, my cousin, he my family, and he one give me job, help me here in America. I owe him everything. I never speak against him."

Robert sighed, reached across the table, and patted the clasped hands. "I understand. He is family, and family comes first. But that still doesn't relieve you of telling me what you know about Suten-Mdjai."

Carlos looked up. "Mr. Suten-Mdjai is hero, saved cousin's life."

Robert pulled a pen from his pocket and a small notebook. As always, he would take a few notes for quick reference. "Saved his life? How?"

Carlos glanced around the empty room, as if checking to see if anyone else was listening. "My cousin went visit his estate in Bolivia. It right on border with Brazil. He comes and goes there as he pleases, no one bothers him. It very large—many, many acres of farmland and rubber trees."

.Robert smiled but held his peace. According to the file, the government believed the estate to be populated with coca plants, not rubber.

"Mr. Suten-Mdjai was guest at mansion when it happened. A large group of men burst into grounds of estate. They had lots

51

guns…shooting everywhere."

Robert lifted his pen and raised one eyebrow. "Who were these people, members of a rival drug cartel?"

"I not there. I not know. My cousin not tell me. All I know he afraid his life, but Mr. Suten-Mdjai saved him. That all I know."

Robert set the pen next to the pad on the table and frowned, vexed. "What happened?"

"I not know what happened. He stopped men from killing cousin. I only tell you what my cousin told me. Why important I take good care Mr. Suten-Mdjai personally and for free. I failed them both."

Before Robert could question any further, his cell phone rang, his office. "Hello, Bob, I have the State Department on the other line, regarding who issued those passports."

"Hang on." He got up. "Okay, Carlos, I've got to go. We'll talk some more later." Stepping out of the room, he hoisted his phone to his ear. "Put me through."

"Hello, Director Grimmson. I've been asked to contact you regarding the Suten-Mdjais and the State Department's decision to grant them American citizenship. Understand what I am telling you is confidential."

As always. One department never knows what the hell the other one is doing.

"We had a situation in Bolivia that needed resolving. As you are aware, the United States is not exactly on the most friendly terms with their government. You might recall the news about those protesters who went down there who were kidnapped by cocaine dealers.

"Our operatives in the area were directed to Mr. Suten-Mdjai for assistance. He was wanting to leave Bolivia, so in exchange for the safe return of our people, we granted him and his wife citizenship. The man went into the jungle where the drug cartel holds sway and came back with five of the six who had been kidnapped. He personally carried the body of the sixth, as the kidnappers had raped and beaten, then killed her."

Those details had not been in the news reports. Even then the government must have been covering up.

"How he did it, we don't know, nor do we care. Our nationals were recovered, which was what mattered most. We honor our commitments, Agent Grimmson. The Suten-Mdjais are now valued American citizens."

Robert asked a few more questions, but the man from the State Department was not prepared to give any further details. Thanking him, he hung up and decided to get back to the warehouse. The enigma surrounding Alexander Suten-Mdjai continued to grow. Based on the two stories he'd just heard, the probable supposition was the man was somehow involved in the drug trade. How else would he be on a friendly relationship with the cartels such as Carlo's cousin's, or the cocaine dealers who kidnapped those Americans?

When Robert entered the warehouse, it seemed as if nothing changed in the intervening hours. People were still photographing and documenting the weapons and Alexander still at the mercy of Bartholomew Higginbottom.

"Ah, Agent Grimmson, I need you to find a way to convince this young man of the urgency of letting me display his collection. Some of the tales associated with these swords are absolutely fascinating. They are without parallel. There must be some law...you know...things of national interest and all that."

Robert chuckled as he pried free of the sudden grip Bartholomew applied to his forearm. "I'm sorry, Mr. Higginbottom, there's nothing I can do."

He glanced down at the particular sword in front of them. It seemed familiar and then it clicked. An identical blade had been used by the terrorist in the beheading the other night. "What's the story on this one?"

Alexander handed it to Robert for closer examination. "It is a katuttila, a ceremonial sword from India. It belonged to Osgood Suten-Mdjai, who served with the army of the British East India Company.

The Tale of Osgood Suten-Mdjai

Under siege for more than a week, Osgood Suten-Mdjai wondered how he'd convinced himself to get into such a situation.

Having some skill in the medical arts, he helped the company doctor, John Holwell, set up the infirmary.

"How long do you think this siege will last, doc?"

"I don't know, Ozzie. It's not customary for the locals to challenge us. They fear the wrath of the British army."

"But we're not the British army."

"No, you're right. We're the military forces of the British East India Company. That's how a rogue like you got in, not being British and all, but they don't know the difference."

Osgood finished setting the sheets on another cot. "Then why are we preparing for a battle?"

"Because, Ozzie, old chap, these Bengalese blokes, under the command of the Nawab of Bengal, Siraq ud-Daulah, want this fortress. Since we brought the big guns here, Fort William controls the whole area. No ships can go up or down the river without our say so."

"Hmm, then why don't they attack? Why the siege?"

"I can only figure they're hoping to starve us out. Or they're waiting for reinforcements."

"If the fighting starts, I'm not sure how well we'll do. There's hardly a battalion of regulars, and then there's the Dutch contingent. The rest are all local Indian and English businessmen and their families. Not exactly the crowd you expect to put up a fight."

The doctor put the bandages in his arms down to look out the window toward the main battlements. His gaunt countenance made the gesture seem forlorn. "Right you are there, Ozzie. They're here for our protection. The base commander allowed them in when the Bengals started their uprising."

"And taken all the bunks we have. The men are doubled up and none too happy."

"Sorry about that. 'Fraid there's not much I can help you with there. Stiff upper lip."

"Don't fret, doc. I've got a plan."

Osgood grabbed his kit and headed for a rooftop location to bivouac. From there, he got a clear vision of the fort below and its goings on as well as cooling breezes uninterrupted by the buildings and the fort walls. He was surprised by the clarity of sounds without the din of the camp and the closeness of the buildings affecting them. Whole conversations floated up to him, many not meant for his ears. As Osgood prepared to stretch out on his sleeping bag, he saw the fort commander come out on the stoop of the command house and appear to scan the grounds. After a few moments, he called over a couple of regulars. "Prepare the horses for departure."

"How many, Commander?"

"All of them, you dolt. Now get going!"

As the two men hustled off, the officer went back into his office, only to reappear with one of the Englishmen sequestered on the base.

"You're sure, Commander, there will be no problems?"

"I would never lie to an upstanding gentleman such as yourself. Rest assured, all will be as we discussed."

The Englishman produced a small bag and tossed it to the officer. It resounded with the obvious chink of many coins. The commander glanced around then stuffed it inside his tunic.

John Holwell stalked across the courtyard to the stoop. Osgood didn't need the harmonics to hear his outburst.

"What in blazes is going on? I just learned you're taking half the troop to evacuate the private citizens."

The commander purpled but held his ground. "Tut, tut, Doctor. I am performing my duty to insure the safety of these people, and only by making this move can I find the necessary troops to return and break the siege."

"And who, pray tell, is going to run Fort William in your absence?"

"Why, you are, Mr. Holwell. After all, you are the senior East India representative here. You will still have the foot regulars and the Dutch contingent, and with fewer mouths to feed, you will be able to survive this siege until reinforcements come."

Osgood did the math in his head as Dr. Holwell stormed off. The cannon teams, men to man the ramparts, support crew and such— things were going to be pretty thin with the remaining troops. Heaven forbid a sustained attack should come.

***

Within the hour, the train of people on horseback lined up, ready to move out. Osgood, now down on the ground, watched the fort commander lead the parade out the gate and south toward Delhi. It wasn't lost on him that all the troops going were solid Englishmen, and though he didn't speak Dutch, based on the loud muttering around him, the fact wasn't lost on the Dutch either.

***

Night came, and with it, his duty time. Walking the ramparts, Osgood kept an eye on the campfires at the distant encampments of the Nawab of Bengal's troops as they continued to enforce the siege.

He came across a friend at his post.

"Evenin' Ozzie."

"Evening, Mac. Looks like they're partying it up out there."

The soldier spat over the wall. "Why shouldn't they. They watched as the commander left with all the horses and half the troops. They must figure we're easy pickin's now."

"It's the fort they want, Mac. It's a bottleneck here, if you want to reach Calcutta."

"Maybe so, I still aren't likin' it."

Osgood laughed. "Just keep alert. Even with half the troops, this is still a pretty easy place to defend. That's probably why they haven't attacked yet."

He moved on. When he came to a position over the main gate, it wasn't activity out beyond the perimeter, but activity within it that caught his attention. A number of men congregated near the gate. A short run, a couple of leaps, and with a resounding thud, he landed mere feet from the group, catching them by surprise. "Evening, gents, out for a stroll?"

The leader of the Dutch relaxed and lowered his firearm. "Ah, Ozzie, it's you. You gave me quite a fright there. We're making a run for it. The English have left us here to die, the bastards. You aren't one of them. Come with us. You're good in a fight. We could use you."

A number of the others voiced their agreement. Osgood sighed. These were good men, and they had a right to be upset about the day's events, but desertion wasn't in him. "Gents, I won't be coming, but at least let me get the gate. Someone has to lock it after you're gone."

The Dutch leader clapped a hand on his shoulder. "You're too good for them, Ozzie. I'll pray for you."

The Dutch opened the gate and all one hundred and twenty of them slipped out into the night. As he resecured the gate, he shook his head. *Another fine choice you've made for yourself, Ozzie. Best go wake the good doctor.* It would be morning soon, and some tough decisions were going to be needed.

***

By midafternoon, the Bengals swarmed at the base of the fort.

Osgood joined Dr. Holwell and one of his Indian aides by the front gate. "Walk with me, Ozzie."

"Where're we going?"

"To have a wee chat with our friend out there, Siraq ud-Daulah."

"If we do that, he'll expect us to surrender."

The doctor glanced up. "Do we have a choice? Right now, we still might have a chance to negotiate some terms."

Osgood followed the doctor's sight line to see the walls, bare of troops.

The doctor held a white hankie in the air and they strode toward the opposing forces. At about fifty paces, they were met by a number of Bengals. Doctor Holwell nodded to his interpreter. "Ask them which one is Siraq ud-Daulah. I would speak with him."

After a moment of discussion between the interpreter and the Bengals, the one in a jeweled turban did all the talking. After a moment, the Bengal waved off the translator and faced the doctor directly. "I speak English. The Nawab has retired for the day. I am his second, Mir Madan. You will deal with me."

The two men negotiated a deal. While they talked, he watched the body language of Mir Madan and listened to the Bengal's tone. There was nothing conciliatory in the man's stance. The way he leaned forward and constantly fisted his hands told Osgood all he needed to know. For a brief moment, their eyes locked, and in Madan's, he could recognize disdain as the fellow sneered at him and his uniform. *There's something I don't like about this fellow.*

The doctor agreed they would be held prisoner for the night and released in the morning. The surrender of the fort would be immediate.

Soldiers, civilians, and Indian servants were treated the same by the new masters of Fort William. The main building was constructed in such a fashion where its cellar operated as the jail with a barred door facing out into the yard and two small barred windows. The Punjabi troops began to herd everyone into it for the night.

Osgood stayed next to Doctor Holwell as they were jostled and shoved down into the darkness. As more and more entered, it became apparent the room was inadequate to house everyone, yet Mir Madan did not stop. Like sardines in a tin, he continued to cram the people in. Bodies pressed against bodies, and in short order, the air became stale with the smell of sweat and fear.

Osgood grabbed the doctor by the arm. "Stay with me, doc. It's going to get ugly in here."

Pulling Doctor Holwell along, he managed to claim a location along the wall near the door. The dirt floor in the cell bowled and lipped up against the wall, giving those standing there a good one foot height advantage over the middle of the pack.

Soon many cried they could not breathe and shouted for the soldiers to let them out. Doctor Holwell started to sob. "This is horrible, horrible! They must let us out of here!"

"Focus on your breathing, doctor. There's not enough air in here. Inhale slowly, and don't get excited. It's the only way to survive."

They watched the crowd battle for space and air. Over time, the noise diminished, the flailing abated, and people died. It was going to be a challenge to survive the night in the black hole of Calcutta.

**

Morning came not a moment too soon. When the jail door opened, Osgood Suten-Mdjai stepped out into the fresh morning air, dragging Doctor John Zephaniah Holwell with him. Of the one hundred and forty-six who had entered the cell the night before, twenty-three survived.

He sat down in the square and watched the Punjabi soldiers haul out the dead. They stacked the bodies like cordwood in the yard.

As tears rolled down his cheeks, anger began to burn inside at the horror these people had committed. There would be a chance for retribution, deep down he knew it.

**

Despite the agreement, the survivors of the night of horror were not released, but kept imprisoned in unbearable circumstances for seven months. Finally, a regiment of British East India Company troops arrived to liberate the prisoners and occupy Fort William again. On seeing the troops, the small contingent of Bengals holding the base fled.

Word reached them of the anger of Siraq ud-Daulah and how he was regrouping his forces in Calcutta to retake Fort William. This time the British army forces were waiting to oppose him.

During the morning, the two sides exchanged cannon fire with small forays back and forth, probing weaknesses in each other's defenses. The British East India Company troops were entrenched in a grove that occupied the last of the high grounds to the left of the fort.

Crouched in the trench with Mac, Osgood watched the sky and the sudden tempest bearing down on the field of battle, when Mir Madan led a charge against their position.

"Look, Ozzie. It's that bastard who locked us up!"

"So it is, Mac, so it is. It appears like we're going to get a chance to get even."

As they neared, the order was given to shoot and Osgood made sure to pick his first target with great care. A Bengali soldier rushed toward him with sword raised, a kattutila, He fired and the man dropped to the ground. As Osgood hurried to reload his weapon, the clouds broke open and a torrential downpour ensued.

"Shit, looks like they're retreating Ozzie, and this rain makes our muskets no good. Guess we'll have to wait until later for payback. It's so damned dark; it's almost like night out there."

"You wait, Mac, I'm going."

"Going? Going where?"

Osgood jumped up and raced out to retrieve the kattutila.

61

Scooping it up in his right hand, he continued toward the enemy line.

"Ozzie! Where the hell you going? Get back here!"

Osgood glanced over his shoulder. "Light a candle for me, Mac. I won't be long."

Running bent nearly double, and taking advantage of rocks, trees and bushes for cover, he advanced on the milling Bengali. In the deluge, he ran right into their midst.

He cut through the first few men with ease. Others pointed their muskets, cursing as the rain made them misfire. He spun to face a half-dozen swordsmen, his lifelong training taking over. His movements and strikes were all one fluid motion as those who dared to oppose him, died.

As the Bengali fell one by one, others broke and ran. Stopping for a moment, he yanked the tarps off the Bengali cannons, exposing them to the storm.

A spate of harsh Bengali cut through the panicked forces, slowing their retreat. A bejeweled turban met his searching gaze, and he charged, the path to vengeance clear.

Mir Madan's widened eyes met his, recognition in their depths before he turned to run. Too late. Osgood struck him down. Normally he would find distaste in striking a man from behind, but the grim satisfaction in this assassination felt justified. The balance of the attack force, upon seeing their leader dead, broke and ran.

The adrenalin rush of the anger faded. Plucking the ruby jewel from the dead man's turban, he stumbled back to his trench, slid in, and landed with a splash in the muddy water at the bottom. He tossed his trophy to Mac. "A present for you, from Mir Madan."

Mac looked at the jewel, wide-eyed. "Jeezus...Ozzie! Good show!"

In the ensuing silence, broken only by the drizzling rain on the muddied field and a sharp boom of thunder in the distance, the troop commander came by to check on them "Ozzie, where'd you get that sword? You didn't go out there, did you?"

Osgood hoisted the kattutila, allowing the rain to rinse away the last of the blood along the blade. "Not too far, sir. The man I shot before the storm started dropped it. I thought I'd retrieve it as a memento."

The officer scowled. "Well, stay in your position. It's almost impossible to tell friend from foe in this weather. I wouldn't want one of the other boys shooting you by mistake."

"No, sir. It's dark as hell out there. Hopefully, the Bengali make the same mistake and kill each other off. Make our job a lot easier."

The commander stalked off. About fifteen minutes later, the sky cleared. Mac spat from the trench. "Damn monsoons! They come and go and leave hell behind."

The troops of the British East India Company uncovered their cannons and fired again on the enemy. Instead of the boom of returned aggression, strange silence came from the opposing side. The British troop commander climbed up a small hillock to get a better view of the enemy positions. "The bloody fools forgot to cover their cannons! The day is ours, boys. Let's at 'em!"

Chapter Eleven

Robert retrieved the sword from Bartholomew Higginbottom to examine it. "I must admit, Mr. Suten-Mdjai, you have a gift for storytelling. Out of curiosity, what are you going to be doing with all of these collector's items? Surely, you do not use them."

Alexander took the sword and settled it into its case, snapping the lid closed. "Of course not. I display them in my studio as testimonials to my clients. They are far too precious to allow any harm to come to them. For the same reason I have been hesitant on Mr. Higginbottom's request. But perhaps we could work out an arrangement whereby I might lend him a couple of swords at a time, under security arrangements I deem acceptable."

Bartholomew thanked him repeatedly, wringing his hand, and promised a complete written report on what security measures would be provided, along with a visit by his chief of security. He would provide Mr. Suten-Mdjai with a priority list of the swords he would like to display as well. When he left, a wide grin creased his face and he was raving about what he had seen on his cell phone.

Robert reviewed the report illustrating the final catalogue of the weapons and turned to Alexander. He still had reservations, but he wasn't prepared to detain the man any longer. "You are free to go, Mr. Suten-Mdjai, and take your swords with you. Correct me if I am wrong, you mentioned a studio, do you have one already?"

Alexander heaved a heavy sigh. "You must excuse me, Mr. Grimmson. It has been a long day and Mr. Higginbottom was, to be polite, tiresome. Yes, I have a studio up and ready to go. My realtor secured it for me in advance. I wanted to hit the ground running. You know what they say about idle hands."

From the corner of his eye, Robert noticed one of his agents standing near, waiting to talk to him. "All right then. Give me your contact information should I need to get hold of you, and we'll call it a day."

Alexander reached in his pocket and produced a business card. "These were waiting for me at my hotel last night. Good day, Mr. Grimmson. All the best to you."

He walked away and the moving company, waiting by, snapped to it and began to hustle all the cases into waiting trucks.

Robert turned his attention to the waiting agent. "Alright then, what else have you got for me?"

The agent handed over a clipboard, stacked to its limit. "We photographed in detail every sword and scanned them all both in infrared and ultra-violet. In the process, we found seventeen minute traces of blood and took samples from all. They are on the way to the lab for DNA analysis. We tested metallurgy, and as best as we can figure, all are authentic, except the wood ones, of course."

Robert, stopped leafing through the clipboard. "Seventeen? You found seventeen traces of blood? How long until we get reports back?"

"Two to three days, sir, without crossing them all with the national registry of crime samples. That would take weeks, maybe even months. But what would be the point? He just brought them into the country. There's no way any of these could have been used in a past crime in America."

Robert dragged his open hand across his face down to his chin then wagged a finger at the agent. "Alright, do what you can. I know the higher ups would freak on me spending a ton of dough on lab research for nothing. In the meantime, check out the guy's business. I want a complete list of everyone who visits his studio. Let's set up a

65

surveillance team on it—pronto."

Robert handed him the business card and waved him away. Either Suten-Mdjai would check out, and the blood on those swords just a hazard of his business or he faced a dangerous criminal, a cartel hit man, perhaps, with a penchant for swords.

Robert's phone rang and pulled him out of his reverie. "Bob, another video popped up with the Sword Masters at it again, a real messy job. We blocked it quick. It couldn't have been up more than fifteen minutes or so. They used a different approach this time, an independent web site with links. The tech is pretty sharp. No one in North America is going to see it, we blocked all the portals, but it's out there, and sooner or later word's going to get out. We've notified the police should they discover the victim to contact us. So far, no dice."

Robert hung up and headed for his car. Annoyance filled him. With no real leads on the killers, the coincidental ties to Alexander Suten-Mdjai were all he had to work with.

Chapter Twelve

Steven Bishop sorted through the news odds and ends posted on his computer, trying to find something exciting. In over twenty years as an investigative reporter, change in his methods was radical in finding a story. He didn't go out in the field anymore to find dirt. He sat at his desk, reading over reports from other men around the world, searching for answers.

A bell chimed. He clicked find a new email from a fellow reporter overseas. *Steve, what the hell is this all about?*

Steven clicked the link underneath, but got a message, *URL not found.* He sent an IM to the reporter. *What's on this? The link doesn't work.*

Really? Let me check. Nope, still active here. It must be blocked where you are. Hang on. I'll download it and send it as an attachment.

A few minutes later, a new email popped up. He opened the attachment and watched a video of the brutal, inept beheading of an older woman by a trio of masked guys calling themselves the Sword Masters. Rhetoric demonizing the United States accompanied the murder.

No longer half asleep, he pulled his chair up tight to his desk. *Check out what you can from your end. I'll see what I can find on mine.*

He dialed the phone with one hand while beginning new searches online for news regarding beheadings in the USA and terrorist groups in America.

The phone was answered on the third ring. "Detective Brown here."

Without a lot of details, he would bluff his way and see how far he got. "Larry, it's Steven Bishop. How come there've been no reports on this beheading? You know you guys can't keep this stuff quiet."

"How'd you hear about that? Come on, Steve, you know I'm not supposed to talk to you."

Bingo. "Okay, okay, but the cat's out of the bag and unless you give me a reason not to, I'm going to run with the story."

"Keep your shirt on. All I can tell you is when the guy got whacked and his head cut off, the feds asked us to keep a lid on it until they could get a handle on the situation."

He sat in stunned silence. The video he'd watched showed a woman. Were there multiple decapitations?

This is going to be big.

"Okay, here's the deal. Get me the file so when you get permission to release details on this guy getting his head cut off, I'll have a head start, and I won't publish anything until you give me the go ahead."

"Come on, you know I can't do that. Besides, I really don't know much anyway. Homeland Security is handling it. You'll have to get your info from them."

He cradled the phone between his ear and his shoulder so he could keep talking while he typed. "So it's terrorists then, on American soil. Why else Homeland Security? Overall, a tad too big to keep under wraps. You'll get crucified by the press if this goes south."

"Good-bye, Steve. I'm done talking. I need to go report this call. Don't call back."

He figured he would have an hour before his editor called, better make good use of the time. He needed all the info he could gather to win the argument on why they should go to press with the story.

The few beheadings he found were all old news and mostly family disputes. He marveled at how one spouse could so hate their partner as to commit such a crime, and what values and morals must be exhibited to consider such an act.

That's a possible angle. The American moral value system—is it being corrupted by our enemies?

His search for terrorist groups was coming up as a wash also. He came across a couple of interesting articles about some bad guys getting hit and cut up. Seems the coroner was most impressed at whatever weapon was used, a sword of superior caliber to cut so well.

He posted requests on a couple of chat sites, hoping somebody on line knew something.

As expected, the phone rang, and his ID showed the number from his editor.

Almost forty minutes. Boy, those guys work quick.

"Bishop speaking."

"Steve, it's Hank. Listen, I just had a short conversation with the chief of police asking me to sit on whatever you're working on. "What in God's name is it?"

"Hank, I'm sending you a video. Make sure you're sitting down when you watch it. Terrorism in America. Not something in some far off country the average Joe can't pronounce, but right here in New York. They call themselves the Sword Masters. They've cut off the head of not one but at least two people, so far. Yeah, that's right, decapitation." He continued to surf online, as he spoke.

"Okay, pack up, get down here. I'll stall the police. I'm putting together a team right now. You'll be in charge. Let's get this right."

He hung up, and then searched one more term that seemed likely. "Sword Masters." An intriguing website for an Alexander Suten-Mdjai, Sword Master headed the list. He emailed the information to his office, shut down his computer and headed out the door.

Chapter Thirteen

In his office conference room, bright and early, Robert met with his team on the Sword Masters case. The techs were providing him with a whole load of nothing but techno-babble about what steps were used to download the first video, how the second one was set up, how they were blocking it at all the North American portals but it was still visible overseas. Nothing to help him catch the criminals at large. "What about Suten-Mdjai? Have you set up the monitor on his shop?"

One of the agents smiled and handed him a printout. "Even better, boss, we tracked everyone who signed up through their credit card transactions. He has two hundred and twenty people registered for classes. We're vetting them for priors and anyone matching the psychological profile we've added to our investigation list."

Robert leafed through it. "What have the geniuses in psych come up with for the profile?"

The tech handed him a second printout. "Let's see, male, ages 18-40, most probably immigrants of Arab-Muslim origin, educated, most likely post-secondary, above average wealth, self-assured, good looking."

Robert put down the pages with a slam. "Good looking? What the hell kind of report is that? You've described about ...what, half a million people in the greater New York area? Get out of here and get to work on those people you have from Suten-Mdjai."

Two agents left the room, but before they could close the door, another stepped in. "Hey, Bob, just got a call from the chief of police. Seems a local reporter is onto the beheadings. They talked to his editor yesterday evening, but we're not holding out hope they'll keep the matter quiet. The editor's giving us double talk. It's a good thing today's Sunday. Otherwise, it would be out by now. They'll probably go to press today for the morning edition. What do you want us to do?"

The day couldn't get any worse and it was only eight o'clock in the morning. "Call our lawyers, use the anti-terrorism provisions, and get a judge to slap a cease and desist order on them. I don't want to see this in the morning paper."

The agent waved and headed back out. "Right, I'm on it."

So far, two and a half days had passed since the first beheading, with the second one about thirty-six hours ago. Was the plan to kill a person a day? The police still hadn't found the second body, and there were no clues to work from. The best they could hope for from the judge would be a week. More than likely, they could expect a couple of days. And if the editor refused to comply, the shit would really hit the fan when word got out.

Maybe he needed to start thinking of a public statement to control panic. He addressed the agent to his left. "Get a hold of public relations. I need a speech for the press on this, pronto."

Robert skimmed Suten-Mdjais customer list. Just about everybody on it met that psych evaluation. A couple of women and a few elder guys rounded out the list. "I still want that place monitored, what about walk-ins?"

One of the agents seated, raised a hand. "We're setting up a van to work from, but it won't be easy. The studio occupies a third story warehouse space with two other businesses operating on the floors below him. We won't know who're whose customers."

He threw his left hand in the air and brought it down with a slap on his desk. "Great, effin' great. Okay, what about the leads on the first victim?"

One of the agents pulled his own list up. "We interviewed all of

71

his co-workers, known associates, family and friends. We did our best to retrace his steps for the previous couple of days and ran the best history check on him as we could. The Malaysian authorities still won't provide any details. The US embassy there reports we shouldn't expect any, either because the Malaysian government is not interested in helping or they simply don't have adequate records worth examining. And as a footnote, the victim had a trace of opium in his system."

Robert leaned back and put his feet up on his desk. "Being a drug user, he might have fallen in with bad company, or maybe didn't pay his tab. Okay, so let me sum this up. Everything else comes up as a bunch of zeroes. No one knew the victim well. He had no family here in the area. He wasn't a member of any terrorist group like the Tamil Tigers. In fact, he probably didn't even have so much as a parking ticket."

"Well, Bob, that last's an easy one. He didn't own a car."

Everyone chuckled for a moment then Robert waved a hand to get them to stop. "Okay, okay, so the victim right now is a dead end." More chuckles. He waited until everyone calmed down. "What about the perps?"

"As far as the Sword Masters, prior to our current situation, they were unheard of. We've found no links to any other terrorist organization and no forensic evidence to give any indication as to who the members are."

"The only solid clue is the sword used is of East Indian origin, lending credence to the possibility one or more of these Sword Masters is of such nationality."

He brainstormed with his team, throwing ideas out as fast as they brought them up. Two hours later, the agent who'd brought the news of the reporter returned. "Good news, boss. We got a restraining order for seven days from the date of the event, which gives us four and a half days. Unless the paper is going to put out a special edition, we have five. Though I suspect they'll post it on their website the moment the injunction ends. But the paper can apply to have the injunction lifted early if new details arise."

He thanked the agent on a job well done and got back to the brainstorming session. "Somebody pull up Suten-Mdjais website."

One of the agents sitting at a computer retrieved the site. "What do you want to see, Bob?"

He pulled out his wallet and retrieved a credit card. "If you can't beat 'em, join 'em. Get me registered for the earliest class you can."

Chapter Fourteen

Amazing how quiet the streets were on a Sunday. Hours passed as David and the other Sword Masters drove around a number of neighborhoods, talking as they went and listening to the radio.

Miguel had changed. Had the others noticed as well? He wore a furtive expression, eyes darting to and fro. When he laughed, it seemed forced. And then there was the nervous tick he exhibited. Miguel had suddenly started scratching at the back of his neck like he suffered head lice or something, stopping only when people were watching him. Once no longer the focus of attention, he would go to it again.

Lakshanthan, on the other hand, appeared cooler than ever. Prior to the event, he had become argumentative when his views weren't taken. Now he was relaxed, without the edge. Diametric opposite reactions.

Ivan drove, as usual. Saleem rode shotgun, with David and the others seated in the back. Saleem leaned over the headrest, his narrowed eyes focused on David. "So how come this hasn't hit the news yet? Why isn't our cause publicized? You are the one responsible for getting the message out. I went online to find the website and there's nothing there. We are starting a revolution, David. We need the masses to support us."

"I'm responsible because none of you idiots has the tech savvy to do it. Both videos have been posted, the website was up and running. I can only assume the government has blocked them. But what do you expect of me? I'm one person. They probably have a roomful of tech guys catching those kinds of things. Would you like me to go the local news and ask them to run it? Or better yet, you want me to paint it on a sandwich board and walk downtown? The idea was mass media, the Internet. The old fashioned plan of handing a video to a local news authority wouldn't work. There's no guarantee they would show it, and it might end up local anyway."

Ivan poked Saleem. "Easy, buddy. David's right. Stuff like that, the government can control if they want to. Remember the Olympics in China? The reporters there couldn't access half the stuff they wanted. But don't worry; sooner or later the word's going to get out."

David listened to all of the different theories being expounded as to the why and wherefore, but he knew they were all just conjecture. He concurred that, though there would be a lot of negative impact, there would be enough public support to call for an end to American foreign policy the way it was so that attacks in America would cease.

David sought a distraction. A tall, well-built black call girl trying to wave down customers fit the bill. "Pull over here."

Ivan pulled the car up and hit the power windows. Saleem's scowl was less than enthusiastic. "What the hell are you doing?"

Ivan nudged him. "Come on; don't let that religious bunk of yours interrupt a little fun."

The girl sashayed up to the window and leaned in. Her very large breasts all but spilled out onto Saleem. "You boys looking for a good time?"

Saleem purpled. "Get away from me, you whore!"

The girl popped up into a stance of indignation, hands on hips. "Say what?"

David leaned out the back window. "Ignore him. He's just pissed because he's a eunuch. Think you're up to handling four of us?"

"What we talkin' 'bout?"

David peeked in his wallet. "Five hundred?"

"Five?! Hell, for five it's just one of you."

He glanced around. A couple of negative head shakes and one, "I got no cash" met his silent query. "If it's only me, then two hundred."

"Hmm, you're cute, three."

David climbed out of the car. "Three then, where to? I'll see you guys later."

The girl hooked her arm into his. "I have an apartment in the building behind me."

He followed the girl up the stairs. Watching her ass twitch from side to side gave him a real hard on. He promised himself to make sure he got his three hundred dollars' worth. When they got into the unit, he headed for the worn leather sofa but she stopped him. She demanded payment up front, but he protested. They settled on half and she was all business, stripping David down while she got undressed.

He pushed her down into a doggy position on the sofa and was plowing away in earnest when the door burst open. Saleem, sword in hand, followed by Lakshanthan and then Ivan hovering in the doorway. He espied Miguel staying out in the hall. As the girl began yelling obscenities, in a quick aggressive swing, Saleem cut her head off. Blood spurted everywhere—the sofa, the floor and David's shed jacket.

David struggled to stand, but his pants were around his ankles, hobbling him. He yanked them up. "What the hell! Jesus, Saleem! Why'd you do that!"

Saleem spat at the girl's severed head. "She is a whore, an example of what is wrong with Americans."

Ivan shushed him, grabbed David and ushered him out the door. "Come on. Let's go before someone comes. Look at it this way. Saleem saved you three hundred bucks."

Lakshanthan stopped in the doorway to take a picture with his cell

76

phone. "I will send you this pic to post, David. Another strike for the Sword Masters."

The five of them piled into the car and peeled off. David's clothes were spattered with blood, his jacket soaked. "Jesus effin' Christ! I hope nobody saw us."

Ivan chuckled. "Holy shit, David. You should have seen your face. You, with your pecker hanging out. Now that was a pic we should have taken."

Lakshanthan and Miguel snickered as well. For a moment, David felt steamed, but then he calmed, no point in arguing the issue. It was over. "I guess you're right. It must have been funny as hell." *Though at the time, I didn't find it so.* "Take me home so I can get cleaned up." In the future, he would need to keep his private life out of the Sword Masters' circle.

Chapter Fifteen

Would he ever get any sleep? At 2:24 in the morning Robert got the call about the dead prostitute and at 6:11 they found the body of the woman from the second video. No video had been posted on the prostitute, yet. Getting dressed, he decided to investigate the nearby crime scene of the hooker first. The older woman's decaying corpse had alerted the authorities. Without at least a couple of cups of coffee, he didn't feel ready to test his constitution so early.

The crime scene comprised a one bedroom unit over a five and dime store. The tenants of two of the three other apartments on the same floor had been roused by police. The death had been called in by another hooker, the deceased's roommate. She'd been out working at the time of the decapitation.

The other tenants were an old couple who'd slept through the entire thing, a young couple who heard the noise but ignored it, and a single fellow who returned home at about three in the morning, after the police arrived. Detectives were still in his apartment, grilling him on his evening's activities, when Robert made his appearance. He took one look at the red-eyed fellow and turned to one of the officers. "Did anybody bother to take a breathalyzer on him? It seems pretty obvious to me, and I just got here. His claim he's been out drinking all night with his buddies should hold up."

One of the detectives said they believed he was intoxicated as well, but no, they hadn't tested him. They thought maybe the guy acted in a drunken rage. Robert kicked everybody out of the apartment. "Let him sleep. If we need to interview him again, we know where we can find him. I have grave doubts about his involvement. You guys are

78

barking up the wrong tree. What about the couple who ignored things? Where are they?"

He went down the hall to find the people sitting at a kitchen table, drinking coffee. "Gee, that looks good. Would it be too much for me to ask for a cup?"

The girl got up to pour him some as he sat down at the table. "Thank you very much, I truly do appreciate it. It's going to be a long day." The woman got a container of cream out of the fridge and held it over his cup. He put a hand on top of the rim. "No, no cream or sugar, I drink it black... So, the two of you were woken by the noise, and then what?"

The young man turned to his wife, got a consenting nod, and then leaned forward. "Like I've been telling the detectives here, noise comes from that apartment all the time. Between the johns and the drug dealers, we're so used to the racket that when we heard the noise, we figured, just another night of those two acting up again."

Robert sipped his coffee, thankful for the steaming hot liquid to sharpen his wits. "Okay, so you decided to ignore it. What did you hear then?"

"We heard a bang, and then a lot of yelling and swearing, then people running down the steps. That's it."

Robert took another gulp. "Alright. I want you to slow down and think for a second. Remember the steps and ask yourself...how many people went down them? Two...three or more?"

The young couple looked at each other in a quizzical fashion. They mouthed numbers to each other. Finally, the girl spoke up. "More, I think. At least three for sure, but something tells me more."

He downed the last of the brew and stood. "Well, thank you for the coffee. I think that's it for now. Let's leave these people be. If we

79

need to talk to you again, we'll contact you."

Once again he ushered the policemen from the apartment. Out in the hall a couple of his people stood near. "Listen, I'm pretty sure this is our gang. Did any of you go to the other site?"

The agent nearest to him nodded. "I was there, Bob. That one was more like the first, victim tied and all. She was a Venezuelan ex-national, lived alone. We're canvassing the neighbors, but so far, no one heard anything."

"Alright, I'm going to the office. Finish up here and bring me the reports on both killings as soon as you can."

***

Robert sat down at his desk. The public relations guys had dropped off a draft copy of his statement for review. After reading it, he balled it up and threw it in the trash.

Two points...nothing but net.

He feared the case might be spiraling out of control. With a fresh cup of coffee in hand, he stretched out and put his feet up on his desk to think. It didn't take long for his reverie to be disturbed by the phone. "Grimmson here."

"Bobby, me boy, we'd better talk. Ya think things might be getting a bit out of hand here? I got detectives all over me 'cause ya keep steppin' on their toes with these killings. Dun't ya think it might be time we teamed up?"

"Hi, Seamus. Are you sure you want in? Once the media gets loose on this, the shit's going to come down on us like a ton of bricks. Maybe you should wait until after I do my press announcement."

"Whatever ya think, Bobby-boy. *Just* don't take too long. I got to answer to some people, too, ya know."

"Alright, I get the message."

"So when then do you think?"

"Right after class."

He hung up the phone on a probably befuddled Chief Flaherty. He needed to get to his first lesson at Alexander Suten-Mdjais school for swordsmanship.

***

Robert strode into the studio with unsure expectations. An attractive woman greeted him. "Welcome to the Suten-Mdjai school of swordsmanship. You are our first customer. Mr. Robert Grimmson, am I correct? I'm Jasmine." A mix of Asian, Indian, and something more—Persian, maybe?—with large dark brown eyes that pulled him in. "Pleased to meet you, Jasmine. It's good of Mr. Suten-Mdjai to hire such a pretty receptionist. Your beauty takes the edge off my nervousness."

"There's nothing to be nervous about, Mr. Grimmson. Alexander is the finest teacher in the world, I can assure you. Allow me to show you in."

He followed her into the main hall, surprised at how large it was.

Spying Alexander across the room, he went over to say hello.

"Mr. Grimmson, I am honored by your presence. I will be with you as soon as I can, In the meantime, sit down and relax for a few moments. I have a special guest to attend to first." Alexander glanced behind him at a man in a white outfit. "I've been challenged to a sword duel. You might enjoy it."

Alexander wore a similar outfit to the other man, who waited on a long runner. The other man wore a helmet with a metal mesh mask, however, while Alexander didn't.

The challenger wavered in his stance for a moment. "No mask?"

Alexander pulled on a small black mask and smiled. "As you wish, a la Zorro. In Bolivia, they still play all the reruns. He is a Latin American hero. En garde!"

He took up a position opposite the stranger. The two men began to test each other out. But in moments, the pace picked up in intensity. The two fencing swords flashed with such quickness, Robert had trouble following the tips to see if any found their mark. The tips must have been electronically sensitive and whether he could see the hits or not, the computer continued to register them on an electronic scoreboard hung on the wall. Minutes later, the match ended and the two men bowed and walked off the mat. The scoreboard showed 15-0, a shutout.

The other fellow yanked off his helmet, broke his sword over his knee, tossed the pieces down, and stomped out.

Alexander sat down next to Robert and peeled off his protective gear. "He is very good, very good indeed. I probably shouldn't have put on the Zorro mask and added insult to injury. But he *was* the one who challenged me. I suppose he was expecting to win and thereby defuse the possibility of losing clients to me."

Robert picked up the sword Alexander had used. "So is this the sword of your preference?"

Alexander finished pulling off his Kevlar outfit and took the weapon. He strode to a rack on the wall and placed it in one of the slots. "No, not this one, merely a hobby. Competition attracts me, but I never enter tournaments, just one on one matches such as this, and usually discretely. I do not wish to embarrass anyone in front of their peers, so these clandestine matches are my forte."

Robert pointed up to a mounted glass case on the wall with another sword, very similar to the one Suten-Mdjai had just used. "Well, what about that one? Somebody must have used that one."

Alexander looked up. "Yes, that's the sword of Balwar Suten-Mdjai."

The Tale Of Balwar Suten-Mdjai.

"Tell me, Ozzie, why'd ya move the school to Luxembourg?"

"Quite simple, Mac. It's a central European location with no political ties, quiet, quaint, and easy access to Switzerland, the Netherlands, and the German republics all around."

"But I thought you were doing well in France. After all, your family was established there for a long time."

Osgood broke from his practice. It had taken him some time to master the epee, but in true Suten-Mdjai fashion, he'd become unequalled in the art. "Things have changed since we were in India. The country is going through some tough times, and one thing my family learned a long time ago is get out while you can. Go to where the opportunities are."

Mac rubbed his chin in thought. "Hmm, well if that's so, why aren't you teaching how to use a gun? Swords are going outta style."

"One word. Dueling. This age is full of a lot of puffery. Personally, I find it hilarious. But many fine men of the court come to learn the craft and skills of swordsmanship. They arrive in clothing of the highest quality, in designs both outlandish and impractical. Their garb limits movement, which makes them easy prey to any good swordsman. Then, rather than admit to inadequacy in their skill with a sword, they laud me with even higher honors than I deserve."

"I hear ya. Though it seems kinda silly to me."

Osgood winked and smiled. "It allows me to raise my fees even higher."

A frown settled on Osgood's face. His oldest son, Balwar, twenty years old, approached, dressed no different than the fools who came to be trained in dueling.

He glanced over his shoulder to see Mac approach. Mac chuckled. "Of course, you have another reason, getting that lad of yours away from the crowd he's been hanging with."

The temptation to lash out passed. His old friend spoke the truth.

The boy better grow up soon.

***

New arrivals rode into the yard, inductees into the Gardes Suisses for the castles of France. Balwar groaned. "I'm never going to get out of here."

"You'll have plenty of time to go running off with your pompous buddies after today's classes," his father chided. "Now go get into some proper work clothes. You can help Mac get these guests situated."

In the middle of the afternoon, some of his friends rode in.

"Come on, Balwar. The soiree won't wait all night. You going to get ready or not?"

"Just give me a moment, I need to get changed."

Balwar did not want to miss the party he was supposed to attend that evening and decided not to finish the current session with the Swiss. He went to get into some of the finery the event required. In the process of buttoning his vest, he became aware of a lot of shouting out

84

in the yard. *What's going on?* While trying to yank on his boots, he hopped his way outside to see swords drawn and his group engaging the Swiss.

"What's going on?'

One of his friends nodded him over. "Balwar! You're just in time to help us teach these foreigners a lesson in civility. They insulted us."

His friends, though better swordsmen, were outnumbered. He finished pulling on his boots in time to see one of them nicked in the arm. Leaping in, he caught the Swiss by surprise as an attack from a new quarter. With speed, he stabbed two of them in their arms, causing them to retreat and regroup. Balwar was just about to renew his attack when he was clubbed on the side of his head and sent sprawling.

His father stood above him, between the combatant groups. He glared at Balwar and his troupe, his face purpled in anger. He then turned and bowed to the Swiss. "My pardon, good sirs, for this most grievous event. Allow my physician to attend to your wounds. Your stay is, of course, without charge. In the meantime, allow me to deal with these ruffians."

The Swiss group, unhappy but without the gumption to continue, acceded and withdrew toward the physician's quarters. Balwar rose from the ground, rubbing the lump on the side of his head. "Why'd you do that?"

His father reached out to take Balwar's sword from his hand. "You idiot! These are our guests. Whether right or wrong, you had no right to engage them to do harm. Even if your friends were in the right, at most you should have fought to disarm only. You're skilled enough. You know better. Hopefully none of the injuries you caused are serious. It appears as though they were small wounds, but one never knows. I only hope the school's reputation is not severely damaged. Now take your friends and get out of here before I turn really angry."

***

Balwar and his four pals crossed into France by horseback. During the entire two hour trip, he listened as they derided the Swiss and bragged about the fight.

"Cowards, the Swiss, attacked us when they had numbers."

"They turned and ran quick enough when Balwar joined the fray."

"Still, I think we could have taken them. Hanging around Balwar, we've learned more than enough sword play to show those bastards a thing or two."

The banter continued until they neared the town and upon seeing the outpost, one of the fellows pulled his epee and waved it in the air. "You know what we should do? We should sign up for the Gardes Francaises. The pay is less, but we're only called to active duty if there's a war. In the meantime, we can show up the Swiss!"

Balwar joined his troupe in a hearty laugh at the notion, but as they rode, the discussion continued and he recognized the more serious tone the others began to discuss it with.

As Balwar dismounted at the gates to the grounds where the party was to be held, a few beggar children approached him. "Coins, sir, for the hungry?"

"Certainly." He reached into his pouch and placed a number of small coins into the outstretched hands.

The gate guards rushed over, brandishing clubs. "Off with you!"

The children scattered, and one of Balwar's friends grabbed him by the shoulder to pull him inside. "Peasants, such a nuisance."

Sometime later, Balwar, feeling the effects of a long evening and plentiful drinks, leaned against an out of the way balustrade, when his friends walked up.

"Balwar, there you are. We've been searching all over for you. Look who we've found!"

Balwar took in the stranger's military uniform. "You appear to be a soldier of some type. I'm sorry, do we know one another?"

The man harrumphed. "Not just some common soldier. I am the Captain of the French Guard, and you will address me by my title."

"My apologies, mon Capitan."

He harrumphed once again. "Well, that's better. I'll need your name, lad."

"My name? My name is Balwar Suten-Mdjai. Why do you need my name?"

"For the roll record. I need to submit it to officially enroll you into the service. Just like your friends here. Welcome to the French Guard."

The man walked off and his comrades huddled in. "Isn't it exciting, Balwar? We're soldiers now."

***

He fretted all the way home over the decision he'd made the night before. As he rode into the camp, his father met him at the gate. "And how was your evening romp?"

"Father, it was—"

"Was what? Another excuse to get out of work? Get changed. We've more new students coming in today, and you're to spend time training the Swiss in conditioning."

"But, I..."

"No but's, get going."

He moved toward the house, trying to think how to explain about the enrollment. His father stormed off in another direction, leaving Balwar to decide whether to pursue him or do as he was told. For the moment, he chose the latter. As the weeks passed and spring rolled along, he all but forgot about it.

On the first day of summer, one of his friends rode in at a fast pace. "Get dressed. We've been called to duty. We're to report to Paris."

Balwar excused himself and stepped up to his friend's horse. "Is France at war?"

"No, but we are required, nevertheless. I'm not aware of the details, but apparently it has something to do with the new National Assembly."

His father strode over in time to catch the tail end of the news. "What matter to Balwar? He is not French. Hell, we do not even live in France."

Balwar turned to face him. "I signed up for the French Guard a couple of months ago. I tried to tell you. I was told I would only be called upon in a time of war."

His father scanned around, as if trying to find something in the very air about him. After a moment, he sighed then returned his gaze to Balwar. "If you have made a commitment, you must honor it. Remember to do what is just and return home safely."

Balwar found his mother and hugged her and his siblings good-bye, packed provisions and left the school grounds with his friend. They met up with the others along the long, hard ride to Paris.

***

Arriving in two days, he and the other new recruits were set to guarding the perimeter of the town. Balwar and company were required to check the papers of people entering and leaving the city. There were a lot coming and going, with a definite disparity between the two. Many of those leaving were of the nobility and upper echelons, while most of the new arrivals were of the common people.

Their commander showed up with new orders.

"Listen, men, we have a job to do, and it isn't one you're going to like. There's trouble brewing in the city center. The National Assembly is continuing to act in defiance of the king, and the common folk are rioting in the streets, mostly over food. It's our job to arrest the lot."

Balwar leaned in. "On whose orders?"

"The Duc du Châtelet, on orders from Governor Marquis Bernard de Launay."

Balwar and his friends marched into town to find the mob made up of ordinary townsfolk, without weapons. He felt disgusted at having to make any arrests.

Catching hold of one poor fellow, the man he caught crumpled to the ground. "Have mercy!" Balwar glanced about; no one was watching. "Quickly, leave the square and go home. This is not a place to be at this time."

The man scrambled onto his knees, then got up and ran.

***

That night, Balwar and his friends sat together in a local tavern, listening to the conversations swirl around them.

"This is crazy! We're fighting our own people!"

"Yeah, but if you don't do it, they throw you in a cell. A couple of

89

our pals got imprisoned today."

"We ought to do something."

"What? Go against orders? They'll hang us."

As the debate raged Balwar remembered his father's last words. *"Remember to do what is just…"*

He stood up and kicked over the table of drinks. "Tomorrow is the fourteenth of July. Before the day ends, we are going to do what's right."

He balled his fists in fury, awaiting a challenge. None came. The man next to him tugged at his sleeve. "What do you want to do, Balwar?"

"It is simple, really. We get up early, go down to the Bastille Saint-Antoine, and liberate our friends."

"From the fortress?'

"Yes, and from the madness."

***

They rose before dawn and eluded roll call with little difficulty, as hundreds of others were abandoning their posts as well.

When they reached the Bastille Saint-Antoine, crowds were already gathered. Balwar gauged the growing mob mentality. It would not be long until things got out of hand. "We must get inside before this throng loses what little control there is now."

Balwar and his comrades slipped past the crowd and into the fortress, their uniforms giving them access. Once inside, they raced through the corridors toward the cells.

As they rounded a corner they came face to face with a regiment of the very same Swiss Guard who were at his father's school.

Their ranking officer used his epee to point their way. "Look, it's the same puffed up boy from the school. You won't catch us unawares this time, boy."

Another pulled his rapier. "This time you won't have your father to save you."

Balwar pulled his own weapon. "It wasn't me my father saved." He took the middle front position between his friends. "Stick close. Keep the corridor blocked so they can't encircle us."

The Swiss attacked together, but the narrow hall took away their advantage of numbers as many were crowded behind those in front. Balwar would see an opening in the guard of one of those in the lead and strike in lightning fashion before he could counter. One by one, the Swiss fell, injured or dead. In the beginning, they faced a regiment of thirty-two. When only six were left standing, the Swiss broke and ran.

Exhausted, Balwar leaned against the wall. One of his friends whooped in jubilation. "We beat them! Come Balwar, let's make haste and free our comrades before those Swiss bastards return with a larger contingent."

He tore a few strips of cloth from his shirt. "I must bind these wounds first. You should do the same. All of us are bleeding from numerous cuts and will fall from fatigue if we do not tend to them."

They finished their bindings, made their way to the cell, and released all the French Guard they could find. When they were finished there were only seven prisoners remaining.

"What should we do with these others Balwar? Let them go?"

"No, we know not what crimes they've committed. If the people of France decide to release them, so be it, but I for one will not be responsible. Let's go, before the masses break in here. I would rather not be part of whatever happens next."

They headed for the exit and slipped out into the crowd as the first tendrils of the mob were working their way in.

***

Later that day, the mob decapitated Governor Marquis Bernard de Launay, placed his head on a pike and paraded it around the town. Balwar followed along for a while then decided to head home. Taking off his sash of office in the French Guard, he gathered his belongings and rode out of town.

He reflected on how he'd pledged an oath of allegiance to country and king and in the end killed many of those who were there to uphold the monarchy, tearing asunder his allegiance, with the country being the benefactor, and he wasn't even French. His ride home was a lone one, as his friends remained behind to continue the French Revolution.

Chapter Sixteen

The ringing of Robert's cell phone broke the reverie of Alexander Suten-Mdjais tale.

"Bob, bad news. The newspaper has been able to get our injunction lifted. They've been holding back the morning edition, waiting, and are releasing the beheadings under the headline, *Terrorists in America*."

He closed the phone. "Sorry, Mr. Suten-Mdjai, work calls. I'm afraid I'm going to have to postpone my first lesson."

The other man rose to shake his hand in farewell. "Call me Alexander. I hate to let you go without a lesson, so I invite you to come back any night this week to one of my group sessions, no charge."

He accepted the handshake. "Okay…Alexander, you can call me Bob. Maybe I'll take you up on your offer. In the meantime, I need to run."

He raced out and got into his car. Once rolling, he phoned Chief Flaherty. "Seamus, you're on. I'm on my way to see you. Announce a press conference for, oh, an hour from now. Have as many detectives as you can round up in your office in thirty. I'll get my people there in twenty."

He rang up his office and found out which paper would be printing the story. Chances were he knew some of the people involved. He might be able to work the fences, so he made a call.

"Hello, Steven Bishop please… Steven? …Robert Grimmson, Homeland Security…Hold on, hold on, I know you have a right to publish and the judge has lifted the injunction. I just want to negotiate an exclusive for you in exchange for one hour…Okay then, let me speak with your editor… Hello, Hank? …Bob Grimmson, Homeland

Security. Has Steven got you up to speed? Alright, here's the deal, the complete files, everything, you give me an hour...Yes, I know the word is out and your competition will be all over you. But you'll have the exclusive, all the inside stuff. Now, of course, I'll call my office to fax it over pronto...Thank you, Hank. I owe you one."

He pulled up to the police station. Not willing to wait for the elevator, he took the stairs two at a time. People along the way directed him to the briefing. Chief Flaherty had managed to get a lot of people there, detectives and blue shirts alike.

Robert's people were also filing in and giving out handouts. He joined Seamus at the podium. "Alright, everyone, here is the scenario. We have a string of murders by beheading, three we know of. Though we're afraid there may be a fourth out there, undiscovered. Things began three nights ago and we have a group calling themselves "The Sword Masters" doing the dirty work with demands American foreign policy be changed. So far, we believe there are five males in the group, fitting the general descriptions provided. We need to find these people, pronto. The media is expected here momentarily, and I need to tell them we have things under control.

Starting today, we will be initiating a door-to-door contact with approximately thirteen thousand potential suspects. This is not a joke. Thirteen thousand is the initial number. You will have special search and seizure powers under the anti-terrorist legislation. Plain and simple, anybody with a sword in their possession is suspect and to be brought in."

Chief Flaherty took the mic. "Alright, boys and girls, you have your assignments. We ain't gettin' through this any faster sittin' on our arses Get out there and find these bastards!"

The room cleared with the exception of a couple of Homeland

Security techs. It wasn't long before the first of the media began to show. The room, once crowded with officers, filled with reporters and cameramen. Word had spread fast about the killings. As a result, the reporters in the room weren't just the run of the mill bunch, but the cream.

Robert straightened his tie, and Seamus pulled on his jacket. Tech people positioned a large stack of microphones next to the podium and fitted the two men with portables.

He nodded to Seamus. "You go first. I'd like to give the impression this is a local investigation with Homeland Security only called in as a helping hand. With the importance of public perception, we want people to believe there is nothing to fear in the way of terrorists in America."

"I hear ya."

As Chief Flaherty took the podium, the room quieted. "Ladies and gentlemen, thank ya for coming today. As ya might have heard, there been a few coincidental murders involving decapitation. Understand this; the department is diligently searching these criminals out. I wouldn't be surprised if my men caught some of them before we leave this room today. We have a number of good leads, and it's just a matter of time until justice is served. You're gettin' handouts now that'll give you all we can tell you at the moment. I'm prepared to answer a couple of questions."

Seamus pointed to Steven Bishop in the second row, as arranged. "Mr. Bishop?"

The room quieted again as Steven rose. "My question is for Mr. Grimmson. In light of the videos and the website, are you prepared to admit Homeland Security has failed to protect the people of America from terrorists?"

Seamus glanced at Robert and then back toward the reporter. "I said *I* was prepared to answer questions. Do you have one for me? If not, sit down, and I'll go on to the next one."

A clamor arose and while Chief Flaherty began asking for the next question, Robert edged in at the mic. "No, Chief Flaherty, it's okay. I'll answer that."

The room quieted again and he breathed in to collect himself. "Your question is a good one, Mr. Bishop. The mere idea of terrorists on our shores is both abhorrent and frightening to most Americans. And it is with this in mind that we work as hard and as diligently as we can to prevent such an occurrence from happening. It is why people such as me stay up nights so people such as you can sleep soundly. It is why your government conducts itself in the manner it does to curb terrorism. Not just in the United States, but also around the world. After 9-11, when President George W. Bush declared the war on terror, it was said then, and I repeat it now, this is a war not like any war ever fought before.

"This struggle has been fought since that day, and will continue to be fought for many days to come. It is not a battle where you can read headlines and see how well goes the struggle. Are we gaining ground or losing? It is a contest of wills that is being pressed against us because we, the United States of America, stand for everything these people do not like: freedom, justice, and democracy for all. As much as I would like to, I cannot promise terrorists will never come to America. I can only promise we will do everything within our power to make sure it never happens."

As Robert moved to sit down, Steven Bishop popped up once more. "I'm sorry, did I miss something? I should have asked if you were running for office."

The room broke into laughter, and Chief Flaherty took over the podium once more. "Alright, you've had your fun. This is officially a police matter, so from now on; I would appreciate if you would direct your questions to me."

The rest of the session dealt with innocuous questions about the victims and the terrorists. Seamus fielded them as best he could, with Robert answering a few as well, and then called the interview at an end.

The reporters filed out, and Robert got up to leave. Seamus grabbed him by the arm. "Bobby, me boy, you waited a little too long on this one. That fine little speech you gave there is only going to make 'em to wanna prove ya wrong."

Robert looked him straight in the eyes. "Heaven forbid if they do."

Chapter Seventeen

Stretching at his desk, he was preparing to call it quits for the day when Lakshanthan called his cell. "David, have you seen the news? We're meeting at the bar for drinks at six. The news should be on there. In the meantime, check out the report by Steven Bishop online. He has all the details."

David hung up and searched for the story. It didn't take long to pull it up. *Terrorists in America* blazed the headline.

They said it could never happen. Foreign terrorists could never again penetrate the steel curtain of defense installed by Homeland Security. 9-11 was an aberration, never to be repeated. Once caught unaware, the United States was now on guard against intrusions with deadly intent. Americans could sleep at night knowing their government was on the job, protecting each and every one of us.

Many of us were skeptical, but in the years since 9-11, it seemed as if the promises they made were going to be kept. Until today. Today, a group known as "The Sword Masters" is attacking American citizens in their homes, committing atrocities only known to occur overseas, the decapitation of people. That's right; they are cutting off the heads of their victims, and videotaping these cruel acts for all the world to see. Not once, not twice, but three times, so far, that authorities are aware of.

Originally posted here, you can now only view these videos overseas as government officials have blocked all website portals to view them. I thought this a tactic employed by totalitarian regimes as exampled by China did during the 2008 Olympics. How many other events have occurred without our knowledge? Is our government on the slippery slope toward controlling all we hear and see? Is this the new

98

American way? Pray to God it isn't so. It is merely the overzealous actions of a few like Homeland Security Director Robert Grimmson trying to use anti-terrorism legislation to cover his own failures...

The story went on to describe the three murders in detail and delineate the demands of the Sword Masters in regard to American foreign policy. The picture accompanying the story came from one of the videos showing the group before they killed the woman from Venezuela.

David packed up and headed out the door to meet up with the others.

***

David entered the bar and spotted Ivan who waved him over. "Sit down, the news is about to start. Want a drink?"

When the waitress came by, he ordered a perfect Manhattan then turned his attention to the wide screen television above the bar. The drink arrived just before the news began. The lead reporter wore a grim expression.

"Terrorism in the United States, something we've all dreaded since 9-11 has finally happened again. Reporters this morning learned of a new terrorist group that has been reported by other media as "The Sword Masters," though not confirmed by this station. The previously unidentified group has been committing murders throughout the greater New York City area by beheading their victims. Apparently they have posted a list of demands regarding American foreign policy. Earlier today, Police Chief Seamus Flaherty, held a press conference releasing few details except there have been three decapitations over the past few days."

The news cut to a clip of the Police Chief addressing the media. "For now, this is a local police matter. We're pursuing these criminals with haste. We'll bring them to justice; ya can have my word on that."

"Homeland Security Director Robert Grimmson was also present at the briefing. When questioned as to whether these were terrorists, he responded with the following."

The news cut again to the podium with Director Grimmson in front of the microphones. "We do not believe these are foreign nationals who have infiltrated our country, but people already here, perhaps even American citizens. To our knowledge they are neither affiliated nor associated with any other organization or government. Merely, misguided souls on a path of destruction. Our involvement is here because of the declaration of these individuals as terrorists, not because we believe it."

The newscasters bantered back and forth as to whether they were terrorists or not and then the program moved on to other news.

David hoisted his drink. "A toast then, to success."

Saleem refused to raise his. "What success? You heard them, they aren't taking us seriously. They didn't even mention our demands on the broadcast."

Ivan clinked away with David. "Relax, it's the evening news. Everything they report on television is kept to a minute or less. They don't have the time to cover everything, just what they consider most relevant."

Lakshanthan leaned in. "I believe Saleem is correct in his analysis. We need to step up the pressure. They need to be convinced. What do you think, Miguel?"

Miguel sat a distance away, in his own world. "Me? You mean more killings? I...I don't know. Why don't we wait first and see what happens?"

David ignored Saleem's scowl. "Alright, the majority has it. We wait for a while, see what happens. Besides, I expect the police will be trying very hard to catch us for the next little while, so staying underground is probably the smart thing to do."

After the quintet finished their drinks, Saleem and Ivan left. Miguel and Lakshanthan remained for another drink then offered David a ride. He eyed a pretty girl at the bar. "No thanks. I think I'm going to stay for a bit longer." As the two left, he walked over and introduced himself.

***

Robert breathed a sigh of relief to be home after another late night of answering to his superiors and local politicians, coordinating the sweep with Seamus, and fending off more media attention. Slumping into his Easy-Boy, Robert turned on the ten o'clock news. As expected, the beheadings topped the agenda. Getting up to get a beer from the fridge, he stopped when the announcer blurted, "And now some breaking news on this story!" The scene switched to a room he recognized, and the reporter continued. "A huge inventory of swords recently arrived in the United States last week."

He was surprised to see a close up of airport inspector James Munroe wearing a smug grin. "Yeah, I was working days last week when I personally intercepted this guy from Bolivia bringing in all these weapons. Doing my job, ya know. I turned him over to Homeland Security, and then they just let him go."

Robert cursed himself for stopping the baggage worker from attacking the fat bastard. Now there was going to be more hell to pay.

He made it to the fridge and pulled out a cold one just as his cell rang.

Chapter Eighteen

Mohamed El-Barai arrived at his mosque for prayers in a foul mood. He hoped *salat* would free his mind of its troubles.

The invasion of his home by reporters had caused him to react in anger. They demanded to know how many swords arrived in the shipment a few days before. It was his decision to physically oust one of them that now caused his distress. *I must atone for my actions and pray for Allah's forgiveness.*

Despite the late hour, there were still a number of people in the mosque, including a group of young men who eyed him as he came in. As he knelt on his mat and conducted his *salat* prayers, it bothered him to hear whispers behind his back.

This is a place of worship. The imam will hear of this. The youth of today have no respect anymore.

When prayers were over, Mohamed rose and stretched his aching back, then went to retrieve his shoes. As he sat to put them on, a few of the young men encircled him. "Mohamed, we wish to speak with you."

He looked up into the earnest faces, some of them in full beard, however sparse. "How may I help you young men?"

The questions came fast and furious. "Tell us about the man you met at the airport."

"Is he some sort of Jihad leader?"

"What type of Muslim is he?"

"What did you do with the swords?"

"Can you get me one?"

"Did he have any message for our people?"

"What is—"

"Enough!"

He slumped and collected himself, remembering his faith. It was not right for him to raise his voice in the mosque.

Once calm, he held up a hand in defense. "I did not meet the man, I only saw him from a distance. I do not believe he is a Muslim. He has a name I never heard before, though it seemed familiar to me in a strange way.

"As for the swords, I delivered them all to the men from Homeland Security. What they did with them, I do not know. But you should not concern yourselves with the matter. If the man is involved with these killings, then he should be put in jail. It is not for us as good Muslims to invite these troubles into our lives."

One of the older ones sneered. "You call yourself a good Muslim? If this is a calling, we should heed it, not hide from it."

The loud talking had drawn the imam to the room, waving an admonishing finger. "Allah will call you when he decides you are ready. Do you want to bring the wrath of the American government down on us? Do not be fools. Listen to Mohamed. Go home, be with your families, and pray to Allah no harm comes to our people."

The youths filed out, some with confusion on their faces, most apologizing, though one or two showed unrepentant of their opinions with their sneers. The imam put an arm over Mohamed's shoulders. "Do not worry for them. They are young and easily swayed, but they will not act against my wishes."

He stood up to go. "Thank you, Imam. As always, you are right, but I fear whether they act or do not act, we will be once again branded as terrorists merely for our faith."

The imam smiled and met his eyes. "It is our faith which will see us through. Just like it did after 9-11. Just like it always has, ever since

Muhammad brought us the word of Allah."

Chapter Nineteen

David turned the key and entered his apartment, the girl from the bar hanging all over him. She oohed at his furniture and artwork, announced how impressed she was with his taste, and gave him a wink. The furnishings had cost him dearly, but David could afford it. And a few excesses such as the Monet artwork on the walls and the designer furniture gave the opulent look one would find in a high fashion magazine.

David segued into the kitchen, the girl following him in. He hardly ever ate at home, but like the rest of the apartment, the kitchen sparkled with high end finishes. Granite counters graced elegant dark wood cabinets. The stainless steel appliances included a six burner commercial gas stove and a built-in fridge, freezer and glass-door cooler. He knelt in front of the cooler to make a selection from the rows of bottles of wine lining the shelves while his date draped over his shoulders to watch. "Champagne?"

"Oh, yes, please."

David brought up a bottle of Dom Perignon and placed it on the counter. He pulled down a couple of glasses from the overhead rack. After a few twists, the wire cage holding the cork came free. No sooner did it pop than the telephone rang.

He picked up the receiver. "Hello?"

"David, where have you been?"

He held up a finger, and his date extricated herself and wandered back into the living room. "Hi, Mom, I've been out. What's up? Why are you calling so late?"

"I've been worried sick. Your father and I have been watching the late news about all these terrible killings in New York. It's horrible. I think you need to get out of the city before things get worse. Come home, where it's safe."

"Relax, Mom, I'll be okay. Besides, you're in Connecticut. That's a heck of a commute."

"But you know how these people are, David. They're vicious, with no morals. And they like to blow up the kind of bars you go to. You need to be careful. Call your work. Ask for some time off until they catch them. Your father and I won't mind, and then we'll get to visit with you."

In the background, he could hear his father's voice. "Mary, leave the boy alone. He can take care of himself."

His date found the sound system and cycled through the stations.

"Say hi to Dad for me. Listen, Mom, these guys aren't blowing people and places up. The bars aren't in danger."

"David says hi... Well, that's the next thing they will do. They run around with those bombs under their jackets, or those, what do you call them...burkas! No one can guess what's under those things. They could be hiding a nuclear bomb, for all I know. I just want you to be safe. I worry about you all the time since last year."

The girl came and retrieved the bottle of champagne and the glasses from his hands.

"Mom, this is New York City. There are like twenty million people here—the odds are pretty small I'm in any danger. I've been here for six years now without any problems."

"That's not all of it, David. I'm worried you might be bothered by it, that it might affect you."

His father's voice carried through once more. "Mary, quit talking. He's fine, the doc said so. Hang up the phone and come back to bed."

David frowned at the phone. He didn't like the way this was going. The girl walked back into the kitchen and hugged him from behind, her hands roaming his chest. He'd opened his mouth to retort to his mother when the girl's hand found his crotch. "Listen, Mom, I gotta go, I have...company."

"Oh...oh, okay... I'm sorry, David. I'll let you go. Call me in the morning, will you?"

He turned to see the girl head toward the bedroom and drop her dress at the door as she entered. "Okay, Mom, I'll call tomorrow. Bye for now."

David stared at the receiver for a moment before he hung up the phone. He would worry about things tomorrow. Right now, his mind was otherwise occupied.

Chapter Twenty

No amount of tossing and turning would help. At four in the morning, Robert could rest no longer. Rising to get ready for the day, he cursed the sleep lost overnight and for many more nights ahead if he was unable to apprehend the Sword Masters.

As he drove to work, the radio news focused on the beheadings. Despite the severity of the killings, you could always count on the disc jockeys to make fun of it.

"How many Homeland Security people does it take to catch a terrorist?"

"I don't know, how many?"

"No one knows, they haven't caught one yet!"

He reached over and shut off the radio. As the day went, he would likely hear much worse.

In the office, he focused on the first duty of the day, getting a cup of coffee from the staff kitchen. A couple of the overnight guys were relaxing there. "Morning, Bob."

"Good morning, guys. How's the java?"

"I put on a fresh pot five minutes ago."

"Great. Let's see how long it takes me to drink the whole thing."

Mug in hand, he was striding down the hall toward his office when he heard his name on the overhead. "Robert, a Mr. Higginbottom on line two, says he knows you."

He reached for the telephone with his free hand as he entered the room. Plopping into his chair, he jostled the cup and a small splash landed on his left knee. "Damn!"

"Pardon me?"

He lifted the phone to his ear. "Sorry, I was talking to myself, just spilled my morning coffee. How can I help you, Mr. Higginbottom?"

"Oh, er…uh…sorry about that. Well, good morning, Director Grimmson. I'm wondering if I might ask a favor. It seems the directors at the museum are concerned about the sword display from Mr. Suten-Mdjai. I was wondering if you could stop by and assuage their fears."

"Mr. Higginbottom, I really am quite busy right now. Can't we do this another time?

"I'm sorry to disturb you. I just didn't know who to call."

Robert patted at the stain on his trousers with a tissue and sighed. He had been sloppy with the coffee and sloppy when he answered the phone. "Look, Bartholomew, isn't it? I'll tell you what. *If* my travels bring me near the museum, I will stop in for a minute, but a minute only. Do you understand?"

"Oh, thank you, Director Grimmson. Any of your valuable time would be most appreciated."

Robert hung up the phone. He hoped Mr. Higginbottom heard the big "if" in that statement. He dragged his team in to review everything since he'd gone home the night before.

Overseas, news stations like Al Jazeera were making great hay out of the Sword Masters. A complete review of all foreign broadcasts and websites still found no link to the beheadings, despite the bravado claims of a couple of extreme terrorist groups. Local police search and seizures had recovered a half a dozen swords already, with the owners being questioned. Hundreds of tips were coming in to the hotlines and staff members were following up as fast as they could.

Still no word from the Malaysian government. His guess—one would never come. Internet chat on the beheadings was rampant; it would take forever to follow all of the possibles.

He checked his watch. *Damn, almost time.* "Let's go, everyone. The deputy secretary is waiting for our report at his hotel, and it doesn't seem like we have a whole lot to tell him. So I'm counting on all of you to baffle him with bullshit while we give the people on the street more time to come up with results."

***

Two hours later, Robert stepped out of the meeting. So far he'd wasted half a day reviewing reports and giving them. His phone rang, which gave him the excuse he needed to leave the balance of the reporting to his team. "Hi, Seamus, any news?"

"Bobby, me boy, nothin' but a sore arse from lookin' at more crap than I care to. Would you care to join me for a sandwich? I've got a hankering for some corned beef on rye."

"I don't want to sit in a restaurant. I've been cloistered all morning. How about something on the street?"

"I've got an even better idea. Let's talk a walk in the park, pick up a dog or two."

***

Robert reached for the mustard. "So, Seamus, I see they haven't skinned you yet. I left my hide with the Deputy Secretary this morning."

Seamus chuckled. "The only reason I still got mine is I've been avoiding the mayor's call all morn. This ain't a good one, Bobby. So far, we haven't sniffed a thing that looks like a solid lead."

Robert took a bite of his hot dog. "We've got hundreds of tips but

111

so far, none of them appear solid."

Seamus was still in the process of squeezing a huge portion of ketchup on his lunch. "I've got every man I can spare working on this. We're stretched to the limit."

A large drop of mustard dripped onto Robert's lapel. "Damn it! First, the coffee this morning, and now mustard. At this rate, I'm going to need a bib."

"Tell me, Bobby, since this thing started a few days ago, how much have ye slept? Based on the bags under them eyes of yours, I wouldna' be guessing much."

He was wiping desperately at the mustard with the paper napkin that came with the dog. "You're right, Seamus. Four, maybe five hours a night. I can feel the drag on me already."

"Go home, take a couple of hours. You'll need to be fresh for the media scrum planned for five. It'll give ya a chance to change as well. Don't worry too much. We'll catch these SOBs sooner or later. It's fate."

Seamus was right. The two of them talked a bit more about steps being taken and then Robert got in his car. Driving down Fifth Avenue, he noticed the Metropolitan Museum coming up on his left and recalled his promise. With a sigh, he pulled in.

Bartholomew Higginbottom displayed great enthusiasm to see him in the suffocating way he grabbed hold of Robert's arm. "Director Grimmson! I'm so glad you could stop by. Come, come, you must meet the directors here."

Robert once wondered about the implausible expression of being swarmed by someone. With this man, he finally found the meaning of the definition. "I only have a moment, Mr. Higginbottom. I need to be quick."

"No, no, no. The situation has changed, Director Grimmson." He shook his head. "Most distressing, these murders—by decapitation, no less, very medieval. It's been all over the news. Mr. Suten-Mdjai has come by and solved everything. No swords on display now."

Robert followed Bartholomew into a room titled *The Dark Ages* and Mr. Suten-Mdjai came into view. "Good day, Alexander."

"Ah, good day to you Director Gri...Bob. There was some concern by Mr. Higginbottom as to the swords being on display due to the beheadings. So I have come and replaced the swords with a few other items from my collection."

"They've taken the same moniker as you, the Sword Masters." He watched Alexander carefully, hoping to see some sign of recognition, but instead, Alexander.

"They are but name thieves. My title is hereditary. It is a title of honor, and they sully it."

"Well, with the tales of your family you've told me so far, it sounds like there was a lot of killing in your history."

"Killings with honor. These ruffians have been preying on the weak and helpless. They take no risk that might result in the ultimate sacrifice, their own lives."

Alexander led them toward a couple of elderly gentlemen standing in front of a glass case, filling him in on the way. "Senior members of the board of directors." To Robert's surprise, the case held a large axe.

"I thought all of you Suten-Mdjais only used swords?"

Alexander placed a hand on the glass. "That is true, for the most part, but sometimes fate interferes. This weapon was used by Dagoné Suten-Mdjai."

The Tale of Dagoné Suten-Mdjai

"Two meat kebabs, Salaan!"

The street vender wiped his hands on his apron. "Ah, Dagoné, how is my favorite Suten-Mdjai today?"

Dagoné chuckled. "You only say that, because I buy the most kebabs from you."

Salaan reached out and up to grab at Dagoné's bicep. "That's why you are the biggest. My kebabs treat you well. You stand a full hand taller than anyone in Constantinople. Only those northern men who make up the Royal Guard can come close. And even then, you must have a good two or three stones on them, and muscle at that!"

"Father says all this muscle and size are slowing me down in training."

Nonsense. Did I not see you win at the games last year?"

"Last year, neither of my brothers were old enough to enter."

Salaan held out the two kebabs. "Hmm. I take it the school continues to prosper?"

"Ever so much so, or where would I find all the coins to pay for your food?"

They laughed together, and then Dagoné glanced about him. The Constantinople markets were bustling as usual. And why not, here in the hub of the Byzantine Empire, with goods from all lands flowing through its shops. And people from countries far and wide visiting to indulge in the opulence.

He breathed in the aura of the square. Spices, meats, fruits, and humanity all blended into a cacophony of smells assaulting his senses. He noticed several men across the square scanning the crowd and speaking to each other with their heads close together.

114

Dagoné tried to follow their sightline but a number of veiled women and their bodyguard—a large fellow with arms clasped across his chest—blocked his view.

A second glance at the group of men showed him the women *were* the focus of their attention. Dagoné chuckled. *Ah, the veil, tantalizing in its mystique. Are they pretty, or are they hags?*

When the women shuffled off, he turned his attention toward a display of sweets. Though he'd consumed the kebabs, hunger was still upon him. Purchasing some figs and dates along with some bread, Dagoné decided to head toward home. Checking the square one last time, he noticed the group of men was gone as well.

After a few blocks, free of the market crowd, he headed down a narrow lane. He ignored a scream—something common in the streets—but hurried his steps at the clash of weapons ahead. He turned a corner just in time to watch the bodyguard cut down by the men he'd seen before, and the women grabbed and bound.

Two of the assailants charged him. Dropping everything, he ducked under the attack of the first man, pulled his own weapon and cut deep into the belly of the second. The others turned and ran with their prizes. Dagoné whirled and finished the first man in an instant.

Anger welled up in him as he set off after the others. *My food lays spoiled on the pavement!*

Despite the head start, the men, burdened by struggling females, didn't get far. Dagoné descended upon him the last one in line and killed him with a single stroke. The others dropped their hostages and drew weapons. Only five remained. They lunged at him in tandem, with Dagoné able to avoid the back attackers and strike severe blows to those caught in front.

In the next moment, half a dozen of the Royal Guard appeared to his left. As they did not jump into the fray, he focused on the remaining attackers before him.

He struck again and again until two more men lay dead and one moaned, wounded, on the street. The remaining two fled. In six long strides, Dagoné set upon them from behind, hamstringing the first, and then cleaving the other one through the shoulder. He returned to the hamstrung man, who held his hand upstretched, as he plead for mercy. The severity of Dagoné's stroke sent the man's head flying in the direction of the bound females.

Chest heaving, he wiped his weapon on the dead man's tunic, sheathed it and stepped back toward the women. For the deeds he had committed, he felt entitled and ripped the veils from their faces. Just then, some of the City Guard arrived and a shouting match ensued between them and the Royal Guard. In the end, the City Guard arrested him for defiling the women's honor. As they led him away, he stopped to pick up what he could from his lunch. When one of the guards clubbed him as he rose, he popped a date into his mouth and grinned at the man.

Well, at least the women were pretty!

At the magistrate's office, the man ceased his writings to watch Dagoné being brought in by the City Guard. The Royal Guardsmen followed. "What is the crime?"

The lead guard stepped forward. "Magistrate, this man damaged the honor of the wives of Prince Abdul, a guest of the king."

"These are serious charges. Has the accused anything to say?"

Dagoné shook himself free. "I only sought payment for my deeds."

"Payment? What deeds?"

"Why, saving their lives, of course."

The City Guard interrupted. "Magistrate, though we found a number of dead men, we saw no rescue."

A tall, blond man from the Royal Guard joined in. "Magistrate, allow me to intervene. My men and I witnessed more than the guard. It is as this big fellow says. The women were bound, and he dispatched those ruffians with great skill."

The magistrate focused his attention on the new speaker. "And you are?"

"Harald Signurdsson, captain of the Royal Guard."

The magistrate purpled. "Captain of the Royal Guard, you say? This crime merits the death penalty. I know not if my authority supersedes yours."

"Then let me solve your dilemma for you. I will induct him into the Varangian Guard to serve your king and Constantinople."

The magistrate waxed relieved. "Alright then, I release him to you, captain. Are you sure you can handle him?"

Harald laughed and clapped a hand across Dagoné's broad back. "His size makes me want him even more."

In the following days, Dagoné informed his family of his forced induction into the Varangian Guard. But after a few months, he actually came to enjoy the exemplary pay, respect, and royal treatment.

In time, as Harald served as a bodyguard for the king, so did he serve as a bodyguard for Harald.

***

Marching orders came down. Rebel forces of Bulgars were haranguing the Bulgarian provinces, and the Royal Guard was ordered to accompany the army in eradicating them.

117

During the fighting, Harald held back Dagoné and the Varangian Guard. "Let's wait for the enemy to tire itself out." After a short battle, the Bulgars fled.

Harald whooped. "Come now! After those vermin!"

Dagoné raced alongside him as they pursued the rebel forces. "Why not just let them go? They've lost."

"Because, lad, it's not our way."

With fresh legs, Harald, Dagoné and the rest of the Varangian Guard caught up with the tired rebels and laid into them. *It's like lambs to the slaughter.*

Despite pitiful resistance or none at all, the bloodlust rose in him. With countless strokes he hacked and slashed at the men as they ran. Any who dared try to defend himself suffered the full fury of his attack.

In a few hours, hundreds lay dead or dying. Dagoné lost count of how many he killed. The blood spattered across his armor and leggings had all but dyed his outfit red. There were no more to kill. As the roar in his ears subsided, Harald came and clapped him across the shoulder. "Dagoné, you're going to make a fine Viking!"

***

Dagoné accompanied Harald to the king's court when the blond man announced his resignation. His title and position awaited him at home. By now, the two were close friends. They said their goodbyes to friends and family and sailed around Europe until they reached the shores of Norway.

Throngs of cheering people lined the wharf at Harald's return. As they disembarked, Dagoné caught up with him. "They seem pleased to see you. I am glad. You were worried we might have a fight on our hands when we got here. Why were you were so nervous about coming home?"

"I feared there might be resistance to my claim on my title."

"And what is that?"

"King."

Dagoné froze. He'd always known Harald was high born and would hold an important position upon returning, but his friend had withheld high nature of the title he claimed.

During the following years, he watched and helped as Harald entrenched his position as king. He joined the Vikings as they raided the coastal towns of England. During these years, his skill in battle proved Dagoné faced no equal.

Unseasonably hot weather accompanied one sortie. Harald, Dagoné and the rest of the Viking force stripped down from their armor as they began the process of transporting supplies to their ships.

"I worry, Harald. We travel too far from our ships and armor. What if we should cross with Englishmen on the way?"

"Don't fear, Dagoné. We have routed the English. A contingent of my men wait at the transfer point to hand over what they have been able scour from the countryside and those towns now under our sway."

As they approached the crossing at the Derwent River, the clashing of swords issued from the opposite shore. The handful of Vikings, waiting with the supplies, was under attack by a large force of Englishmen. In moments, they would come over and catch Harald and his men unarmed.

Dagoné grabbed a long handled large axe from one of the men who hesitated in the face of so large an enemy. "Get Harald to safety. I will hold them here."

The king tried to stay him. "Are you crazy? One against

119

hundreds? They will cut you down. Come, we must try and run."

He shrugged free. "Then run. They will cut us down if we don't halt them here."

As the last of the Vikings on the other side fell before the onslaught, he squared himself in the center of a bridge wide enough for a single cart. With the river swollen from yesterday's rain, there was no way across except through him.

The enemy rushed onto the bridge, swords brandished and men packed tight. He smiled. They had no room to maneuver. He waited until they were two strides away and then charged, closing the gap in an instant. As the front men tried to lift their shields in defense, he swung the axe in a high arc and severed the head of the first man, with the axe carrying though into the shoulder of a second. In the ensuing mayhem, some men tried to scramble past the fallen, others scuttled backward into the crush of those still trying to enter the bridge. Dagoné swung freely. Some screamed, others cried, and the remainder wore looks of shock as each in turn fell before his axe. At ten men dead, the English pressed hard. At twenty dead, they tried to press harder. At thirty dead, they became tentative, and at forty, they broke ranks and retreated.

Dagoné glanced back to see Harald and the others regrouped and forming a shield wall to meet the English assault. Wearily, he turned to smile with grim satisfaction at the English approaching the bridge anew. Yet again engaged with the enemy, it was impossible for him to find the coward thrusting the spear up from below the Stamford Bridge.

Chapter Twenty-One

Bartholomew Higginbottom clapped his hands together. "Amazing! Simply amazing!"

As the curator expounded to the directors on the marketability of this fine weapon, Robert stifled a yawn. "How did you ever regain the thing?"

Alexander chuckled. "I suppose the statute of limitations must have passed by now, so I can tell you. Dagoné's brothers searched for him for two years before they unearthed the entire story. They found an English lord displaying the axe in his home. When his brothers arrived and asked for it, the man set his dogs on them. The two brothers killed all the dogs, the lord, and his servants and took the axe home."

"Well, I won't arrest you for that one. However, I must get going. I've been here too long already."

Alexander shook hands with Higginbottom and the directors. "I'm afraid I must be off as well. My next appointment will be arriving soon." He caught up with Robert as he left the gallery. "May I walk with you?"

"Sure, why not. What's on your mind?"

"My apologies for bothering you, Mr. Grimmson. Things lately have become a bit more…complicated. Perhaps, if you get the chance, you might stop by and see for yourself."

Robert calculated what remained of the afternoon. The studio was not too far out of his way. "Alright. Jump in. I'll give you a ride there now."

Alexander climbed in the passenger side. "In all actuality, many of my appointments have cancelled. The media attention has been unfavorable, to say the least."

"How bad could it be?"

"Bad enough."

With the traffic clear, Robert arrived at the warehouse complex in no time at all. Pulling up, he was astounded to find an angry mob milling outside the building. Police were there, as well, trying to cordon the protesters away from the entrance. Reporters recorded the whole thing, cameras rolling.

As he stopped in front and exited the car, he grimaced at the chants from the crowd. "Swords are sick! Swords are sick!" Robert looked over the hood of the car at Alexander. "How long has this been going on?"

"Since about eleven or so. They seem to be well organized."

He scanned the crowd. Yes, many toted placards, and one carried a megaphone, leading the chant. Upon closer examination, he determined the man wore a collar, and behind the crowd, the parked bus proved the final dead giveaway. Robert pulled on the arm of one of the police officers and flashed his ID. "Who are they?"

"Evangelists, sir. Pastor Wamsley and his congregation. We got wind of it before they got here so we were able to set up in time."

Just then, the man with the megaphone pointed at Alexander. "Is that him? Is that the sick one who calls himself the Sword Master?" The crowd surged toward them. One of the protesters rushed Alexander with his placard raised over his head like an axe to chop at him. Robert interceded and the fellow brought the sign down with a crash against his head. He engaged in a shoving match with the man as police came to his rescue and the door closed behind Alexander Suten-Mdjai.

Robert's reflection in the glass door showed a small gash as an ugly red mark on the top corner of his forehead. Blood trickled down to catch the crow's feet by his right eye and spread as a gruesome fan across his cheekbone. *I can't believe this shit.* "Get these people out of here now before I have them all arrested!"

He left it to the police to argue with the man with the megaphone. In time, the protest group withdrew into the bus with a shouted promise they would be back tomorrow. Robert requested the police release the man who hit him, and they hustled him onto the bus.

He rubbed at the blood by his eye with the side of his index finger. One of the officers produced a med kit and cleaned the wound. Looking in a car side mirror, at the superficial cut, he spotted blood on his collar.

Just great. Coffee, mustard, blood, what next? At this rate, it probably makes more sense to take the suit off and burn it.

As he climbed back into his car, his cell rang. Seeing it was from the office, he placed the cell next to his ear and turned his head up to the third story. Alexander Suten-Mdjai stood by the window looking down at him. "What's up?"

"Bob, you better get back to the office, the shit has just hit the fan."

"What's going on?"

"A member of the senate oversight committee is here."

"On my way." He closed his cell and took one last glance upward. Alexander waved and Robert feebly returned his salute. Starting the ignition, the doubts in his mind continued to grow.

***

Steven Bishop watched the Homeland Security Director pull away.

123

What an interesting development. Grimmson's protecting his prime suspect in the beheadings. Things are definitely developing into a great story. The public is going to eat this up.

He emailed the picture to his editor. The paper would soon be uploading the shot of Grimmson's confrontation with church members to their website. He needed a few more details and then off to Stan for approval on his story.

Typing away in fury on his notebook, he tried to ignore the flash on his cell. After the first two calls, the third went to voice mail. Someone wanted to talk...badly.

"Bishop here."

"Mr. Bishop, I'm calling to confirm what we discussed earlier."

"You have my word, Pastor Wamsley. No derogatory remarks about your church or congregation."

"I am expecting you, as a man of faith, to adhere to your promise."

"Yes sir, though there is some difficulty with regards to the fellow who struck Director Grimmson."

"That should not be an issue. The police decided not to press charges, provided we were willing to vacate the premises. I expect you to show that Grimmson surprised our people. Our intention was to chase this Sword Master character, to rattle him. The church member saw someone coming at him and acted defensively, nothing more."

"Yes, I suppose we could show it in that light..."

"Suppose nothing, Mr. Bishop. That is what happened. Period."

"Right, right. An innocent misunderstanding."

"Good. Have you learned where Alexander Suten-Mdjai is staying? Is he in a hotel or a residence?"

"He *was* at the Marriott, but he checked out already."

"Too bad. A protest outside the hotel would have been most effective."

Steven finished his edits, but hesitated before hitting send. "So what's your next plan?"

"Not sure yet. Let's see how the American public reacts to what we accomplished today. Sinners cannot go unpunished. With your help, we will spread anew the gospel of Jesus and his commandments. The almighty Lord will recognize our good work and surely strike this heathen down."

"Okay, listen, I gotta run, get the story up. I'll call you later."

"May God be with you."

"Yeah, right."

Stephen broke the connection. Though not cold, he shuddered. *Damn! Those religious guys freak me out.*

He would ride this one through. It made great copy and was giving him another exclusive advantage on the story of the decade.

Stephen added one more edit to the story and hit the send button. Hank had promised he would give it top priority and would be waiting at his desk for his email.

He strapped on his seat belt, checked the traffic, waved to the police officers and pulled out of the lot.

"Look out, Pulitzer, here I come!"

***

Alexander watched the comings and goings of people below the window. He easily recognized the photojournalist. He made it part of his extensive training to be cognizant of everything around him and everyone. He found the eye contact the reporter held with the leader of

125

the bus group most disturbing. There could be no mistaking the recognition between the two.

Combining this problem with the van, which would sometimes occupy the lot, and the men who never got out, perhaps it might be time to take some action of his own. Though what action was something he still needed to fathom out. He did not know the city. His movements were being followed. A final, inevitable, decision was clear, he needed help.

Chapter Twenty-Two

"Another vodka!"

"You're going to be drunk before the afternoon is half over."

Ivan Gregorski leaned forward to wave his empty glass at the waitress. "Don't worry, honey, I know my limit."

He settled back in his seat once more. Since his arrival in America, he found himself enjoying many of the benefits of his new country. Of course, securing employment with the Russian mob didn't hurt. Even for a lowly foot soldier, the perks were excellent. Such as this restaurant in the Brighton Beach district. The place offered all of the feel of home, right down to the samovar on the table.

As he poured himself another cup of tea for his vodka, Nikita sat down beside him. "Bring me one of those as well."

Ivan lifted the steaming cocktail to his lips. "Nicky, how goes?"

"Don't get drunk. You have work tonight."

"What gives? Is everybody my mother today?"

Nikita waved the waitress over. "Bring us something to eat."

"Don't worry, Nicky. I'm not going to get drunk."

"Good. The police are everywhere right now doing road checks because of those terrorists, and if you appear even a little intoxicated, they will pull you over."

"Ha! They will never catch them."

"Let's hope they do. It's bad for business having many police around." Nikita frowned at him. "Why do you say that? Don't you want them caught?"

"They're just like us. Criminals."

"No, they are idiots! When we take care of someone, we do it

127

because they have crossed us in business. These...Sword Masters, they kill anyone. Old women, whores, janitors for God's sake! Who are these people to them? Nobody. Just in the wrong place at the wrong time. It makes the whole world go crazy, and then police are everywhere and we can do nothing."

"I'm quite sure they aren't nobodies. They got offed for a reason."

"Why? Is there something you know? Or are you just full of bullshit like usual?"

"Nicky, my friend, what's so hard to understand? They kill for a cause. You kill for money. That's all."

"Ivan, I never know when you are kidding me. Someday you will get into some real trouble with your thinking, and then what? Forget these lunatics and their craziness. Tonight you need to be there when the goods arrive. Once you get that done, you can go back to your drinking."

"Okay, okay, I get the message. Not too late though. I got plans. I'm meeting up with my friend Saleem."

Nikita banged his cup down. "Why do you associate with that Muslim dog?"

Ivan drained his cup, put it down, and smacked his lips. "Ah! Well, if you must know, I get a kick out of his lunacy. His craziness makes me laugh."

***

"Good day, everyone. I thought I would do something a little different today. Rather than continue on the macroeconomic implications of imported foods, I have decided to discuss the economic implications of terrorism. The events in our fair city over the past few

128

days lead me to think there must be a significant factor in the economy. For the United States, it's increased spending in security; for countries where terrorism is a daily occurrence, the costs to infrastructure must be astounding."

The professor moved from the podium to where his computer station was set, allowing him to display things on the screen behind him.

"Now what I'm looking from all of you are suggestions as to the economic factors and their calculations as you identify it. Put it into a formula that can be debated on. All of you have your economic models from your theses. I want to see how you factor it in."

Saleem groaned.

The professor focused on him. "Mr. Al-Najjar, you have something to say?"

"Do we really need to do this?"

"Terrorism is a very real cost to developing countries. If I recall, your thesis was on Yemen. You must recognize the financial implications there. Yet I don't recall it in your economic model."

The professor scanned the room. "Come to think of it, I don't recall it in anyone's model."

"It is so American to talk of terrorism in such a trivial manner."

The professor chuckled. "Well, this isn't a psychology class. We are here to study Third World Macroeconomics. We analyze and design macroeconomic formulas here. But I am willing to indulge you for just a bit. What makes you think I am being trivial?"

Saleem pounded his desk. "Certainly you don't think subjugating terrorism to an addendum to an economic formula is trivializing? It is no different than American viewpoints on third world countries. Terrorism is a symptom of what ails those countries that doesn't occur here. Pity those poor countries and all their homegrown terrorists. Let's go over there and impose American doctrines to eradicate the problem. If a few domestics die along the way, they're just collateral damage. In American viewpoints, there are no people involved, just statistics." By the end of his tirade, Saleem was on his feet. He realized every eye in the room was on him and sat down.

The professor pushed his glasses up his nose. "Well, Saleem, I'm glad to see you have a passion for the issue. But do you not think the current situation here in New York with all the public attention to it, let alone the three people killed, puts a human face to it?"

"The only human face to the story I see is the speculation the terrorists must be foreigners. Why can't they be Americans?"

"Well...I suppose they could be, it's just that...until proven otherwise, Americans would rather believe it's foreigners. They aren't prepared to accept any of their own would be involved, as it's not part of our culture."

"So what are you saying? That terrorism is part of mine? You are merely proving my point and until you comprehend the truth, there is no point arguing with you."

Saleem stood and packed up his books.

The professor's voice followed him as he marched out the door. "Well then, where was I? Oh yes, terrorism as a calculated factor in the macroeconomic formula of third world countries. Does anyone else have something to say before I continue on?"

***

"Jesus! You almost killed a guy!"

Miguel rubbed at the back of his neck. "Sorry, it slipped."

The foreman worked his way across the steel framework. "Okay, it slipped, was that any reason not to yell look out below?"

Four stories down, one of his co-workers was waving a fist up at him while yelling a few choice words and brandishing the hammer that had missed him by inches.

As the foreman closed the gap, Miguel turned his attention to the sky. It was a clear blue day and a few birds passed across the heavens in a cluster, their wings beating furiously. *I've never noticed the birds before.*

"Miguel, are you listening to me?"

"Sorry, Eddy. I guess I was daydreaming."

"Daydreaming? Daydreaming! You're thirty feet up in the air. This isn't the time to be daydreaming."

Miguel studied the beam he sat on and reached back to rub his neck again.

The foreman sighed. "Pack up; you're done for the day."

"I'm done?"

"Just for the day. I can't have you working here when your mind is elsewhere. You're going to kill someone, most likely, yourself. What's the matter with you lately, problems at home? With money? What?"

Miguel got up from his position on the beam. "No, I guess I just haven't been sleeping well."

"Go home and sleep the rest of the day if you have to. I don't want you back until your mind is clear, understand?"

"Yeah, Eddy, I got it. See you tomorrow."

Down in the yard, he was packing his gear when his friend, Cesar, came over. "Miguel, where you going?"

"Eddy sent me home. Says I need to pay better attention at work."

131

"Will you be back at work tomorrow?"

"I don't know, maybe. We'll see."

"Watch the news for me. I want to find out if they catch those guys who are doing the beheadings. Can you believe they killed that old woman from the protest? Talk about luck. Right now, those guys are heroes. I'm cheering for 'em."

"Yeah... luck."

Cesar gave him a funny stare. "Geez, I thought you'd be happy about that. She had you pretty pissed that day."

"Yeah, whatever. Killing her was a bad thing...I think...killing...is bad."

"Miguel?"

He walked away. "Bad."

As he left the yard, he reached one more time to rub the back of his neck.

***

There were voices in the hall. Policemen were announcing themselves to the other tenants. He had picked a bad time to come home. Should he head out right away or do his best to ignore them? Perhaps, if he kept silent, they would think no one was home.

A knock at the door. "Hello, anyone there? This is the police. We would like to talk to you."

His nosy neighbor's voice followed. "You looking for Lakshanthan? Knock harder, I saw him come home not half an hour ago."

Sensing defeat, he made his way to the door, as a harder rapping began. "Hold on, I'm coming."

Undoing the lock, he popped the door open the three inches the safety chain allowed. "Yes?"

In the hallway were two men, one a uniformed police officer, the other in a dark patterned suit, reading from a tablet. "A Mr. Lak-shan-than Vair-a-vi-yar?"

He rolled his eyes at the slow pronunciation of his name. "That's me."

"I'm Detective Brown. Do you mind if we have a word with you?"

"I suppose. What can I help you with?"

The two policemen exchanged glances. "Do you think we could come in?"

Lakshanthan hesitated. *Better to answer than not. They'll think I have something to hide.* After a moment, he slipped the safety chain free and stepped into the hall. "What is it you want?"

Detective Brown glanced up and down the corridor. "Now, Mr. Vairaviyar, you don't want us to do this out here for everyone to hear and see, do you?"

He poked his head out the door and noticed at least one neighbor watching the goings on. "Oh, all right, come in, if you must. You still haven't told me what this is all about."

He led them into his living room and plopped down into a high-backed chair leaving the sofa for the others. Brown sat down, but the uniformed officer stayed standing, craning his head around to take in the apartment.

"I'm sorry to disturb you, but we're conducting an investigation into the death of a janitor who worked in the building from time to time. I have a picture of him I would like to show you."

Lakshanthan took the photo and gave it a cursory glance. "Sorry, I

133

never pay attention to the people around here. I wouldn't recognize him from my next door neighbor."

Brown retrieved it. "That's funny; your next door neighbor sure does seem to know you, even called you by name. Are you sure you don't want to take a second look?"

He shook his head. "No. I'm certain. Is there anything else?" Lakshanthan rose, hoping the man would do the same.

The fellow smiled up at him, but remained seated. "Actually, there is. I was wondering where you were from."

Uneasy, he sat back down. "Why do you ask?"

"Well, this fellow was from Malaysia. Are you from there? I thought you might know him from your community. You know, at church or something."

"First of all, I'm Hindu and we don't go to church, we go to a temple. And *I* don't go to the temple much anyway. In fact, I don't think I've gone in ten years. Besides, I'm from Sri Lanka, not Malaysia."

"Really. I find that a little surprising, as I have it you're a fund raiser for Feed The People." Detective Brown clapped his hands down on his knees. "Well then, thank you Mr. Vairaviyar. I guess we'll be going. Here's my business card, should you think of anything to help us. Sorry to have troubled you."

Lakshanthan ushered the men out the door and closed it behind them. Then he peered through the peep hole and listened closely.

The uniformed officer asked, "Which one next?"

Brown pointed down the hall. "That one, just give me a sec." Holding his tablet, he talked as he typed. "Pos-si-ble…sus-pect."

134

Chapter Twenty-Three

Back at headquarters, staffers directed Robert to where the senator sat waiting. "Good afternoon, Senator. How can I help you today?"

Senator Joshua Pallabee remained seated for a moment then rose, eyed Robert up and down and extended his hand. "Director Grimmson, sorry to intrude. I realize you must be very busy. I appreciate you taking the time to meet with me."

With a bandage on his forehead, blood on his collar and sleeve, mustard on his lapel and coffee on his trousers, he was simply a mess. *What a sight I must make.* "No problem, sir. I understand the oversight committee must be apprised of the situation. Have my people brought you up to speed?"

Senator Pallabee pursed his lips and folded his hands behind his back. "Show me around a little, would you please, Director Grimmson."

Robert waved the senator ahead of him down the hallway "Well sir, perhaps we might start in logistics. I could use an update myself."

As they walked, Robert told him about the steps taken so far on the case. The senator just nodded and added "Uh hum" a number of times, with a smattering of "I see."

The two men ended up in his office. On the way in, Robert asked his assistant to get coffee for him and the senator.

Robert took a sip from his coffee and moved his legs under his desk to hide the stain. "So, tell me, Senator. Is there anything else the oversight committee is looking for? I'm quite sure our report to the Deputy Secretary will make its way to your desk."

Once again, Senator Pallabee pursed his lips before responding.

"I'm not really here on behalf of the oversight committee, Director Grimmson. This is more of an exploratory investigation on my own."

Robert sat up straight and plopped his cup back onto the desk with a significant splash landing on his paperwork.

While Robert grabbed a napkin to swab at the spill, the senator smiled and took a sip from his own coffee. "Oh, have no fear; I will be reporting my findings to the committee when next we meet. As for your report to the deputy secretary, I have already glanced through it and found it somewhat...lacking, hence the visit."

Robert tossed the soaked paper napkin into the trash, picked his coffee up one more time, and used the long drink to think. *Politics is not my forte. What game is the senator playing?*

His best action would be to shut up. If the senator made any more interpretations on his own, it wouldn't be from Robert giving him further ammunition.

He stood up and extended his hand. "Thank you for coming in, Senator Pallabee. I will have someone show you out. As you said before, I am very busy and need to get back to the task at hand."

The senator hesitated, but took the clue and rose to accept his hand. "Thank you for your time, Director Grimmson. Until next we meet again. Good-bye."

Robert opened the door and instructed an agent to escort Senator Pallabee to his car. Once the senator was out of sight, Robert stormed back into his office with two of his agents hot on his tail.

"Hey Bob, what did Senator Pallabee want?"

He plunked hard into his seat. "That son of a bitch!"

The two agents exchanged glances. "The senator?"

"That S.O.B. wasted two hours having me drag him around here, and the whole time I thought he came on behalf of the oversight

136

committee."

One of the agents sat down. "What do you think he's up to?"

"I can't say for sure. I'm just pissed at myself for not questioning him."

"What do you want us to do?"

He grabbed the telephone. "Nothing. We'll deal with whatever fallout happens from Senator Pallabee when it does. In the meantime, get back to work and catch these Sword Masters before anyone else gets his or her head cut off. Otherwise, it will be our heads rolling."

The two agents returned to their own desks and Robert sat back in his chair, pulled up the reports on his desktop, and dialed police headquarters. "Hi, Seamus...no, I never made it home...yeah, I'm looking at it right now...1,135 possibles...okay, we'll do complete backgrounds on all of them... we have to start somewhere...I know that's a lot of work, but between the undersecretary and now Senator Pallabee...yeah, that's him...yeah, I know he's a pain in the...yeah, I know. Listen, Seamus, I need a favor...no, I'm not going to ask you to do anything like that...no, now listen, you're about to give today's press release right?...yeah, now here's what I need you to do...yeah, you guessed it...okay Seamus, thanks...yeah, same to you...bye."

He hung up the phone, exhausted. For once he would head home on time, enjoy a nice relaxing shower and take things easy until the evening news came on.

Chapter Twenty-Four

David sat at a table where he could see the wide screen television located above the bar. While enjoying a three olive vodka martini, he fended off others hoping to steal seats until Lakshanthan and Miguel made their entrance and occupied two of the four empty chairs.

Lakshanthan pulled in closest. "Evening, David. Thanks for staking out a table."

"No problem. I came straight from work, wanted to get a good spot." David nodded to the far seat. "Hi, Miguel."

Miguel gave a halfhearted wave. "Order me a drink, will you?"

"Sure, what'll you have?"

"Anything, just make it strong."

David waved the waitress over and ordered two more martinis then, spotting Ivan and Saleem approaching, expanded it to three and a Diet Coke.

David waved them to seats. "The six o'clock news should be on in a few."

The drinks arrived as the news came on.

"Good evening, this is your six o'clock news. More today on those gruesome killings over the last week. Police chief Seamus Flaherty announced they believe they are close to making arrests."

The camera cut to a shot of the police chief in front of a number of microphones. "Today I want to give the criminals in this case a last chance to turn themselves in. Our offices have been flooded with over thirty thousand tips that we have sifted through very carefully. We are narrowing down our suspect list. So, fellas, do the right thing. Come on in, we know who you are. It's just a matter of time until we come fer ya. If you wait, it'll only make matters worse."

The station returned to the anchorman.

"In other news on this, reporter Steven Bishop was on the scene when members of the Church of the Redeemer protested outside the business of Suten-Mdjais School of Swordsmanship. A confrontation occurred between members of the congregation and Homeland Security agents."

The news cut to the part where a man wielding a sign reading SWORDS ARE SICK, crashed it down on the head of another man in a suit while police officers milled about trying to move back the protesters from the area.

"No one was injured and no charges were filed. When contacted later, Pastor Wamsley had this to say."

The scene switched once more to the reverend standing on the steps of a church. "God says in the sixth commandment, 'Thou shalt not kill.' Anyone owning a sword and or learning the art of swordsmanship can have no other purpose in mind. We must cleanse them of their evil ways."

The picture cut to the anchorman again.

"The pastor's congregation seemed out to prove the pen was mightier than the sword with the way they wielded that sign."

"In other news…"

Ivan broke out laughing. "Did you see that guy get hit on the head?

Miguel, on the other hand, looked frightened. "Do you think they know who we are?"

Saleem slammed his Coke down. "Shut up, you spineless coward."

David placed his drink on the table and stretched out his hands.

"Easy, guys, let's not get rattled. I'm quite sure it's all a bluff to get you to jump."

Lakshanthan interjected. "I'm not so sure. They came to my apartment today to question me. I did my best not to arouse any suspicion, but one never knows."

Miguel threw his hands in the air. "Oh that's great, just effin' great." Through you, they'll catch the rest of us."

Lakshanthan sneered. "That's enough. Hold your voice down, people will hear you."

Miguel cast about wildly in an obvious effort to scan the room and see if anyone overheard. David followed suit but no one around appeared to be listening in. "Relax, no one's looking, but you do have to calm down."

"Easy for you to say. You haven't killed anyone."

Lakshanthan steepled his fingers. "But I have, and I agree with David. We need to take things easy. We knew from the beginning there would be risk. We were prepared to live with that risk then. We need to live with it now."

Ivan elbowed Miguel in the side. "Come on, relax! Let's get another drink. Life is good. Things are good. If you keep worrying like that, you will get an ulcer."

Saleem jumped into the conversation. "I think the time is not one of relaxing, but stepping up our agenda. Did you just watch the same news I did? Barely three minutes. Then the reporter began telling jokes. And they're on to the sports. We have not had enough of an effect."

Things quieted when the waitress returned. David and the others ordered another round with Ivan making his a double, then everyone settled back into their seats. Only when the news was nearing the end did they perk up once more.

"And now back to our top story. In the studio with us today is Senator Joshua Pallabee, a sitting member on the Homeland Security oversight committee."

The camera picture widened to include the senator in the frame next to the reporter.

"Now, Senator, is this a terrorist attack or not? That is the burning question on everyone's mind."

Senator Pallabee straightened and stared straight into the camera, pursing his lips. He appeared more concerned about his appearance than his message.

"It is too soon to say for sure, as the perpetrators of these deeds have not yet been captured. My major concern is whether Homeland Security is addressing the situation properly or not."

"Senator, are you implying Homeland Security is not doing the job?"

"Let me put it this way. As a member of the oversight committee, I need to be proactive in my approach to Homeland Security. That's why I took the initiative to visit with Director Grimmson at his offices this afternoon. A step in order to keep myself abreast of things. Should I determine measures need to be taken, I will involve myself at a committee level."

"So is Director Grimmson up to snuff? I seem to recall him earlier in our reporting getting hit on the head by a protest sign."

"The very same question occurred to me. Again, that is not a decision for me to make, but one for the committee as a whole."

"Well, thank you for visiting with us, Senator Pallabee."

"Thank you for inviting me."

The camera focused again on just the reporter.

Tomorrow on *Viewpoint*, our panel of experts will debate the situation, terrorists or no, and focus on the list of demands they published. Are steps by Homeland Security working? All this, and more, tomorrow morning at eleven."

Ivan started laughing again. "So that guy getting conked on the head was Director Grimmson of Homeland Security? Based on the way that senator was talking; I think that Grimmson fellow better start worrying about his job security!"

The others at the table joined in the chuckle and a lot of the tension left the air. Still, David did not believe Director Grimmson to be the buffoon they were making him out to be. But maybe, just maybe, he wasn't up to the task.

Chapter Twenty-Five

At seven in the morning, Robert finished getting ready for another day. With yesterday's suit in the cleaner's bag, he opted for something in black. Should he have a repeat of yesterday, at least it would hide the stains better. He'd stayed up to watch the late news and then the episode with the protester on the Late Show with the host making the quip, "Now that's using your head!"

He climbed into his car and called the office for an update.

"Morning, Bob, not a lot to report since last night. The usual ton of bad tips once the news ended. Forensics concluded its report on the Venezuelan woman. No luck. These guys just aren't on the grid. We've tried to trace the downloads, but the trail leads nowhere. The police say they still have another five thousand people to interrogate. The night sergeant called to ask if they could cancel the rest after hearing Captain Flaherty on the news. I told him no. So far, anyway, it looks like your ploy didn't shake anything out of the bushes."

"Don't get too excited. It takes a little time for the perceived pressure to sink in. We just need to keep it up, and sooner or later, one of the five will crack."

"Whatever you say, Bob. You're the boss. In other news, you remember that driver we grabbed from the airport?"

"Yeah, what about him?"

"The State Department sprang him last night."

"I don't get it. I thought we were going to deport him?"

"So did I. You want us to follow up on it?"

Robert thought for a moment. "No, I've got a hunch. Let me check it out."

"Okay, see you when you get here."

Robert disconnected and changed course. Twenty minutes later, he parked his car and took the stairs two at a time to the third floor and Suten-Mdjais studio. Though only about seven-thirty in the morning, the unlocked doors and glowing windows told him someone would be in. Stepping through the glass doors, it took just three paces to clear the foyer and enter the main room to see Alexander and another man together.

"Good morning, Mr. Grimmson. It's nice to see you bright and early. I've only just finished my morning routine. I'm sorry there was no one to meet you at the door. My receptionist, Jasmine, is away right now…business trip."

"Good morning, Alexander. I thought we agreed you'd call me Bob."

Alexander bowed. "I apologize, Mr. Grimms…Bob. Old habits are hard to break."

"Well, never mind that. I came to see your friend." He pointed to the other man. "Hello, Carlos, I didn't expect to find you here."

Carlos Santiago cowered back a step. "Hello, Mr. Grimmson, sir. I work now…Mr. Suten-Mdjai."

"Yes, I see that. I was just wondering how."

Alexander stepped between. "Allow me to explain. When it became obvious I would need some time to acclimate to life in New York, I decided I needed a driver, one who knows the quick ways around town, and one I could trust.

"After a conversation with Carlos' cousin, I made a phone call to the State Department and called in a favor."

Robert exaggerated a deep breath. "That is some kind of favor."

Alexander chuckled. "I suppose it is. Nevertheless, it's done.

144

Carlos knows the streets, his loyalty is unquestionable, and I could use the company."

Robert stood nose to nose with Carlos. "I believe we still have some unfinished business, Carlos and I. No matter, it can wait. But I expect you to be on your best behavior. State Department or no, if I hear one thing wrong, I'll personally kick you off the island."

Carlos swallowed hard and nodded.

Robert strolled to the window and looked out. "Yes, I suppose with the protesters, company may be hard to come by. Few of your clientele will chance it."

Alexander joined him at the window. "The protests will end. They will tire of them soon enough. They fail to see the honor in a sword compared with the weapons of today, the guns that proliferate in your streets. In the meantime, I'm not always alone."

Alexander pointed to a blue van parked at the far end of the lot then walked away.

Robert studied him for a moment. "Say what you will, I would rather have a gun in my hand. You come out the loser bringing a sword to a gunfight."

"You must excuse me, Mr. Grimmson. I have completely forgotten my manners. "Make us some coffee, Carlos, would you?" He set off across the room, Robert following. "If I recall correctly, you drink yours black."

"Um, yeah, how did you know? I don't recall telling you."

"In our first meeting at the airport—you were drinking one then. I prefer espresso."

Robert was impressed with how Carlos handled the coffee machine, a high end piece of equipment that appeared capable of producing coffee in a number of ways. At this time, it was easily handling both a regular black and an espresso.

Alexander waved to his left. "While Carlos is busy with the coffee, walk with me a while, will you?"

They circumvented the gym. Alexander pointed out different things as he passed them, describing their purpose. The floor area was about twenty thousand square feet, with various workout stations around the periphery and a large open area in the middle. Along all the walls, countless swords were mounted for easy access with others enclosed in closed displays. Carlos presented them with their coffees as they passed him. Alexander stopped in front of an elegant case. "Ah, this is the one."

The display held a long blade so fraught with dents and nicks; it gave the impression of scrap metal. "What happened to that one? It looks like it's been through a war."

Alexander opened the latch and handed Robert the sword. "This is the sword of Amadeus Suten-Mdjai."

The Tale of Amadeus Suten-Mdjai

"It's time to relocate the business."

The announcement caught Amadeus by surprise. "Relocate! Why, Father?"

"When you are older and wiser, you will understand."

He tried not to let the disappointment show in his face. "Father, I am eighteen years old. If I'm not to know your reasons, then how am I to gain the wisdom you preach?"

He braced for a sharp retort or a stinging slap to the side of his head. Instead, his father's shoulders slumped. "Because you will not listen anyway, as you have not listened to me these past couple of

146

years."

"Our only argument is why we do not add guns and marksmanship to our repertoire. The day of the sword is over."

A fire lit in his father's eyes. "There is always a need for the sword, something you will one day discover. Unfortunately, if we stay here, that day will come sooner than I would like. War reveals such truths. For it is in war when one gleans the truth about things."

"What war?"

His father put his arm around him. "The one about to set upon us. Look hard, it's in front of you. Open your ears. You can hear it on the wind. You can smell it. It's in the air."

"I neither see, hear, nor smell anything."

"Your lack of awareness is why I am the one who decides whether to stay or go, not you." He turned his son to face him, placing a hand on each shoulder. "I will explain this once and hope you comprehend. You see it in the men who visit our school these days, military all, not a noble or a commoner among them. As they train, they grumble about the political situation and their reassignment to front line locations. They sense the impending conflict.

The older ones nod knowingly, they have lived it before. And the smell... is fear. It permeates their bodies and leeches out of their pores, for each one fears when the fighting begins, he will be the first to die."

Amadeus listened. As he examined things in his mind he recognized the signs that had eluded him before. But unlike these men who grumbled and sweat out their fears, he felt a different kind of emotion, though he didn't quite know what it was.

His father broke his reverie. "We will be taking on no new clients in this location. By this time next month, I intend to move the school to South America. The strong Spanish and Portuguese influence still

147

bodes well for the training in the arts of the sword."

Amadeus shook his head. "Surely you don't expect the war to encompass all of Europe?"

"All of Europe, and more."

Amadeus worked hard with his family to complete the schooling of the present clients and begin the task of packing up. As the last of the trainees left, he found solace walking with his younger brother. The newfound silence gave him a sense of momentary grief over leaving. Many generations of Suten-Mdjais once walked these grounds. The breeze rustled through the trees, and he stopped to breathe in the aromas.

Closing his eyes he could still imagine the bustle of men working through their maneuvers. Even as a young boy, he'd helped, show grown men the proper techniques. He chuckled to himself as he recalled the surprise some of the men showed when a mere child bested them in practice.

His brother tugged on his arm. "Amadeus! Someone's coming. I hear trucks on the road."

They raced to the front courtyard just in time to watch four trucks filled with men in uniform pull up. His father blocked their progress. "I'm sorry, the school is closed."

An officer with a chest full of medals climbed out of the lead truck's cab and approached his father. "We are not here to go to school. I am here to exercise my orders to use these grounds for the German army."

"But no one has asked me for permission."

The officer produced a document from his vest and handed it over. "No more. This property and its immediate proximity to France is required."

His father scanned the papers. "This is preposterous. I'll file a grievance with the local authorities. Last I recall, Luxembourg is not a vassal state of Germany, but is a neutral country."

"It is now under our protection. But as for you, Mr. Suten-Mdjai, you and your family are not nationals, but secondary citizens. All men of age are required to report to be recruits in the German army."

Armed men poured from the trucks Amadeus managed to stay his father from pulling his sword. "No, father, I am not afraid. I will go."

***

After a very short training, Amadeus was sent to Tanga in German East Africa to serve under Lieutenant-Colonel Paul Emil Von Lettow-Vorbeck. Despite having been forced into the German army, he still found the idea of possible combat exhilarating. He joined a force of less than a thousand men, most of African heritage.

He liked the lieutenant-colonel right away. He was someone who found the time to introduce himself to all new recruits. "I am pleased to have you. Welcome to the Tanga. What is your name soldier?"

"Amadeus Suten-Mdjai, sir."

About to move on to the next man, the lieutenant-colonel paused. "Amadeus, a good German name, but Suten-Mdjai, I am unfamiliar with it. What is your nationality?"

"I'm from Luxembourg, sir."

"Luxembourg? I have family in Luxembourg, There are no such names there. Is it Arabic?"

"No, sir. It is a title awarded to my family a long time ago."

"A title? A title for what?"

"It stands for royal warrior. I come ready to assassinate your

149

enemies."

Von Lettow-Vorbeck appeared amused and smiled. "Well, you have a new title as a member of the Schutztruppe, Africa's best fighting force."

"I shall try and do the name honor."

"Yes, I think you will."

***

Amadeus and the rest of the troop rushed to the main square. When the men were assembled, the waiting commander began. "The war in Europe has started. Every country has taken sides. Many will die and, in the end, this will be remembered as the Great War. I cannot account for how the battle will fare back home, only for how we present ourselves here, in Africa. Our scouts tell us the British are preparing an amphibious assault against our position here in Tanga. They outnumber us eight to one. It's a shame they're coming so ill-prepared."

A chuckle rippled through the company.

Von Lettow-Vorbeck smiled and raised a hand for silence. "I have faith in each and every one of you to make a full accounting of yourselves in the coming battle. We have prepared ourselves for this moment, let's not waste it."

The local African contingent, the Askaris, let loose their war cry. Amadeus, posted with them, found the shout contagious and joined in.

The sun had set by the time the British attacked the town, giving Amadeus and his comrades the cover of night. With the Askaris yelling out their war cry, they fell upon the British troops in the dark, attacking from behind and drawing them from the main battle.

As Amadeus and the Askaris charged, many of the British troops tried to break and run but one soldier directly in his path remained unfazed, raised his rifle and took a steady aim at him. With no chance of avoiding the shot, Amadeus angled the broad side of his sword just as the English soldier fired. The flat of the blade banged against his chest, as it caught the bullet mid-blade. The hard Damascus steel withstood the impact and in the next instant slashed through the surprised enemy, severing his head.

As he ran along, Amadeus noted the large number of beehives in the area and an idea flashed through his head. Hacking through each hive as he passed, the bees became infuriated and chased after him and any others in the area. The British troops in close proximity were set upon by the buzzing swarms. Amadeus chuckled. Tens of thousands of bees filled the air, stinging the enemy. Flailing away, the British dropped their weapons and ran for the shore and the transport boats they'd come in.

Amadeus joined up with Von Lettow-Vorbeck in town. "What news from your quarter, Amadeus?"

He licked at the honey coating his sword. "A stinging victory for you, Commander!"

Chapter Twenty-Six

Robert rolled the sword in his hands, checking it over from all angles. "Why is it so beat up?"

Alexander retrieved the weapon from him. "He used it against all manner of enemy armaments; guns, bayonets and the odd vehicle, with his weapon bearing all the marks of the long campaign.

On November 13th 1918, they captured the town of Kasama. Only then did they learn the Great War was over. Throughout the years, they had battled against vastly superior forces which kept them on the run with little chance to resupply, but in all that time, they never lost the field. They were the only German forces to go undefeated."

Robert lifted his coffee and glanced at his watch. "Look at the time. I gotta go." He took the last sip and smacked his lips. "Carlos, you make a mean cup of coffee. Must be in the blood."

On the way to his car, he stopped by the blue van and rapped on the door. It slid open to reveal the two men he'd assigned to watch Suten-Mdjai. "Pack it up, guys. He made you. See you at the office."

The driver nodded. "Sure thing, boss. See you there."

He made one more stop at the newspaper where Steven Bishop worked. He wanted to have a little chat with the editor.

***

Alexander watched both Director Grimmson and the blue van pull out of the lot. He turned from the window and found Carlos holding a fresh espresso. "Ah, thank you. Director Grimmson is correct in his assessment—you do make a great cup of coffee."

He took a sip of his espresso and then looked out of the window one more time to make sure. "Alright, Carlos, you know what to do."

"Yes, Mr. Suten-Mdjai, sir. I go now."

***

Robert walked right past the reception desk on his way to the editor's office. "Tell Hank I'm on my way up."

As he neared the editor's door, Hank stepped out to meet him. "Hi, Bob, what can I do for you?"

"Cut the crap, you know damned well why I'm here."

Hank stopped in front of his personal secretary. "Sally, be a sweetheart and get me and Director Grimmson a couple of coffees, will you?"

"Right away, Hank. What do you take in your coffee, Mr. Grimmson?"

"Thank you, black would be fine."

Hank waved toward his office. "Come on in. Let's sit and chat for a bit shall we?"

Robert followed Hank into his wood paneled office and sank into a large, heavily padded leather chair. "Ah. Hank, you got the best office furniture in town."

Hank sat down behind his desk. "So what do you want, Bob?"

Sally walked in and handed them their coffees. Taking a sip, Robert waited until she left the room. "Listen, I know this story is great copy and helps sell the odd paper, but something's a little fishy here. Yesterday, when those Baptist zealots beat me on the head, your man Bishop was there, front and center. Now I know what you're going to say, but hear me out. I'm not here to give him or you a hard time. I pulled my men off Suten-Mdjai this morning. Though I still have a few

153

unanswered questions, I need all the manpower I can lay my hands on to find these killers. And if I keep men on Alexander, the higher ups are going to start to wonder why I don't bring him in."

"I thought I heard yesterday you were ready to make arrests. Wasn't Chief Flaherty saying just last night they were closing in?"

"You heard right, and no, we aren't, not unless you consider 1,135 possibles closing in. And something keeps telling me there's a connection between these killers and Suten-Mdjai. A connection I need to figure out."

Hank tugged at his short goatee. "Thanks for the inside info you gave us earlier. You have no idea how we need to sell papers. With the Internet and all, our industry is doomed. But until such time as the owners pull the plug, I'm going to do my best to keep my circulation up. If I'm reading between the lines correctly, you want my people to tail the guy for you. My people are reporters, not cops, for heaven's sake."

Robert chuckled. "I know that. No, I just want your people to keep up the heat, that's all. Let the public think we're focused on this guy. I'm hoping the real killers will think they're in the clear and let their guard down."

"How am I going to do that?"

"Hey, you're one of the panelists on *Viewpoint* aren't you? The killings are supposed to be today's topic. I'll leave it to you to figure it out."

Robert finished his coffee and got up, Hank rising with him. "I'll see what I can do, but no promises."

Robert shook his hand and headed for the door. "Thanks. I'll call in a renewal of my subscription tomorrow."

Hank laughed and made a mock kicking motion at his behind.

"Get out of here!"

***

David sat down and pulled the lid off a large caramel Macchiato. Taking his first sip, he logged onto his work station and prepared to start another workday.

The phone rang, and without looking away from his screen, he picked up the receiver. "Good morning, David here."

"Good morning, David. How are you doing today?"

He froze and read the caller ID.

"Hello...David...are you there?"

"Oh, sorry Dr. Bellemore. I was drinking my morning coffee."

Dr. Bellemore chuckled on the other end. "Yes, yes, yes. We all have our priorities."

David scowled at the mouthpiece. "Uh, Dr. Bellemore, why are you calling?"

"I wanted to find out how you were doing. It's been three months since your last visit and you were supposed you come see me yesterday. We need to reschedule your missed appointment."

"Do I have to, Doc?"

"Yes, unfortunately you do. I need to provide a quarterly report."

"I feel fine."

Dr. Bellemore sighed. "We've been over this before. The terms of your release require quarterly checkups. When you can demonstrate to me a complete recovery, I can recommend a change when I file my findings, but until then, our visits will continue. And if they don't, then I am required to report that as well. You wouldn't want that, would you?"

"No, I wouldn't." David fidgeted with his pen for a moment then sent it bouncing across the room. "Alright, when would you like me to come in?"

"If it will make you more comfortable, how tonight, same time as last time, after all my other clients have gone home."

"Yeah, I would like that."

"We'll see you then."

"Okay, Doc, good-bye."

When he heard the click, David slammed the phone down. For the rest of the morning, he brooded at his desk. Just shy of eleven o'clock, Lakshanthan showed up to take him for an early lunch.

They headed down the street to one of the local eateries and found a table where, after some coaxing, Lakshanthan managed to get the waitress to change the channel from *Sportsbeat* "There's something on I think we'll want to see."

"Welcome ladies and gentlemen to *Viewpoint*. Today's topic, terrorism in New York. Is it real?"

"With me today are my usual panelists and special guest is Senator Joshua Pallabee of the Homeland Security Oversight Committee."

"As we are all aware, New York City and its suburbs have been hit by a crime wave with one very troubling issue. The perpetrators, who call themselves The Sword Masters, are decapitating their victims and demanding American foreign policy changes. Local and federal officials claim they are not foreign terrorists but misguided Americans. Senator, I'll give you first crack at this. What's your take?"

Senator Pallabee straightened in his chair, stared into the camera and pursed his lips before answering. "Thank you, Michael, for the opportunity to address the American people here today. Let me begin by pointing out that since 9-11, no foreign terrorists have been able to penetrate American soil. The numerous failsafe measures we have instituted since the inception of Homeland Security have more than met the challenges posed from outside.

"Nevertheless, no system is infallible, and perhaps one day our defenses may be penetrated. Heaven help us if that ever happens, which is why we must stay strong in our resolve.

"But that day, in my opinion, is not today. More than likely, what we have is an incongruence in the management of this situation that needs retuning."

The host interjected. "Okay panel, you've heard the remarks from the senator, what say you?"

The panel, news people from both sides of the spectrum, right and left wing, erupted into a debate over what constituted a terrorist, and whether they need be from other countries. Arguments raged over the videos and the demands, the police efforts and the efforts of Homeland Security. As a result of the senator's comments, Director Grimmson and Police Chief Flaherty's names were bandied about.

"Senator Pallabee, do you think the United States should reconsider its foreign policies in light of what has happened here this past week?"

The senator puffed up in his chair. "American policy is to never give in to demands, whether from terrorist organizations or from elsewhere."

"But surely, Senator, you must now and then have misgivings about our always being the target."

"I answer to my constituents, and until they direct me otherwise, I will maintain the status quo."

The focus of the conversation changed again, and David became

157

bored with the debate. Concentrating on his turkey sandwich and soup, he half listened as he ate.

"What about this fellow caught at the airport with all those swords. The Sword Master is his moniker as well. From what I understand, he arrived here courtesy of the State Department."

David refocused on the television.

An interesting note dealt with no known terrorist organizations being affiliated with the Sword Masters. The discussion changed to a possible conspiracy theory and cover up. Senator Pallabee was queried as to what the State Department's involvement a question which the flustered senator tried to side step.

The half hour program soon came to an end with the host looking for summations. The lack of an affiliation, the localization of the attacks and the targets being non-traditional Americans—the first an illegal alien—led the panel to the conclusion that the assassins were not terrorists but homegrown radicals.

Lakshanthan tapped the table. "So? What do you think?"

"It's like Saleem feared. They aren't taking us seriously."

"Perhaps, or perhaps they are just afraid to admit it. Don't you think he hinted at a change in policy if his electorate was behind it?"

David tapped the side of his nose. "Hmm…maybe so. The only thing that caught my attention was the mention of the guy importing the swords. It rings a bell with me."

"So who do you think he is? A copycat?"

"No, my instructor. In fact, I have class with him tonight!"

***

Ivan gunned the engine and laid on the horn. "Come on, Saleem!

158

I've got somewhere to go!"

Saleem pounded down the steps, threw his duffel bag in in the backseat, and then climbed into the front. "Are we meeting the others?"

"Nah, it's just you and me. Miguel isn't feeling well, Lakshanthan's busy with somethin', and David says he has class tonight."

"Class? What kind of class?"

"How the hell should I know. I didn't ask him. Who cares, anyway?"

"And Miguel isn't sick."

"Maybe he's just sick of us. Ha ha!"

Saleem grimaced, and Ivan elbowed him in the ribs. "Lighten up. Being grumpy ain't good for ya."

"So where are we going?"

"I have to take care of some business, and then we can go out and get drunk."

"You know I don't drink."

"Yeah, but I do."

"Okay, but I hope we have some fun on this trip."

Chapter Twenty-Seven

Steve wanted to milk every aspect of the story as far as it could go. With Hank detailing the part about the imported swords on television, people would be clamoring for all the little details. The local news station always paid him well. Between the paper and the television coverage, this was going to be his sweetest freelance story ever, with his name attached to every byline.

It hadn't taken a lot to convince the two airport inspection officers to do interviews. "Listen. Before we start, I need the baggage worker, Mohamed El-Barai."

Munroe sneered. "Jesus Christ! What the hell do you want him for?"

"Is there a problem?"

"Yeah, since you ask, I think there is." Jim motioned to his partner. "Tim, go get that camel jockey in here."

While Steve set up his equipment, Munroe continued to rant. "You wonder why we let these people into our country. They're terrorists, every one of them. It's in their blood. They're so used to killing each other back home, they bring that same mindset with them when they come here. If it was up to me, I'd deport each and every last one of them."

Steve tilted the camera so Munroe filled the screen. He doubted the fellow knew the thing was on, so he decided to goad him a little further. "Isn't that the whole thing why they come? Our door is open to new immigrants, no matter where they originate. Didn't Alexander Suten-Mdjai come here as a new American? I understand he and his wife were granted citizenship by our State Department."

160

Jim looked at him as if he'd just found a new compatriot. "Exactly my point. What's wrong with us that we let in every crazy who wants in? One of these days the normal people just aren't going to take it anymore."

"What's normal?"

"People like me…and you." Tim and Mohamed entered the room. "Not him."

Mohamed glanced about for a second then frowned. "I thank Allah every day I am not like you."

"Ya see what I mean? No respect for this country and the people who built it. They bang on our door to come in, promising to become good Americans. We make a place in this world where everyone wants to come, but once they get here…phht!...the promise of loving America goes right out the window. Guys like him should be thanking guys like me for giving them somewhere safe to be, unlike their homelands where they blow each other up every day."

He rolled his eyes as Mohamed and Jim started to yell at each other while Tim tried to intervene. Steve's cell rang. "Hold up, guys. We'll never get done with you arguing. Everyone take a breather while I answer this call."

Mohamed, Jim and Tim all shut up and sat down, glowering at each other, while Steve pulled his cell out of his pocket. "Bishop here."

"Mr. Bishop, I'm calling to tell you of my disappointment with your cohorts on *Viewpoint*."

"Hello, Pastor Wamsley. What upset you about the show today?"

"In short, they wrote off those heinous acts as nothing more than common crimes by common Americans."

"Pastor, you must remember, they don't want to unduly scare the public."

"Scaring the public is exactly what is needed. It is often through fear that wayward sheep return to the flock."

"Hmm, point taken. But the show has already aired. What can I do about it now?"

"Be at the Sword Master's gym in an hour. I'll make sure you get good footage of the evils this man represents."

"One hour, got it. Will you be there?"

"I have other matters to attend to. I am continuing to take you into my confidence, Mr. Bishop. Don't disappoint me again."

"I'll be there."

Pastor Wamsley hung up.

The arguments began again. "Okay, guys, let's get through this without killing each other. I only have time for one take."

***

Could Bishop could be trusted? A knock on Pastor Wamsley's door disturbed his reverie. His assistant, Alan, poked his head into the room. "Excuse me, Pastor, your guest is here."

"Thank you. I'll be there in a moment."

He stood up and brushed his outfit with his fingers, making sure it appeared as crease-free as possible. Glancing in a mirror he checked to see if his coiffure was in place. Satisfied, he turned to ensure the backside of his robes had no rumples.

Striding through the double parlor doors, he found a tall man with salt-and-pepper hair standing with his hands behind his back and pursed lips. Two dark-suited men hovered in the background. Pastor Wamsley held his hands out in welcome. "Senator Pallabee, thank you for coming to see me on such short notice."

After hesitating, the senator unclasped his hands from behind him and offered one to the Pastor. "I'm on a tight schedule. I just finished a television show and must soon be on my way to Washington, but there is always time for a man of the cloth."

Wamsley clasped the senator's within both of his and held firm. "Yes, I know. I just watched the program myself. A troubling issue, I must say, very troubling."

Senator Pallabee tried to pull free but Wamsley held firm. He looked at his captured hand then returned his gaze to Wamsley. "So how may I help you, Pastor?"

Now I have his solid attention. He smiled. "No, Senator, it's the other way around. It's how I can help you." Letting go of the Senator's hand, he led him toward his quarters. "If you wouldn't mind, I prefer to discuss this in my private office."

The senator nodded. "We won't be long." The two men in suits glanced at one another, but remained where they were.

***

Steve pushed the speed limit, trying to meet the deadline. The interview had degraded into a slur session and almost resulted in fisticuffs. Once he turned the camera off, Munroe lost all interest and stormed off, defusing the situation. Nevertheless, Steve had lost several valuable minutes getting his video finished and sent off to the station.

He arrived at Suten-Mdjais building just in time to notice four men jump out of a dark sedan and go into the building. He was not surprised that one was the protester who had hit the Homeland Security man over the head the day before.

Grabbing his camera, he raced into the building, cursing as the

163

elevator doors closed before him. He took the steps, instead, two at a time. He entered the foyer in time to hear the protestations of the receptionist as the men brushed past her. He followed them into a large open room with equipment stations around the perimeter. His jaw dropped at the large number of swords mounted on the walls in glass cases with racks of weapons lined up below.

The receptionist came to stand beside him and nodded toward the four men a few steps ahead. "Are you with them?"

"No, I'm a reporter, here to cover a story."

Camera aimed to the middle of the room, he recorded Alexander Suten-Mdjai surrounded by a dozen or so men holding wooden swords. The intruders approached them. Suten-Mdjai stepped away from the others. "May I help you gentlemen?"

At that moment, Steve noticed the group carried baseball bats, held close to their bodies. The lead man smashed his weapon into the nearest table, sending it crashing down and its contents to the floor. "We're here to shut you down, you freak!"

The others followed suit. Alexander waved his students back, "Jasmine, call the police please." The receptionist fled to the outer office.

One of the men approached him. "Call the cops on me, will ya?" He swung his bat at Alexander's head.

Alexander dodged the blow with ease and rapped the man hard across the shoulder with his wooden sword. The man cried out in obvious pain.

Alexander stepped back. "If this were a real sword, you would be dead."

Another man joined in the fray and both set after Alexander, swinging wildly. He stepped between them and dealt two quick blows with the sword before either could react. A smile crossed his face. "Dead and deader."

The four men closed in, circling Alexander. As they tensed and lifted their bats, he feinted at the two in front of him then, when they stepped back, he spun and attacked the two to his rear. The only sounds were the thwacks of his wooden sword hitting the men and their groans. In short order, all four assailants lay on the floor with the sword master in the middle, unscathed.

The students broke into a round of applause. Alexander flourished the sword and took a deep bow in their direction.

The intruders helped each other rise then stumbled out of the room. Once they were gone, Steve turned back to find Alexander Suten-Mdjai next to him.

"Mr. Bishop, I believe. I've seen your news reports. How can I help you?"

Caught off guard, he fumbled with his camera. "I, uh, would love to interview you, if you wouldn't mind."

Alexander squinted one eye at him and tilted his head as if studying him. After a pause, he smiled. "You can see me after my classes are finished." He rejoined his group to a fresh round of applause while Steve retreated to a corner next to a large espresso machine to sit and wait. He connected his camera to his notebook and fired off the footage, adding his comments. He would wait the rest of the day, if he had to.

Chapter Twenty-Eight

The lighting fizzled in a ghostly manner, making odd shadows in the stairwell, and Cesar held the rail to be sure of his footing while he climbed.

He reached the door to his friend's apartment. From inside, he could hear the television. *Good, he's home.*

He rapped on the wooden door. After a few moments with no response, he pounded again. "Miguel, open the door. It's me, Cesar."

A few more seconds passed before he heard someone plodding toward the entry. The sound of the lock unlatching seemed to take forever until the door swung open halfway. "What do you want?"

"What do ya mean, what do I want? I come to see ya. Can I come in?"

Miguel opened the door the rest of the way then headed back into the apartment. Cesar closed the door behind him and followed.

Miguel went straight for a sofa and slumped into it, facing the television. Picking up the remote from the cushion beside him, he scanned through the channels. Cesar found an empty chair and sat on the edge of the seat, leaning forward so as not to sink back into it. "So watcha been doin'?"

Miguel continued channel surf. When he passed the same station for the second time, he stopped. "Nothin' on."

"Hey, forget that! How ya feelin'? We was wonderin' when ya'd be comin' back ta work?"

"Work?"

"Ya work, stupid! You feelin' okay?"

Miguel shrugged. "Eddy told me not to come in until I was feeling

166

okay."

"Yeah, well Eddy says if ya don't come back soon, you ain't got no job no more. What's wrong with ya anyway?"

Miguel looked at him then back at the television. Cesar began to be concerned. "Come on, out with it. What's eating you?"

"You ever wonder about anything you did and wish you hadn't?"

"Sure, every time I get drunk." He laughed, hoping to lighten the mood.

A small smile passed over Miguel's face then it returned to the grim expression. "Naw, I mean, important stuff, stuff that changes you. Life and death stuff."

"You dying? What's wrong with you?"

"No, I'm not dying. Never mind, you don't understand."

Cesar scratched behind his ear. "I don't get it. You talking about that bitch who got killed? She had it comin'."

"I don't know anymore…maybe…maybe not."

Cesar caught himself from sliding backward into the lounge chair. "Miguel, you didn't have something to do with killing that bitch, did ya?"

Miguel waved a hand in dismissal. "No, I'm just saying, uh, maybe you better go. My show's coming on."

He glanced over to the television and back to Miguel. "On the shopping channel?"

"Never mind. Listen, I just want to be alone tonight. I'll see you tomorrow."

Cesar got up. "Okay, see ya on the job. Make sure ya show. That Eddy's a bastard and might can ya."

Miguel walked him out. "I'll be there."

Heading down the weirdly lit stairwell, Cesar scratched at his head one more time and headed out into the street.

***

A simple, hand-painted FEED THE PEOPLE was scrawled across the door, with a mail slot below. When Detective Brown tried the knob, he found it locked, so he rapped five times then stepped back.

He glanced up and down the hallway at all the other, identical doors sharing the floor. Each one with a hand-painted name and a mail slot, all of them closed. At least forty, and this, the fourth of seven floors. He chuckled. "That's a lot of doors."

The one he stood in front of remained closed so this time he pounded five times instead of knocking. This time, a scraping sound was followed by footsteps drawing near. The lock clicked and the door swung open.

The slim East Indian man stuck his head out. "Can I help you?"

"Lakshanthan Vairaviyar, perhaps you remember me? Detective Brown, NYPD. I need to ask you a few more questions."

"Ah, yes, Detective. I do recall. Come in, how can I be of assistance?"

He stepped into a single room office, maybe ten by twenty, or perhaps a little smaller. A desk and three chairs comprised the furniture. Hung along one wall were a large number of photographs of people, all Asian. Probably people helped by the charity. Along another wall was a lopsided stack of large boxes. Overall, the room appeared in some disarray. "This is your headquarters?"

Lakshanthan smiled. "It is only, how would you say, a necessity. I am required to maintain an office for my charity status."

"Hmm, pretty Spartan. What's a unit like this run you?"

168

"Everything included...almost four grand a month."

"Four thousand a month!" He thought back to the door he just entered, thinking of all the doors out in the hall. "Someone's got a sweet deal running here. Gotta be cutting into the donations pretty good." He whistled long and low, and a small scowl appeared on Lakshanthan's face.

"I'm sure you didn't come to assess my office space." He sat on one of the wooden chairs by the desk. "What's on your mind?"

"Huh? Oh, sorry. Actually, I'm following up another lead. From the beginning, we believe the perps, or at least one of them, knew the victim. I discovered when I went and visited the temple that they have a complete data base on all their members. When I asked who would have access to it, I found out that, days before the murder, you took a copy with you. Now why would you do that?"

Lakshanthan rose, went to the boxes lined against the wall and pulled a flyer from the one on top. He handed it to Detective Brown. "Mailing lists. Some of our best contributors are people from back home who have made it here in America."

Brown sat down and stroked his chin. "Yeah, I kinda thunk that myself. But nobody I spoke to has heard from you. So I figured I better come over here and get the answer from the horse's mouth."

Lakshanthan waved a hand around the room. "Do you see all of my hardworking support staff? No? That's because I don't have any. This is a one man operation. I have a part time worker who comes here two days a week to do the books and that's it. The simple answer, Detective, is I just haven't got around to it yet."

Brown got up from his seat and offered his hand to Lakshanthan. "Thanks for clearing that up. Well, best be going, have a good day, Mr. Vairaviyar."

He let himself out and started down the hallway. When he heard the door close behind him he stopped and pulled out his notepad. Scrolling through his list of names he came to Lakshanthan Vairaviyar and typed in SHORT LIST.

***

Carlos slipped into his favorite, dimly lit watering hole. Latin American music accompanied the dark décor, and the menu he glanced at catered to its Hispanic clientele.

From his position at the bar, Carlos scanned the room and focused on a large group of men engaged in a heated discussion in a mix of Spanish with hints of Portuguese, French and English. Grabbing his beer, he slid into an empty chair at the table and nudged the nearest fellow he knew. "What's the yelling about?"

"They're killing us,"

Carlos stopped lifting his beer and held the glass in midair. "Who's killing who?"

"Those terrorists, they're killing our people. They aren't killing Americans. They're killing people like us, immigrants."

He finished lifting his beer to his mouth and took a sip to give himself a moment to think. "That girl, *she* American."

"Phaugh! Maybe so, but she was black. Before her was the Venezuelan woman and they just killed another one of us, this time from Brazil."

"Who died?"

"You remember the guy they called Pinkie?"

"Yeah, I remember him. Stayed clear him, too. He trouble, drugs and shit."

170

"I heard he was running stuff, but that make no matter. They killed him all the same."

Carlos took another sip. "How do you know it them?"

"Who else could it be? They cut his head off."

He sat back to listen as the debate raged on. Some of the guys wanted to arm themselves while others wanted to call the police. Carlos leaned back in. "Wait a minute. Police don't know?"

One of the others waved a hand in disgust. "What do they care? It isn't one of them. He ain't white. They'll blame it on the drugs anyway."

"What exactly happened?"

"Pinkie went to do a deal with some guy. I think he was from the Russian mob. Anyway, I guess the deal went bad, and the guy shot Pinkie twice then cut his head off."

"How you know for sure?"

"His old lady was in the bedroom. She heard the whole thing. When the gun go off, she hid under the bed. Once she was sure they were gone, she came out and found Pinkie lying there, all shot up and headless."

"So she see the guy or no? Can she spot him?"

"No, she didn't see him, but she said the guy kept laughing, like everything was a big joke."

Carlos learned they'd put the girl in hiding. Sooner or later, someone would find Pinkie's body, and the news would get out. He finished his beer and decided to head back to the school. It was getting late, and Jasmine would be leaving soon, so he needed to be there.

Chapter Twenty-Nine

He'd spent the entire afternoon trying to calm down from his argument with the inspector, Munroe. Now home, Mohamed went to turn on the television to find the cable station the reporter Bishop said would air the story.

In the den, Mohamed's oldest son, Khafra, and some friends were watching a horror movie or something. "You kids can finish watching this later. I want to watch the news."

"Aw, Dad, I always watch this show."

"Then you should be spending more time doing your homework. Move."

His son surrendered his spot and handed him the remote control. "What's so important that you need to see the news right away? They'll play it again later, and meantime, I'm missing my show."

"What's important is that I am to be on it."

Khafra hunkered down on the floor in front. "Really? How come?"

Mohamed flashed through the channels. "You'll see. It's about that man I told you about."

"You mean the one—"

"Shh! Here it is."

"…and in other news today, freelance reporter Steven Bishop, in following up the terrorist beheadings, brought us this report from JFK…"

The image changed from the anchorman to one of a reporter speaking into the camera. Mohamed, Jim Munroe, and Tim Jones argued in the background.

"There you are, Dad!"

"Shh!"

"This is Steven Bishop, coming to you from JFK, where tensions are running high after a man imported thousands of swords into the city through this very airport, at the same time a series of terrible killings began."

He stepped aside and the camera zoomed in on Mohamed and the two others engaging in a verbal battle. Mohamed was trying to defend himself with Jim Munroe hurling insults and posturing in a threatening manner.

After an awful lot of yelling and name calling and what seemed like an eternity, but could not have been more than fifteen seconds, the camera cut back to Bishop.

"These three were on duty then. You draw your own conclusions. This is Steven Bishop, trying to sort it out."

The picture switched to the chuckling anchorman. "Thank you, Steven. It's good to see our airport security in such fine form. In other news—"

Mohamed switched off the television, rose from his seat and left the room. His son yelled after him, saying they treated him unfairly and calling Munroe names.

Khafra burst past him, with his friends in tow. "Come on. Let's go to my room. My computer's in there."

Mohamed was sitting at the kitchen table with a cup of tea when Khafra and his friends emerged from his room, put their shoes on and began to file out. Anger twisted his son's face. "Where are you going?"

"Out."

"Out...where?"

"Just out...with my friends."

173

The nineteen-year-old stood taller than him, but the way he now slouched and turned half away made him smaller. The eyes of the other boys were averted as well. Something was wrong. "You should stay in, Khafra. I don't want you getting into any trouble."

"I'm not the one in trouble. I won't be long." He nodded to his friends. "Come on." The four of them went out the door.

Mohamed tried to drink his tea, but he just didn't feel right. Getting up, he put his shoes and jacket on. Allah be willing, the imam would know what to do.

***

Timothy Jones turned the television off. His girlfriend, Sheila, rubbed his arm. "That reporter made you guys look like idiots."

"What am I supposed to do?"

"You should call the station. Complain about it. He misled you. You were supposed to be talking about the swords, not...that."

Timothy rose and moved to the fridge. He grabbed the open bottle of chardonnay. "Another glass?"

Sheila opened her mouth then slammed it shut in a grimace. As he waved the bottle in the air, she parted her lips again, and then closed them.

"Yes...no?"

Finally, she relented. "Yes. Tim, this is serious. What will they say at work? Will you get in trouble?"

He refilled his glass and brought the bottle over to refresh hers. "What can they do? I didn't do anything wrong. Jim and Mohamed were doing all the yelling. I just kinda sat there."

Sheila waited until he finished pouring. "Thank you. Still, you

174

were there, and it's going to be a black mark on all of you. Racism is something never to be taken lightly when it comes to work. I just don't want you to lose your job, that's all."

Tim put the bottle back in the fridge then sat down again. "Hmm, I suspect if they want to make an example of anybody, it would be Jim, but he does have a lot more seniority than me, so I might be the easier scapegoat."

"Exactly, so what are you going to do about it?"

"Maybe I better give him a call. See what he thinks."

"Jim? He's a big part of the problem. Do you think you should be calling him?"

Tim picked up the cordless phone near him. "You're probably right. Still, I'd like to hear what he has to say."

After two rings, Jim answered. "Hello."

"Hey, Jim, did you see the news?"

"Yeah, I saw that goddamned thing!"

"What do you think we should do?"

"Whatta ya mean, what should we do?"

"Don't you think management is going to be pissed?"

"Screw them! I don't give a goddamn what they think. Ain't nothin' they can do about it. I go outta my way to accommodate that sonofabitch, and look what it gets me. From now on, no more mister nice guy!"

"Okay, Jim, if you think there's nothing to worry about, I'll let you go."

Tim hung up. "He says no problem. He also says 'no more mister nice guy.'"

"Ha! When has he ever been nice?"

***

Three beers and forty-five minutes later, James Munroe still stewed over what he had watched on the television.

All the questions and answers regarding the swords and that Alexander, whatever-his-name-was, never aired. That bastard Bishop!

Noise wafted up from the basement where his wife and kids were watching a movie. He had decided not to join them but instead sat brooding in the kitchen. Jim was getting up to get himself another beer when he heard a loud crash from the living room. Rushing in, he found the front picture window shattered and a brick lying on the floor. A second came sailing in through what glass remained, sending a shower of shards across the carpet.

"What the hell?"

Jim ran to the china cabinet and pulled his rifle down from the top. "I'll goddamn show 'em!"

Running to the front door, he stepped out on the porch to see a car pulling away down the road. Hoisting his gun, he squeezed off three shots before the vehicle turned the corner and disappeared. "That'll teach 'em!"

He returned inside to find his wife and kids huddled in the front hall. "What's going on, Jim?"

"Go back to watching your movie. There's broken glass everywhere. I'll take care of things!"

She shuffled the kids back toward the family room while Jim headed into the living room. As he bent to begin picking up the mess, he could hear the siren of an approaching police car through the now busted window. "Great, just effin' great."

Chapter Thirty

David pulled into the lot, the palms of his hands damp from anxiety, though he couldn't pinpoint why. *It's only a stupid sword lesson. Probably start with something safe like a pillow fight.*

He laughed at his own joke and went to his trunk to retrieve his duffel bag.

In the elevator, he glanced at his watch. *Six forty-six, fourteen minutes early.*

When the doors opened, he found a police officer next to the front desk, talking to a very cute receptionist. For a moment he wondered about the cop's presence, but then his mind returned to the girl. *If she's still here when class is over, maybe I'll ask her out.*

"Good evening. I'm David Crombie, here for my lesson. And you are...?"

"Welcome, David. I'm Jasmine, Alexander's assistant. If you'll follow me, I'll introduce you."

She got up and preceded him into the main hall. David gawked. The room was huge. Jasmine led him toward a man engaged in a conversation with another policeman. "Alexander, one of your seven o'clock's is here."

The officer closed his notebook. "I guess we're done here, Mr. Suten-Mdjai. Thank you for your time. I'll get back to you if there is anything to report."

As the fellow headed out, David offered his hand to the remaining man. "Hi, I'm here for my class."

Before the instructor could answer, a shout came from behind him. "Alexander, are you okay?"

He turned to find the most voluptuous woman he could ever remember seeing standing in the doorway. Tall, with long brown hair and full red lips, he could feel his libido rise.

His host excused himself and went to the woman. "Lucia, don't worry yourself, I'm fine."

The girl placed a hand on his chest. "I heard the news and came straight away."

"It was nothing, merely a little interruption. The men involved are gone, with a few bruises, and I'm no worse for wear. Besides, it was good exercise."

She tilted her head up and placed a quick kiss on his lips. "I should have figured as much, I know you can handle yourself."

"I've just hired a driver—Carlos. Let him take you home. I still have classes to teach. I'll see you afterward."

"Maybe I'll wait here. It's only a couple of hours, and then we can go out for dinner."

Alexander laughed. "So! It's not me you're worried about, it's dinner."

He gave her a quick small spank, and she danced away then turned with flushed cheeks. "You are such a rogue."

"That's why you love me. But now... Lucia, let me get back to my work. Have Carlos make you an espresso. He's a marvel at it."

Lucia diverted her attention to two men sitting near one wall. "Which one of you is Carlos?"

A Latin American-looking fellow stood. "At your service, Mrs. Suten-Mdjai. I make coffee now."

Alexander returned to David, smiled, and threw his arms wide. "Where were we?"

David opened his mouth to speak, but another man walked in.

178

"Mr. Suten-Mdjai, I came as quick as I could. Is everything taken care of?"

Alexander held up a finger to David and faced the new man. "Director Grimmson, so nice of you to stop in. Yes, everything is taken care of. The police have come and gone and I, Jasmine, and those clients of mine who were present have all given our statements."

"Please then, if you wouldn't mind, can you bring me up to speed?"

Alexander sighed and waved David toward the huge commercial coffeemaker. "Why don't you join my wife for an espresso. I shan't be long, and it's still a few more minutes until seven anyway."

The newcomer was the one from Homeland Security. A moment of nervousness passed. The man never looked his way, focused instead on Alexander Suten-Mdjai. David had nothing to worry about.

He walked over to where Lucia stood. Once again, excitement rushed over him at being so near her. He held out his hand. "Hi, I'm David Crombie."

Before she could react, Carlos interceded. "Hi, I'm Carlos. You want a coffee, too?"

The other man, having already risen, shook David's hand. "Stephen Bishop, pleased to meet you."

Lucia smiled. "Lucia Suten-Mdjai."

David gripped the tips of her fingers, bent and brought his lips over her knuckles. "Mine is the pleasure to meet such a beautiful woman."

Lucia pulled away from David's grasp, leaving a sudden chill in the air. "A pleasure to meet you, Mr. Crombie." She spun in Alexander's direction. Did she think he was coming on to her? He thought about it a moment. Yes, he did try too hard, but normally he

179

didn't suffer such rejection. In fact, most women fell for that line.

"How you take your coffee, sir?"

"I'm more of a caramel Macchiato type, is that possible?"

Carlos smiled. "It take just a minute."

David did his best to engage Lucia in idle chat while Carlos toiled away at the coffees. During the next few minutes, a number of other men entered the room.

When a clock on the wall struck seven, Alexander broke off his conversation and walked over to the other men. "Good evening, gentlemen. If you would all follow me into the middle of the room, we shall commence with your lesson."

David hefted his wooden practice sword, surprised at the heaviness. Alexander pointed out that the middle of the swords were hollowed out and filled with lead to give them the appropriate weight.

He took them through exercises involving balance, hand-eye coordination, body positioning, and more. Director Grimmson also participated in the class, to David's amazement.

Near the end of the lesson, they had the opportunity to try out their new skills in disarming each other. Everyone put on headgear so no unfortunate accidents would happen. David got paired with a sorely out of shape middle-aged guy, David discovered the fellow owned a batliff like the Klingons on Star Trek, and wanted to learn how to use it. The only thing David could think of was loser with a capital *L*.

When the call came to begin fighting, it didn't take him long to hit the guy with a sharp whack across the shoulder and send him reeling. Each time he tried to recover, David hit him hard and sent him tumbling again. He still held his sword while on his knees, and David had pulled back to rap the fool as hard as possible when a hard tap against his headgear sent him to the mat.

Alexander loomed over him. "I told you to disarm him, not try and hurt him. It's obvious you're much more skilled than him. You could have accomplished your goal easily."

David got up feeling sheepish and brushed himself off. "I'm sorry. I guess I just got carried away."

Alexander's expression softened as he reached down to help the Trekkie up. "Apologize to him, not me. But in the future, I'll make sure to pair you with someone more skilled."

The lessons ended without further incident, and David waited for the other students to file out before approaching Alexander. Once again, a brief moment of panic overtook him when Director Grimmson stood beside him.

Alexander and Carlos finished putting everything away and came over to the tables near the coffee machine where Lucia and Mr. Bishop still sat waiting. David and the Homeland Security guy joined them.

David rustled through his duffel and pulled out his great-grandfather's sword. "Alexander, I wanted you to take a look at this. It's a family heirloom."

Alexander hefted it, sighted it with a critical eye, and then, across the palms of his hands, offered it back. "An excellent weapon, a US Roby model 1860, I believe. A beautiful saber sword. It's an heirloom, you say?" His left hand swept across the room. "Something I have a penchant for, as you can see."

David took a few steps to his right to focus on the wall and the mounted swords in their cases. "I took a moment to peek around and saw this one here. It appears very similar."

Alexander retrieved the sword from its case, offering it to David to hold. "The saber sword is the preferred weapon of the cavalryman. The French Cavalry Commander, General Chablis is quoted as saying

'The saber is the cavalryman's science of survival.' The history of the saber goes back to the Hussars, where my ancestor got this one. This is the sword of Kazimir Suten-Mdjai."

The Tale Of Kazimir Suren-Mdjai

On Kazimir's thirtieth birthday, his close friend Miloš came to see him. "Kaz, I must talk with you."

Engaged in his fitness exercises, Kazimir paused. "Why have you come empty-handed then, and where is the wine?"

"The wine?"

Kazimir excused himself from the men he practiced with. "Yes, the wine, you fool! Surely you have not forgotten today is my birthday. At thirty years of age, I can finally be treated as an elder with the Hussars."

Miloš put a weak smile on his face. "My apologies. My thoughts were elsewhere."

"What is it, Miloš? What's wrong?"

"News from Maritsa. The Ottomans have slaughtered the king and the Serbian forces."

Kazimir slumped against a nearby post. "My father went with yours to train the king's army. Any news of him?"

"It was a massacre. Almost all were lost. I fear that I am now lord, and you are sword master here."

My father, gone. He pounded the post with his fist. "Why were we not there?"

"Prince Lazar felt it prudent to remain behind."

"What? Is he a coward?"

Miloš reached out and placed a hand on Kazimir's shoulder.

"Kaz, my friend, we would be dead as well. He says we're not ready to fight them. In the meantime, he must unite the Serbian people."

Kazimir's mind raced as he considered what his friend had told him. *I'm just a mercenary, accustomed to carrying out missions, assassinating the enemy. Who am I to train an army?* "We need an advantage of some kind, something the Ottomans don't have."

"Think, Kaz, think. What can we do different? Only then can we avenge your father and mine."

He straightened himself up. "Come, Miloš."

"Come, come where?"

"To get the wine."

***

Miloš waved at the gathered horsemen. "Ten years of training my cavalry, and still Lazar does not think this is the answer."

Kazimir watered his horse in the Dubravnica River. He glanced about at all the others then back at his friend Miloš. "I have done all I can in training and weaponry. These men with the saber swords I have given them are as formidable a heavy cavalry unit as there is. I tell you, they will turn the tide of any battle on open ground."

The hard pounding of the hooves of a scout rider approaching made both men pause as the man reined up in front of them. "My lord, a contingent of Ottoman soldiers, just beyond the bend. I estimate several thousand, mostly on foot."

Miloš signaled to his men to mount up. "Well, Kaz, it looks like King Lazar is about to be proven either right or wrong."

Kazimir climbed into his saddle. "My bet is wrong. I'm ready when you are."

"And so, my lord, we routed the Ottomans with ease. I doubt they will so easily foray into our territory again."

King Lazar sat still for a moment, mulling over the news. Finally, he wagged a finger at Miloš and Kazimir. "You're correct in your assumption they'll not easily foray here again. No, next time they'll return with a proper army, not some overgrown scouting party. We must make haste to be ready for such an incursion. Miloš, you're certain the enemy lacked the ability to counter this heavy cavalry of yours?"

"From what we encountered, I would say so. Our sword master Kazimir has trained our men with his saber sword to strike fear in the Ottomans."

"So, Kazimir, can you prepare this force in haste?"

"Yes, my lord, in the name of my father, and all his fathers before him, I'm ready for the test."

Lazar clapped both men on the shoulders. "Then I expect the two of you to get to work. The fate of the Serbian people now lies in your hands. I hope you're up to the task."

I hope I am as well.

***

Miloš entered the room and waved a large flagon in the air. "Why is it, that I must always bring the wine?"

"Because, you are a lord and can command it from your vassals. Where I, an honest working man, must buy it."

Miloš broke out laughing. "For what the king is paying you, you could buy me and all I control. An honest man indeed."

"I never said I was poor, only honest."

"A toast then, to honesty."

Kazimir stayed the hand of Miloš before he drank. "No, it is fifteen years now since Marica. Let us drink to our fathers."

"Harrumph, you are right as usual. To our fathers."

The two men clicked their wine mugs and drained them. A pounding at the door broke the somber reverie as a messenger entered. "My lord, King Lazar calls your men to arms. The Ottomans have entered our lands and are bearing down on Prokuplje. He wishes to intercept them before they get there. He leaves on the morrow with the main army. The Bosnians are sending reinforcements there as well. I am told to tell you, God speed."

So it begins. We'll need more than just God's speed to make it through.

***

The mist rose from the surrounding hillsides. As sunrise peeked over the horizon, Kazimir could see through the fog the Ottoman army breaking camp by the town of Pločnik. King Lazar had been right. This was no expeditionary force of a few thousand men.

Miloš came up from behind him to peer over his shoulder. "It's said Sultan Murad leads this force. Should we kill him and defeat his army; the Ottomans would bother us no more."

"That'll be no easy task. They're ready for us this time. Even with the Bosnians, they must have as many as twenty thousand more men than us."

185

"That will make the victory all the sweeter."

"Miloš, you're crazy."

He jumped up into his saddle. "Crazy? No, I am visionary."

Kazimir mounted his horse. "Let's pray your vision brings us a victory then."

***

Kazimir wiped the perspiration from his brow. The morning mist had given way to a blistering sun making the wearing of his armor uncomfortable in the exertion of the battle. The forces of the Ottoman Empire were broken and running. From across the field, he could hear Miloš yelling. "After them! We must kill Murad!"

He watched as Miloš broke from the battle to pursue what must be the Sultan's retinue. "Miloš! Wait! You cannot do it alone!"

Kazimir whipped his horse in a desperate attempt to catch up with his friend. Striking down fleeing Ottoman's as he rode, the distance closed, but not fast enough for his liking. A team of archers from the sultan's bodyguard stopped to take aim. A hail of arrows sped toward Miloš. Three struck his horse, which tumbled to the ground in its death throes. Miloš spilled into the turf, not to rise. By the time Kazimir got there, the archers were retreating and he could dismount without fear of being shot at. "Miloš, do you yet live?"

Miloš lifted his headed then collapsed back into the sod. "Did he get away?"

As he knelt down beside his friend, Kazimir spotted the broken shaft of an arrow sticking out from the man. "You are indeed crazy. Let's hope this wound is not mortal."

As if noticing it for the first time, Miloš reached for the shaft

186

remnant extruding from his shoulder. "Let's hope you're right. Otherwise, it will really ruin what's been a good day for me."

Kazimir chuckled and helped his friend up. Looking behind him, he took stock of the remnants of the retreating Ottoman force heading south. "I fear they'll be back."

Miloš struggled up into the saddle of Kazimir's horse. "Next time, I kill him for sure."

Or they'll kill you. I fear the worst.

***

Kazimir tightened the straps holding his chest plate in place. Three years since Pločnik and the Ottomans were once again knocking on the Balkan door. The year before, they'd tried to come in through Macedonia, only to be repelled. Each time, they returned with more troops.

I'm getting old for this. Is their supply of fresh bodies endless?

"Kaz! There you are! Come, we must talk."

"What, Miloš? I'm busy getting ready."

Miloš scoffed. "Why you even bother wearing that stuff, I'll never understand. You go through every fight with nary a scratch. Your armor looks as new as the day you had it commissioned. But never mind that. We'll just be a moment."

Kazimir followed Miloš into a tent to find ten others of noble blood sitting around in a circle. "What is it? Why are we gathered?"

"We're making a pact. We will not leave the battlefield without Murad's head. In this mission, the others will agree if you're with us. What say you?"

He studied the faces of the lords, one to another. In many, he

187

could identify the nervous expectancy of his answer. Some wanting him there for his sword, others hoping he would say no so the mission would be scuttled. A minimal nod or two mixed in as these men recognized the direness of the decision. Twelve hardy knights to charge the formidable bodyguard of the sultan.

"Miloš, as I've said before, you're crazy."

"These men are willing to try. But they feel you'll make the difference between success and failure. Your skills are special. There is no match to your sword. How many did you kill at Pločnik? Thirty? Forty? And at least that many again at Dubravnica. It's up to you. Tell me you'll agree."

He ran his hand over his face, ending with a grip on his beard and chin. As he took the time to ponder the decision, he thought of the large enemy force waiting for them at Kosovo. *Miloš is right. No matter how many times we defeat the Ottomans, they'll keep returning as long as Murad lives. And sooner or later, they'll win. He must be assassinated.*

"I agree."

A small cheer from some of the men erupted and ended with Miloš slapping him across the back. "It's decided then. When the battle is at its fever, we'll ride and attack the sultan's position before he has a chance to flee."

***

His battle plan appeared to be working. The heavy cavalry succeeded in punching through the lines of the Ottoman troops, which allowed the foot soldiers the opportunity to charge through and attack the archers in the rear positions. The group of twelve stayed close together as they hacked away at the muddled mass of soldiers. The flags waved for just such a charge when the commander of the left wing surprised everyone and left the field.

Dismay ran through the men around him. Yells of "We are betrayed!" echoed across the field. Kazimir found himself beside Miloš. "What now?"

Miloš spat on the ground. "King Lazar has cursed them, *'Whoever is a Serb and of Serb birth, and of Serb blood and heritage, and comes not to the Battle of Kosovo, may he never have the progeny his heart desires, neither son nor daughter. May nothing grow that his hand sows, neither dark wine nor white wheat. And let him be cursed from all ages to all ages.'"*

Miloš stood up in his saddle. "We must do it now. Rally here that we might charge together."

The knights gathered and Miloš gave the order to charge. He and the others burst through the light cavalry trying to intercept them and headed straight for the main bodyguard force surrounding the sultan.

The ensuing crash of the horses and their sabers against the shields and pikes of the defenders fought to silence the cries of the men as they were killed or maimed.

Kazimir swung in madness, as did his compatriots, and the enemy died all around them. But the bodyguard forces were at least one hundred and they were a mere dozen. One by one, the knights were pulled from their steeds and died. His own steed fell from the blows and cuts it suffered, and he leapt free to roll into the midst of the enemy.

Seven of his comrades, including Miloš, remained astride their horses, and Kazimir made his way to their sides. Together they worked to clear themselves of the mass of soldiers.

The command tent stood right before them, and Miloš jumped

189

down to join Kazimir and rush through the opening. Once inside, it took a brief moment to recognize Murad stacked behind ten men. Four rushed, and Kazimir engaged them. Miloš sidestepped the group and charged the remainder in an attempt to get at the sultan.

"Wait for me, Miloš!"

His cry came too late. Miloš attacked the group. His first stroke split a man in half and the second he dispatched just as well, but their swords were too many as they found the weak spots in his armor.

Kazimir finished the last of his four and weighed in to the fight. In short quick strokes, he methodically cut down the rest, and without so much as a hint of a pause, split open the sultan so his innards spilled onto the carpet under his feet.

Pulling Miloš up, Kazimir lifted the man onto his shoulder.

Miloš lifted his head. "Did we get him?"

"Yes, we got him."

"Then I can at last rest."

As Kazimir stepped back out onto the pitch he felt Miloš slump. Putting him down, he placed a hand on his compatriot's face. "Yes, my friend, now you can rest."

A quick glance showed his fellow knights were down to two, and in the time it took him to find a steed and mount it, down to one. What remained of the body guard gave way, and the two sped toward their own lines.

As they rode, keeping low from the arrows singing overhead, the noble called out. "Miloš?"

"Dead."

"And the sultan?"

Kazimir hesitated. "Miloš killed him."

"Then *his* is the glory."

From that point, they rode on in silence, the battle being all but over with the Ottoman Empire emerging victorious.

A single tear streaked down Kazimir's face. *Good-bye, Miloš. I fear it has not been enough.*

Chapter Thirty-One

"Come on, darling. I'm starving!" Lucia tapped a toe showing her impatience.

Alexander replaced the sword into its case. "I'm sorry, gentlemen. But as you can see, I am called away. Mr. Bishop, I promised you an interview. Perhaps you would be kind enough to join us for dinner?"

"That would be my pleasure."

"Carlos, go get the car. Mr. Grimmson, perhaps we can continue our conversation another time. David, it was nice to see you again. I'm glad you are well. Now, gentlemen, if you do not mind, I must close up and get my wife out to dinner before I'm in real trouble."

Robert gathered his jacket and followed the young man out the door. As they waited for the elevator, there was a nervous twitch on David's face. "Are you a friend of Alexander's?"

"Huh? Uh, oh, no. Just a student."

Robert eyed the duffel bag David Crombie carried. "You know, you really shouldn't be bringing that sword out and about."

"Why?"

"Don't you read the news?"

"Yeah, I read the news, but just because I have a sword, it doesn't mean I'm one of them. I bet there must be a hundred guys in this town with a sword. No, wait, make that a thousand!"

The bell rang as the doors opened and the two of them stepped in. "My guess is it's probably closer to five thousand, but that's not the point. The point is you're the only person walking around with one."

David's face flushed. "Are you kidding me? Did you see that great big Klingon thing the one guy brought? What he call it...a

192

batliff?"

Robert held a hand up defensively. "Take it easy. I'm just saying it might be better to leave that thing at home lest anybody get the wrong idea."

The doors opened on the main floor, and David walked out. "Whatever."

Robert stopped and made a mental note to check into this guy in the morning. In the meantime, he figured he'd better phone the office before he called it a night. Once he reached his staff, he got the feedback on everything over the last couple of hours. Lots of dead ends, no real new leads.

"One other thing, Bob. You remember that airport inspector, James Munroe? He shot some Islamic teenager. Kid's in the hospital right now."

"Jesus Christ! What made him do that?"

"Apparently he and his buddies were throwing bricks through Munroe's windows."

"And so he thinks the answer is to start shooting. What's he think this is, the Wild West?"

"I hear the kid's hurt pretty bad, might not make it."

"What started it all?"

"Munroe got caught on the news throwing a bunch of racial slurs around."

Robert lowered the phone to take a deep breath and calm down. *Just great. A crazy mucking things up.* He returned to the call. "That's all we need, a race riot over this. Which hospital?"

"I'll get back to you on that ASAP."

"Alright. In the meantime, we need to work damage control on this. Get the mayor's office up to speed and contact the local Islamic

193

authorities. I want this under wraps, pronto."

Robert hung up and jumped into his car. Before he pulled out of the lot, he got the callback on the hospital and the room number. They had called the police to make sure there were enough blue shirts at the hospital, and a few more at Munroe's house. He also received the information on the Islamic League. The mosque was on his way. *Maybe I'd better stop and recruit a little help.*

***

Mohamed felt a hand on his shoulder and looked up from his kneeling position "Ah, Imam, praise Allah."

"What troubles you, Mohamed? You have knelt at prayers for over an hour now. I know you to be a man of religion, but even I can recognize the difference between a good Muslim expressing his faith and one troubled by his inner soul."

Mohamed rolled up his mat and rose. "Imam, I would speak with you in private, if I may."

The imam gestured toward a private room to his left. "Come this way, my son."

Once ensconced in the private chamber, Mohamed sat cross-legged on a divan by the wall.

"Now tell, Mohamed. What troubles you?"

"It's my oldest, Imam. He no longer respects the authority in my own house."

The imam paused for several moments and stroked his beard. "It is hard to counsel you on this. Back home, I would bring the boy in to recite the Koran until he learned it by memory. But here in America, it is hard to counter the culture of its people."

194

"Then what am I to do?"

"You must put your faith in Allah. He will give you the guidance I cannot. Follow his instructions, and your son will return to you."

There was a soft rap at the door, followed by one of the young acolytes sticking his head in. "My apology, Imam. There is a man from the government here to see you."

"Show him in."

Mohamed recognized the man as he entered. "Mr. Grimmson, what are you doing here?"

"Hello, Mohamed. I have come to have a word with your imam here."

The imam bowed and waved a salutation. "What is it I may help you with?"

"I would prefer to speak with you in private."

"Speak up. Don't worry about Mohamed hearing what you have to say. He is a valued elder of this mosque."

Mr. Grimmson took a deep breath. "We have a situation, Imam. Four Muslim youths were involved in a shooting." He then glanced at Mohamed. "It involved James Munroe."

Mohamed felt the shock run through him. "They shot Mr. Munroe?"

"No, it's the other way around, he shot one of them. They were vandalizing his home, and he took action."

The urge to rush out started him moving, but the imam put a staying hand on his shoulder. "And how am I to help, Mr. Grimmson?"

"I'm afraid of a racial spillover from this. Your presence and leadership would be instrumental in calming things."

"Then I will come with you. Let me get my shoes."

Mohamed jumped up. "I'm coming too."

195

The imam placed a hand on Mohamed's chest. "Why? You have your issues to tend to, leave this matter to me."

"Because, Imam, one of those four boys may be my son."

Chapter Thirty-Two

David arrived at his apartment and threw on the lights. Inside, his nerves were all ajumble and he proceeded straight away to his liquor cabinet to retrieve what he needed to make a Manhattan.

Back in the kitchen, he took the large tumbler, loaded in four ice cubes then splashed in the vermouth and a substantial amount of Canadian whisky. Figuring what the hell, he rooted through the fridge and even managed to produce a jar of maraschino cherries.

Retrieving two for his cocktail, he kicked off his shoes, found the remote for his sound system, located a nice jazz station and sat back to relax. The first sip turned out to be more of a gulp and caught him a little by surprise as he coughed and juggled his drink so as not to spill any.

He wondered what made him so jittery. *I suppose the close meeting with that Homeland Security guy didn't help.*

As he warmed with the liquor and calmed himself, his mind went to other things. He thought of Lucia and wondered why he couldn't get a girl like that. He felt, if given the time, he could woo her to him. After all, he always succeeded with every other woman, why should she be any different? He imagined what she would be like naked and in his bed.

Thinking of her brought on an erection, but he resisted the urge to satisfy it. Instead, he came to the conclusion he should head out and see what he could pick up at the bar.

He went to call some friends, when he noticed the message saved light on his phone. Picking it up, he entered his voice mail to listen.

"Hey, David. Me and Saleem bagged one. Come meet us for a

drink. You know where."

David wondered for a moment whether Ivan meant what he thought Ivan meant, and then decided he'd go find out and headed for the door.

Riding down in the elevator, he met up with Alice, a girl who lived in the building, one David already had tasted. "Hi, Alice. Doing anything tonight? Maybe we could hook up later?"

She gave him a long stare before responding. "I don't think so."

"Oh? Some other time then?"

"Probably not."

They stood silent until the elevator door opened. As she stepped out, she glanced back as the doors began to close. "Never again, David. Not in a million years."

The door closed to continue the elevator's descent catching David unable to respond. *Not in a million years? What's up with her?* Still, as he walked across the street toward the bar, it troubled him. Rejection from a female was a rare occurrence, and tonight he'd felt the effects twice. He entertained the idea, for only the briefest of moments, of losing his touch, and then convinced himself otherwise. He had merely encountered two bitches in one night.

He walked into the bar and found the room almost empty. The after business crowd gone home already, he found it easy to spot Ivan and Saleem. He made his way over and plunked down next to Ivan. "What're you drinking?"

"Vodka and Coke, want one?"

The waitress showed and he decided to order a Manhattan instead, preferring not to change what he'd started with earlier.

As the three of them finished their "How you doings" a man came in and headed straight for them. Ivan looked up and smiled. "Nicky!

Come, sit, have a drink." Ivan hailed the server. "Waitress! Another vodka and Coke!"

Nicky gave a wary stare at both him and Saleem then sat down across from Ivan. "Ivan, where the hell have you been?"

"Right here Nicky, drinking."

"You were supposed to meet me. We had a job to do."

Ivan chuckled. "Don't worry. Job is done."

Nicky scowled at Saleem and David one more time, and David felt the animosity.

Nicky's attention returned to Ivan. "What have I told you about hanging with this cretin? He is effin' scum! And who is this other asshole? So did you collect? So help me Ivan, if you messed this up, it'll be your ass, not mine."

"Relax, Nicky. I collected...both ends. The little spic tried to shortchange me so I made short work of him."

"You killed him?"

"Da, what'cha think? I'm going to let him cheat us?"

Nicky slumped back in his chair, glowered at Saleem and David once more then pushed his chair back and rose. "Okay, fine, you did the right thing. Bring it with you when you get back. I'll leave you with these cockroaches."

"See ya later, Nicky."

As Nicky turned to go he bumped into Lakshanthan walking in. ""What's this, more dog shit?"

He pushed his way past Lakshanthan and headed out the door.

David nudged Ivan. "Nice friend there. We should all hang out some time."

Though Saleem scowled, Ivan broke into laughter. "Ha! That's what I like about you David. Nothing gets you down."

He thought back to his earlier rejections. "Well, not exactly nothing."

Lakshanthan plopped into the seat vacated by Nicky. "What's going on, anyway? Who was that guy?"

"Don't ask me. He's Ivan's friend. I have no idea."

Ivan ran a quick hand through his hair. "Don't worry, fella's. It has nothing to do with you. Just a little business is all."

Lakshanthan paused to tell the waitress what he wanted. "It's not every day I get called dog shit."

David snickered. "You got off easy. We got called cockroaches."

Saleem leaned in. "If it were up to me, I would cut off his head!"

Lakshanthan held up a hand. "Shh! Don't talk out loud like that. With this place nearly empty, our voices will carry, and we don't need people hearing you talking about that stuff. Besides, I thought we agreed no more beheadings for a while. At least until things cool down. I don't need any more visits from the police."

David felt startled. "You got visited by the police? When?"

"Today, again, this is the second time."

"Do you think they know?"

"No, I don't think so. I probably just fit the profile. You know, foreign, from a country where beheadings are usual. It's just racial profiling, nothing you'll ever have to worry about."

Dave took a long drink from his Manhattan then banged the empty glass down. "I got you topped. You'll never guess who I ran into tonight."

All eyes focused on him. "Who?"

"Homeland Security Director Robert Grimmson, the guy we saw on TV. I tell you, the guy is clueless. I even had my great-grandfather's sword with me. He told me to be careful with it and leave it at home so

200

no one would get the wrong opinion of me."

Ivan laughed. "No shit!"

"No shit. He showed up at my class tonight. Must be trying to get an inside perspective on what it's like to wield a sword."

Saleem slammed the table with an open hand. "You think this is all a joke. Maybe he's onto you as well, David. We should not be sitting here doing nothing. We should be out cutting off heads by the dozen, as quickly as we can, to make America change. Just like we did tonight."

Lakshanthan pointed a finger at Saleem. "You decapitated someone tonight?"

Ivan spread his hands in apology. "He was already dead. I shot him full of holes. Saleem just decided, why not cut off his head as well. He had his sword with him. I figured, what the hell."

"David, do not publish this. We can use it to our advantage."

Saleem flushed. "What are we waiting for?"

Lakshanthan steepled his fingers. "Saleem, you must stop your infernal shouting. What we have been waiting for is about to begin. On my way over I heard some Muslim youths got shot up by some redneck American. They say it has to do with the murders. Let them think another group is imitating us, doing decapitations. The political fallout from this is sure to cause a lot of turmoil. The politicians cannot have fighting in the streets over this. They will have to make some changes. We must bide our time."

Saleem slumped back in his chair, biting back whatever he wanted to say.

Lakshanthan pointed at David. "As for you, just be careful. You may think otherwise, but do not expect Director Grimmson to be a fool. He isn't in charge for nothing."

David nodded but smiled. He planned at the next Sword Master session to pair up with Grimmson to apply a few good hits to the Homeland Security Director.

Chapter Thirty-Three

Robert sat at his desk, nursing a coffee as he read over the reports. Having a hard time focusing, he blamed it on a lack of sleep, the night before another example of how this case continued to test him.

Arriving at the hospital, they had encountered a large group of family members and friends of all four boys. The police officers on the scene were using some common sense and had segregated the group into a closed cafeteria. Even still, by the time he arrived, the shouting and verbal threats were at almost a fever pitch. He thanked his lucky stars for having the foresight to bring the imam who immediately took charge and quieted the group by leading them in prayer. The nurse on duty told him the badly injured boy was in surgery in an attempt to save his life. He could sense the anxiety in the crowd, so once assured the imam had things in hand, he made a quick exit.

The workout session with Alexander turned out to be another culprit in sapping his strength. *I've got to make a serious attempt to get back in shape. Yeah, how many times have I said that before?*

Also, he'd just received a severe lecture from the mayor. Nothing pissed him off more than being called incompetent.

Closing his blurry eyes, he rubbed at them, then gave up and called everyone into his office. "Okay guys, I don't have the energy today to read through all these reports, so I want you to give me the CliffsNotes versions." He put his feet up, stretched back and closed his eyes. "Don't worry, I'm listening."

"When it comes to the police searches, they're still going on, and the detectives are working hard to narrow the list, but no concrete leads at this time."

"So far, the Internet traces have come up nil. We've been going back over chat group logs searching for keywords like swords and sword master but nothing really predates these killings."

"We finished cross-referencing everybody taking those classes and have come up with squat. They're all clean."

"In chatting with all of our overseas partners in the war on terror, we have no leads."

"All the forensic reports are in, no traces at any of the crime scenes to tell us who the perpetrators are."

When they fell silent, he opened his eyes and glared out at them, the anger in him boiling over. "So, in other words, these five thousand word reports you guys keep posting for me have nothing to say. Maybe if you didn't spend so much time writing reports you might actually come up with some answers."

Sitting up, he was about to continue his verbal assault on his staff when his telephone rang. "Grimmson."

"Bobby, me boy, I got some bad news. They found another body this morn, head cut clean off and a couple of gunshot wounds to boot."

"That's just great, Seamus, just effin' great. As if my ass wasn't already in a wringer deep enough. My brain trust here just finished telling me they know jack shit and now you call with this crap!"

"Now don't be taking out on me, Bobby boy. We're doing all we can. My detectives are interviewing day and night, everybody's pulling extra shifts and all leave's cancelled."

"Sorry, I guess I'm just a bit frazzled. See you for lunch? Same place?"

"Should I bring a bib this time?"

Robert, despite his mood, chuckled. "Thanks, I needed that. My treat, see you there."

After hanging up the phone he glared at the group gathered about his desk. "Well, what the hell are you all waiting for? Get to work and bring me some answers!"

Once the room cleared, he drafted his own short note to send off to the deputy secretary. Looking again at all the massive email reports sent by his staff, he decided to make them attachments and chuckled to himself. *Let him read through them. It should keep him out of my hair for a couple of days.*

***

In Central Park, he hunted down Seamus at the hot dog stand. "Hi, thanks for coming."

Seamus patted his stomach. "Ya know, this stuff ain't exactly good fer me."

"Gee, I thought you learned from me last time. You don't eat these things, you wear them."

Seamus chuckled. "So what's eating at you, Bobby boy?"

Robert took a moment to put mustard on a dog and wrap his paper napkin around it tight. "These murders, of course. Tell me about the new one."

"I don't rightly know whether this one's done by the same guys. They put a couple of bullets in him before they cut his head off. Coroner's office says he was dead before they did it. The victim has a rap sheet a mile long, narcotics. We're wondering if it was a hit made to look like the Sword Masters."

"Hmm, plausible. There's been no new claims by these guys online."

"We can't keep this one quiet. You know fer sure someone's

gonna talk."

"I figured. Who you got working lead on these cases?"

"Detective Brown. He's a pretty sharp cookie for a blackie."

Robert rolled his eyes. "Seamus, you really got to work on what you say, you old rube."

"Com'on now, give me some credit. I coulda' used the *N* word."

The two of them laughed together and stopped to finish their dogs.

"So what does Detective Brown think? Different perps, or the same?"

"He won't rule anything out. When they examined the cut, they said it was similar to the murder of the prostitute, same type of serrations, which were different from the ones found on the first two victims. But forensics says any number of swords could leave the same marks. It's not an exact science like matching bullets."

"Okay, so what about suspects…any?"

"We have a list, but it's still pretty long. Until we get a match of known associates on the list together, we're not going to pare it down any further. I'll tell you one thing. This last murder, word on the street is, it's a Russian. Funny thing though, there're no Russians on our short list."

"Hmm, so what's the plan?"

"We're going to shake down a couple of places in Little Moscow in a bit, see if we can rattle a cage or two and get some answers."

Robert strolled over to a wall, and leaned on it, looking over at the surrounding parkland. "You know, Seamus, no matter which way we slice it, we're in for a shit load of grief on this one. The Mayor's office is threatening us with the National Guard if this gets out of hand. What with those Muslim kids last night and now this, I'll be lucky if I still have a job come five o'clock."

Seamus joined him and patted him on the back. "Bobby, yer ever the pessimist. We've been through worse before and weathered the storm. Don't worry, we'll catch these bastards soon enough."

"We have? I can't recall when."

Seamus laughed. "Ya, maybe yer right at that. But look at it this way, after all's said and done, they'll probably elect ya President."

Robert groaned. "That's all I need to be happy, surrounded by politicians."

His cell went off, and after listening to the message, he waved to Seamus. "Gotta go, Seamus, time to get back and kick a few asses around the office, get some results."

"Give 'em hell, Bobby boy!"

Chapter Thirty-Four

Carlos entered the bar where he'd heard about the beheading the day before. Expecting to find the same group of guys, he wasn't disappointed to see them gathered round the same table. He purchased a beer and found a seat near the group. Unlike the day before, the discussion at the table was quiet, subdued, and full of furtive glances.

"You with us, Carlos?"

Not even settled into his seat, he noted a few of the men staring at him. "With you for what?"

"We goin' to hit those Russians today. I think your cousin would approve."

He needed time to think. "I finish my beer first?"

"Make it quick, we leavin' soon."

He pounded his beer and followed the others out the back door, where they piled into a couple of cars. One of the guys pressed a gun into his hand. He handed it back. "I don't know how to shoot."

The pistol was replaced by a facão. He rotated the large blade in his hand, memories of home and working his cousin's plantation coming to mind. *This is going to be a messy business.*

***

At his restaurant, Nikita sat with all of his other guys at the table, fuming. He motioned to the fellow to his left. "Have you seen Ivan? He was supposed to meet us here. If that no good sonofabitch is sleeping off another drunk…so help me!"

"He came in late last night. My guess is he flopped in one of the rooms upstairs."

Nikita ground a fist into the palm of his other hand. "I'm gonna have to teach him a lesson."

"You want me go get him up?"

"Naw, you stay here. This is my problem."

"Suit yourself. I think he's in number twelve."

Nikita got up and started to head for the stairs when the front doors of the restaurant burst open and a group of men rushed in brandishing and firing guns. "What the hell?"

His companions broke into different directions, ducking for cover and pulling weapons themselves. The waitress screamed and dodged into the kitchen, bullets ricocheting off the walls around her as she ran. Nikita pushed over a table and dropped to the floor behind it. "Who the hell are they?"

"Damned if I know, boss. They look like spics though."

He pulled his own firearm and holding the gun over the table fired blindly toward the front of the restaurant. The gunfire ensued for half a minute, maybe more. He heard the groans of people getting hit but had no idea whether they were the guys he was shooting at or some of his own men.

It ended as quickly as it began. Nikita peered out from behind the table as the attackers fled and the screeching of tires and roar of engines confirmed their escape. "Anybody hurt?"

One of the guys hobbled up. "I took one in the leg."

He grabbed the nearest man by the shoulder and shoved him at the wounded guy. "Get him to the hospital. Did we get any of them?"

"I think I winged one in the shoulder."

Nikita walked over toward the doors, skirting the tables and chairs strewn everywhere. "I'd say you did. He's right here."

A couple of others came over and they hoisted the dazed man to a

209

chair. Blood oozed out of a shoulder wound. Nikita gave him a small slap to the face to try and rouse him. "Who the hell are you?"

"I'm...Carlos."

"Well, Carlos, you're in a heap of shit now."

The scream of sirens drew Nikita to look out the window as police cars arrived at the scene.

Nikita motioned to two of the men. "Quick, drag this trash out the back door. We'll talk to him later."

***

Miguel watched from his perch up on the fourth floor steel girders as the coffee truck pull into the yard. He could make out Cesar headed for the truck. "Cesar! Get me a black one, large."

Dropping his tools he clambered down to the ground to retrieve his coffee. He did indeed feel good about getting back to work. It kept his mind off things. But a couple of sleepless nights left him tired. As a result, he found himself pumping in a lot of black coffee just to stay awake. At least he wasn't dropping any hammers.

As he reached for the cup, he noticed Cesar eyeing at him. "What?"

"Huh? No, it's nothing."

"What nothing, something bothering you?"

"Nothing...just...I guess I'm just glad to see you back to work."

They sat down at the picnic table sipping their coffees while Cesar continued to fidget. Miguel decided to ignore it, though it looked like he was about to burst.

When they were nearly finished, Cesar opened up. "Miguel, remember that bitch from Venezuela who got killed?"

"Yeah, what of it?"

"After I visited you, I got to thinkin' maybe you had something to do with it."

Miguel stopped drinking his coffee, nervousness once again beginning to overtake him. "And?"

"And, anyway, now I'm not so sure. I was down at the pub last night and the guys were all riled up. Seems another guy got killed, head cut off and everything. This time the guy was from Brazil, and everybody got talkin'. They think it's somebody targeting immigrants like you and me. And get this…they think it was a Russian, from the Russian mob no less."

Ivan.

"So what happened?"

"What happened is the guys are going to hit the Russians today. They wanted me to go, but I said no way, I gotta go to work. Most of those guys got no jobs or what that differ."

"The last thing our people need is a war between us and the Russians. I think a lot of innocent people might get killed on both sides."

"Who's innocent? Not the Russians?"

Miguel paused to try and think. "Maybe they didn't go and nothin' happened."

"Yeah, yeah, maybe they didn't go."

Please, I hope they didn't go.

***

"Argh! Can't a guy get some sleep around here?"

Ivan stumbled out of bed and scrambled down the stairs. He

211

wondered what the hell all the racket was about. He was sporting a hangover, and his head pounded with each step he took.

Bursting into the dining room, he scanned for the waitress. "Is there any coffee?"

All but falling into the nearest chair he finally focused on the room. His momentary surprise at seeing the police officers soon became replaced by a somewhat muddled understanding that something indeed must have happened. His suspicions were confirmed by overturned tables, and a lot of people were milling about. Off to the side, paramedics were treating one of his fellow Russians.

"What the hell happened?'

Nikita came over. "What the hell happened? You big imbecile, this is what happened! A bunch of greaseballs rushed in here, shooting the place up. We're lucky no one got seriously hurt or killed. And you slept through it all like the big piece of shit that you are."

"Come on, Nicky, give me a break. You know me, I could sleep through anything."

Nikita grabbed him by the collar and yanked him up and through the double doors into the kitchen. "Listen to me, Ivan. These spics didn't just decide to waltz in here and start shooting for the hell of it. Now I'm thinking it might be because you killed that one yesterday."

"Aw Nicky, it ain't the first time we killed someone who was cheating us. The guy was just a lowlife. I didn't think anyway woulda' cared whether he got killed or not."

Nikita let go of his collar. "Yeah, I know, that's what so strange. Is there anything you aren't telling me?"

"No, Nicky, it's like I told you. The guy was skimmin', big time. I couldn't let him get away with it. You always said, someone cheating us, send a message."

Nikita gave him a gentle slap in the face. "Okay, go get your coffee. I'll take care of things in there. I want you to stay in the kitchen for now."

"Sure thing, Nicky. Mind if I get something to eat?"

"Sure, Ivan, sure. Just stay in here."

Ivan helped himself to a large plate of beef stroganoff and found a spot to sit and eat. He thought for a minute about the Latinos trying to bump off Nicky and the boys. He couldn't help but laugh, but after a short guffaw, even that hurt. He decided to concentrate on finishing his food then getting back to bed.

Chapter Thirty-Five

He punched the intercom. "Send him in, Susan."

Through his open door, he could hear his receptionist. "Dr. Bellemore will see you now, Mr. Crombie."

Seated behind a high narrow table, Bellemore typed away into a keyboard as David entered the room.

"Good afternoon doc, I'm here as I agreed."

He motioned toward a couple of tall leather wingbacks near the window. "Sit, David. I'll be right with you."

David lowered himself into the chair he usually occupied when he visited. Despite the deep padding, he always looked unsettled.

He finished typing, picked up his notebook computer and walked over. "Comfortable?"

His patient smiled and nodded. "Yes."

"You're sure?"

"Yeah."

He hesitated, and then sat in the opposite chair. "Okay, that's good. As long as you're sure. I want you to be comfortable for these sessions. It's important."

David smiled faintly and nodded once more. "I'm sure."

"Good. Now, this won't take too long. We'll have you out of here in no time."

"Sounds good, Doc."

"Let's begin then, shall we? I'm going to ask you a series of questions and I want you to give me the first thing that comes to mind."

They'd played this game before. The first few questions would be meaningless, just to get David comfortable.

214

"What is your name?"

"David Percival Crombie."

"How old are you?"

"I'm twenty-seven."

"What is your favorite color?"

"Blue."

"What city is this?"

"New York."

He paused before his next question. "Where is the city of Riberalta?"

His patient blinked and Doctor Bellemore could recognize the tension rising in him as his hands gripped tighter on the arms of the chair. "I don't know, Doc, sounds Latin American."

"Have you ever been to Riberalta?"

"How could I have ever been there? I don't even know where it is."

He leaned forward. "Think now, David. Have you ever just passed through somewhere new? I've done it myself a hundred times. You drive along and get off the highway and *presto*, you're in some unknown backwater town you've never heard of before. You don't even stop except maybe for gas and then you're on your way again. And the little town in nowhere fades to the deep recesses of your memory. What I'm asking you to do is search in those deep recesses of your mind and see if you can find that little town."

David sat and appeared to be concentrating hard. After a long moment he threw up his hands. "Sorry, Doc, no can do, coming up blank."

"Alright David, let's move on shall we?"

"Sure." David visibly relaxed again and loosened his grip on the

215

arms of his chair.

"What is my name?"

"You? You're the doc."

"My name, please, David."

"Sorry, okay, Doctor Bellemore."

"And the name of my receptionist?"

David winked. "Susan. She's a hot one, Doc."

"Who is Jennifer?"

David froze and beads of perspiration broke out on his forehead.
"Huh, I don't know any Jennifer."

"This is just like the game with the town. I bet you've run into a
dozen Jennifers in your life. Surely you must remember one of them."

David chuckled. "You know, Doc, I've dated a lot of women in
my life, and damned if I can remember any of them named Jennifer."

"Then think back further, college perhaps, or even high school."

A moment passed while David stared out the window with a blank
expression. "Sorry doc, no Jennifers."

He sat back and sighed. "Okay David, instead of word
association, we're going to try some picture association. When I show
you a picture, I want you to tell me what you see."

He punched a few keys and brought up an image of David.
"Who's this?"

David laughed and slumped into the chair once more. "Me, of
course!"

"Yes, David, that's you."

He repeated the process. This time the image changed to a man
surrounded by American flags.

David tensed again. "The President of the United States."

On the third time, he filled the screen with the image of an older

216

woman.

David relaxed once more. "That's my mom."

"Very good, David, one more."

This time the image featured a pretty girl of twenty-five with long blond hair.

David sat silent.

He waited a bit. "David?"

"I…I don't know her."

"Look again, David. Are you sure?"

David glanced one more time then tried to push the screen away. "I'm telling you, I don't know her."

Doctor Bellemore closed his notebook with a sigh. "Alright David, that's enough for today. You can go now."

David's relief changed him. All the tension lines in his face disappeared and his pupils dilated. "I got a hot date tonight, gotta run."

"You know David, your mother is worried about you being out and about with these killers on the loose, these self-proclaimed Sword Masters, just a bunch of crazed people. If ever there was a group needing my services, it would be them."

David turned and faced him, purpled with anger. His hands balled into fists at his sides. "What would you know? They have a cause!"

He felt taken aback by David's reaction. "Okay David, okay, just a comment. I'm only telling you what your mother has been saying to me, don't take it personal."

David's fists uncurled, he sighed and his shoulders slumped, then he gave a weak smile. "Sorry, Doc, been a rough day. I'll catch ya later."

"Good-bye, David."

He waited until David left the room then returned to his desk and opened his notebook and began to record his notations.

Memory block still firmly in place. As long as I make no references to his past, he seems in control though showing some signs of anxiety when confronted with authority. But I fear what would happen should something trigger his recall. It may be time for stronger treatments; a relapse might cause permanent damage. I would hate to order him institutionalized, but it looms as a real possibility.

Note: Surprised at his reaction toward the terrorists, but in hindsight, I can sense his empathy toward them, another challenge to authority.

***

What now? As he climbed out of his car to head in, Robert looked up to the third story window to find out whether Alexander watched from above.

The police had notified him of Mr. Suten-Mdjais missing person report. When they informed Alexander it was felt a reasonable time frame was required before being acted on, he replied he would call back. The police were required to notify him on any dealings with Alexander right away which was why he found himself required to visit the sword master once again.

He scanned the windows to no avail. *Must be running a class.* He strode in and pushed the button for the elevator, not feeling energetic enough to try the stairs. As he waited, he glanced at his watch. Already after nine p.m. *Must be a late class.*

Robert stepped out of the elevator into the foyer and could hear the ringing of weapons clashing, real swords. He dodged around the corner to quickly see what he could see. At first he found it difficult to spot Alexander. The room, normally wide open throughout the middle, sported hundreds of mannequins. He followed the sound of Alexander's voice to find him in a small clearing in the middle surrounded by four young men, all holding long, curved blades. Samurai swords—he'd seen them often enough in the movies to recognize them.

Alexander stopped and faced him. "Good evening, Mr. Grimmson. How can I help you tonight?"

Robert appraised the four other men; all young, all fit, and all in identical clothing. "Sorry for the intrusion, but word came to me you tried to file a missing person's report."

"Yes, Carlos. He's missing and not answering his cell."

He shook his head. *Carlos. What the hell are you up to?* "It wouldn't surprise me if he's flown the coop. If he's really missing, I'll have to inform the State Department."

"Then let us not rush on this. Perhaps he will show up in the morning."

"Hmm, perhaps." Robert stared at the weapon in Alexander's hand. "Is that your own personal sword?"

Alexander pulled it up to eye level. "This? No, but it is the choice these students wish to learn, and so I have obliged them by using the same. The katana is a powerful weapon. If properly made, it can cut through much, some actually achieving notoriety as a five."

"As a five?"

"Yes, a five is the number of human bodies a blade can cut through in a single stroke. There are a number of famous blades that have reached that distinction."

"How many is that one?"

"I know not, I only recently received this weapon, having had it

219

specially made."

"Specially made?"

Alexander traced the length of the back side of the weapon. "Yes, you'll note the darkness of the blade compared to those handled by the others here. The metal used is most rare, from a meteorite of incredible density."

He reached out to touch the sword next to Alexander's finger. "I seem to recall hearing meteorites are very expensive, *especially* those of a very strong density."

"Indeed, the stone alone cost me almost two million dollars."

He whistled. "Two mil? That's a lot of cash for one sword."

"Actually this is the second. The craftsman who made this one, made another some time ago. He informed me he'd retained enough of the metal for one more."

"Did any of your ancestors use…a katana?"

"A katana? No, but over here…this is a tachi, one of the old style weapons, this blade was used by my ancestor Sakeel Suten-Mdjai.

The Tale Of Sakeel Suten-Mdjai

"Again!"

Sakeel returned to his set stance. The samurai warrior tried once more to penetrate his defenses. Each time, his attacks became more panicked, making the defense against them easier.

In the end, Sakeel once more paused at the point of lethal strike, then stepped back and bowed. "I think today's lesson must end. You grow erratic in your attack, Shoni. There is little being learned today."

Shoni plopped to the mat sitting cross legged with his sword across his knees. "That is good, because I am tired!"

220

Sakeel joined him on the mat. "Offense is fine, as long as your opponent is weaker skilled, but when crossing blades with someone your equal, it is wise to learn his moves and counter."

Shoni smiled. "I thank you for the compliment, but I know it not to be true. I am far from your equal."

Sakeel smiled. "Perhaps, perhaps not, but you grow closer every day. Do not misjudge yourself, you are very skilled."

Shoni got up to get a drink of water from a nearby pitcher. "How is it, Sakeel, that you come here, and in few short months, you are the master of the tachi, a blade you have never held before?"

"You forget, like my father before me and his father before him, and many fathers before that, I have trained with the sword since birth."

"Bah, I played with toy swords as a child as well, yet I am no match."

"That is the difference. You played, I did not."

"Huh. Well it is no matter for now. I must attend to my father's court. Will you come with me?"

Sakeel bowed again. "I am not one of your *gokenin*. I will not be welcomed."

"As the son of the shogun, I am entitled to bring to court with me who I please. And my friends who also use your services will vouch for you as well. You must come. There will be a royal feast. Something you shouldn't miss."

After the workout, food sounded real good. "Alright, as long as you speak for me."

As evening neared, they approached the castle and Sakeel began to feel some trepidation. "Look at all the guards posted. Are you sure of this, Shoni?"

As the words left his lips, the guards jumped in front of Sakeel, ordering him to halt, insisting he could not enter.

Shoni interceded and after some arguing, they allowed Sakeel in, provided he surrendered all his weapons. Grudgingly, he handed them over and followed Shoni inside.

The halls glowed wondrous as hundreds of lamps burned throughout. Artwork and frescos adorned all the walls and pillars and those people he passed in the hall were dressed in their finery, though many gave him a harsh stare followed by many whispers. He became conscious of the simple clothes he wore.

They sat down near Shoni's friends and waited. Sakeel felt a little better as many of these men were also his students. But when the food began to arrive, the serving girls ignored him. Then just as Shoni began to berate them, four guards surrounded Sakeel and hoisted him off the floor.

Shoni jumped up. "What is the meaning of this? Put that man down. He is my guest."

"My apologies, Kanrei, but the shogun has ordered it."

Shoni stormed to the front of the room to where the shogun sat, surrounded by his advisors. "Honorable father, my forgiveness for intruding, but my honor is at stake as you have ordered a guest of mine arrested."

The guards brought Sakeel to stand behind Shoni. The shogun looked around Shoni to stare for a moment at him. "These are dangerous times, my son. War may soon be upon us. The Huns are massing in Korea. How do you know he is not an enemy assassin? Rumor exists of a clan of assassins sent to destroy me."

Shoni glanced at Sakeel then back to his father. "Would the enemy send one so skilled to train us if it were so? His sword has no match from any two of ours."

222

An advisor leaned in to whisper to the shogun, who nodded, then returned his attention to Sakeel. "Why have you come to our land then stranger, and how know you our language so quickly."

"I know many languages, my lord. My father required it of me. Learning a new one is never difficult. I have come because it is said the swordsmen of Nippon-koku are rumored to be among the best of the world and your weapons unrivaled. I wished to learn and see this for myself."

"So you admit then to being a spy."

"Not a spy, but an ardent student of the blade."

"Then before the feast, we shall have entertainment. If what my son claims is true, you shall earn your meal by defeating two of my men in battle." The shogun stood. "Clear the center of the room! Bring him his weapons."

People scattered to the edges of the room while a man rushed off and retrieved Sakeel's swords. Two men stepped into the rough circle of cleared space, weapons drawn. Shoni blocked Sakeel's path to meet them. "Father! Is this fair? You send our two finest sword masters against one man."

The shogun flushed. "You said any two swords and so I have picked two. Should they kill him, then your boasting will have brought his death and I free of a spy in my midst. Should he somehow survive, then I have erred in my appointment in sword masters so replacing them would have been prudent anyway. Now, stand back and let this trial begin."

Shoni stepped out of the way and Sakeel bowed to the shogun and then to his two combatants, who returned the courtesy. He drew his tachi and his wakizashi and squared off. The two masters nodded to each other and set upon him simultaneously.

223

The sheer ferocity of the assault found Sakeel fighting for his very life. In the beginning, he could barely block their attacks. But as he fought, he counted the rhythm of their strokes. Recognizing a similarity in the pattern, he risked a gambit that resulted in his shoulder getting clipped by a blade.

One of the men stepped back and looked down at the center of his tunic where a small bead of crimson appeared. He stared wide eyed at Sakeel, bowed, and stepped out of the combat area.

With only one man to battle, Sakeel went on the offensive and in a few short strokes combined with a twist of his wrist; he disarmed the man, who dropped to his knees, arms splayed wide in surrender.

The shogun purpled and pointed toward the sword master who had bowed out of the fight first. "What is the meaning of this? Why did you stop? You gave up your comrade."

The man bowed then touched his tunic where the bloodstain showed. "My lord, I could not honorably continue. In all honesty, I should be dead. Not only did this man penetrate my defenses, but pulled short his killing stroke intentionally. I would not dishonor him by continuing."

"This fight was to the death!"

"Then to satisfy your blood thirst, I shall finish the job."

The man pulled his short sword and raised it to plunge it into his own chest but Sakeel jumped and grabbed his wrist. "There is no honor in dying."

Shoni stepped back into the circle. "Enough of this. Put your weapons away." He then turned to face the shogun. "Honorable Father, my man has won. All can see that. He has spared you your best samurais to fight another day. I say it is time to sit down and feast, as is justly warranted."

224

His father appeared about to say something when an advisor whispered to him. Nodding, he returned to his seat. "It seems, for today at least, the kanrei is correct, let us feast."

A mild cheer filled the room and everyone sat down. Attendants came to dress Sakeel's wound and the serving maids brought food to him.

As the meal finished, the shogun rose. "If the Kanrei will not object, I would convene the meeting of the war council without his guest. War will soon be upon us and I do not wish his presence unless he wishes to fight again."

Shoni nudged Sakeel. "You best go."

Sakeel rose and bowed. "Thank you for the wonderful meal. After eating so much, I need go lie down anyway."

Laughter rippled across the room as he made his way to the exit. Shoni sent two women with him. "Take care of him!"

He glanced from one maid to the other. "Perhaps I will not get as much rest as I need."

More laughter followed him out the door.

***

"Sakeel, come quickly. Shoni wants you."

He paused in the training of four youths to face the messenger. "What is it?"

"War. All men are to report to the castle at once."

One of the boys stepped forward. "We will go with you, Master Sakeel."

He smiled and knelt in front of the lad. "I am honored at your courage, but you are too young. Go now, your mothers will be looking

225

for you."

The four lads scrambled off, and Sakeel faced the messenger. "Make haste and tell Shoni I will be there shortly."

He ambled up to the castle amid the thousands of men marshaling on the grounds. In the time since the fight at the feast, many of the men now knew him from visiting his school, the first to visit being the sword master who'd resigned from the fight.

"I am here, Shoni."

"Sakeel, the Mongol fleet is in Hakata Bay. So far they have not attempted a landing as I suspect they await the balance of the invasion fleet coming from Korea. Every man must defend a post along the shore. I would have you with me."

He went to the ramparts to look out over the bay. Indeed a large number of ships now occupied the waters. "Shoni, waiting in small groups for them will only mean, where the Mongols land they will be outnumbered and swarmed by the onslaught. I have another idea."

***

Night came and the lanterns dotted the bay as the invaders stayed on their ships. Sakeel and five others pushed out from shore in a small skiff, paddling as quietly as they could. Six other parties followed in their own boats. They rowed past the front line of enemy ships who they would be wary of attack from shore.

They pulled up in silence to a large flatboat. Boarding by stealth proved easy. If not asleep, the men on board were all at ease, unprepared. Sakeel and his team set upon the men with great alacrity and killed many, sending severed heads rolling across the deck while sleeping men scrambled to find their weapons in the dark.

226

Before the Mongols could rouse themselves in sufficient numbers, Sakeel and his team retreated to the skiff and pushed off, the flatboat unable to maneuver and follow.

They repeated this throughout the night. As they neared their seventh target, Sakeel jumped on board to lead the way and parried an instant attack on him. *This one was alert and on watch.* The others rushed aboard and attacked the sleeping Mongols, leaving him to his lone battle.

The man showed tremendous skill. His attacks were quick, yet he showed no evidence of hurry. Sakeel's jaw tensed as he clenched his teeth. He was being tested as he matched stroke for stroke with this challenge. Behind him, he could hear the others already retreating to the skiff. "Come on, Suten-Mdjai, finish him and let's go."

The eyes of his assailant went wide and he stepped back. "Cousin?"

Sakeel allowed his defenses to drop as he stared in surprise at the man. Yes, definitely not a Mongol, and showing some resemblance. His attention drawn to the man before him, Sakeel was caught unaware as an arrow pierced his shoulder. He stumbled back and fell to the deck. The remaining Mongols tried to pounce on him but his combatant interceded, giving Sakeel the chance to jump onto the skiff.

They rowed away while one of the men managed to withdraw the arrow from his shoulder. Sakeel pressed a cloth against the wound to staunch the flow of blood. "Perhaps it's enough for one night. They are ready for us now."

He strained to look back through the gloom at the craft they just left. For a brief moment, he could still see the man standing on the edge, the man who called him cousin.

When they reached shore, Shoni met them. They told Shoni of

their success and those gathered around gave a cheer. "Tomorrow we will finish the job and destroy these invaders."

Sakeel, still holding a bandage to his wound, found the first place he could to sit along the rocky shore. "Tomorrow, I am leaving."

"Leaving? Leaving where?"

"Leaving here, I am going to go home and find my family."

Chapter Thirty-Six

Watching the evening news only made David angry.

After it was over, he sat at his computer. *It should be late enough. By now, everyone would be gone home.* He triggered the sub-routine redirecting his online presence through a number of firewalls to ensure no one tracked him. Being a programmer gave him inside access to a number of guarded sites without having to crack through. He felt sure not even the CIA could track his online movements.

A few more clicks, and he accessed the hard drive he sought. As he had a number of times in the past, he entered the security code and pulled up the file.

It didn't take him long to read it and make a decision to act. Picking up the telephone, he called Vairaviyar. "Lakshanthan, come pick me up, it's my turn."

"David, are you sure? There's a lot of heat out there right now."

"I'm sure. Bring Saleem if you want. He'll support me and Ivan doesn't give a shit one way or the other. God knows what's going on with Miguel, so you'll be outvoted. Now let's go, or I go without you."

He waited through the long pause on the phone.

"I'm on my way."

David hung up. He looked again one last time at the file on the screen. He closed the link and headed for the wall where his great-grandfather's saber hung.

***

Nearly nine hours later, the police still roamed the restaurant, checking things and asking questions. Nikita ordered another vodka and Coke to kill time. *Better be careful, don't want to get drunk like that jackass Ivan.*

When a dark blue sedan pulled up and two more detectives got out, he wondered if they would ever go home. The detective in the lead, a middle-aged black man, came to sit with him. "How's it going, Nicky?"

"Detective Brown. What do you care?"

"Aw, Nicky. That's no way to talk to an old friend."

"You are not my friend."

"No, I'm not. But I'm going to be. I'm thinking you and I need to get real close, chums like, you know what I mean?"

"Why? I have done nothing wrong."

"Are you sure about that? Are you sure? Because me, I gotta be wondering why a bunch of Latinos would come busting in here, shooting up the place, if you didn't do anything wrong."

"Why don't you go ask them instead of bothering me?"

"Oh, don't worry. I will. I will. But in the meantime, I'm here now, so what say we try and figure out what the hell this was all about, shall we?"

Nikita lifted his drink and sat stone-faced, deigning not to answer the question.

Detective Brown chuckled. "Now from what I know, two carloads of guys pulled up and dashed in. At least, that's what your neighbors say. That works out to what...eight guys?"

Nikita still did not reply. *I won't play his game.*

"Neighbors claim they heard a lot of shots, fifty or more, yet just one of your friends got hit. We dug that many out of the wall, but funny, they were in two directions, like somebody was shooting back.

230

Yet, when we got here, nobody had any guns. Isn't that strange?"

Nikita smiled. "Maybe they bad shots."

"Maybe, maybe, but here's where it gets weird, we found not one, but three blood spatters around the room, telling me three people got hit but just one of you is sporting a wound. Kinda makes you wonder what happened to the other two guys."

"Like I said, maybe they bad shots and shoot each other."

"Yes, now wouldn't that be convenient. Might even explain why they hit and run so fast. But what makes a lot more is sense is they didn't expect to find so many of you and your pals here. Maybe they were expecting only you, and when they came under heavy fire, they bolted and ran. But that still doesn't explain why they tried to hit you in the first place."

"So now *you're* going to explain that to me?"

Detective Brown sat back and smiled. "How am I to explain to you what you probably already know better than me? I was just wondering whether the fellow we found last night, one of your dealers, I believe, why he was found with two bullets in him and his head cut off."

For just the briefest of instants, Nikita felt startled. *Ivan never said anything about cutting his head off.* "I no know anything about that."

Detective Brown stood up. "Okay Nicky, I'll clear the place out let you get back to business. You usually have the late crowd anyway, don't you? We'll talk again soon."

The detective walked away and ordered everybody out. Once the room was clear of all police, Nikita called one of his men over. "What did you do with the greaseball?"

"I threw him in the cellar next door."

"Alright, leave him there to rot for a while. In the meantime, find

231

that drunken Cossack, Ivan, for me."

***

Cesar ordered another round of beers. He and Miguel sat at a table a bit off from the main group of regulars. He sensed they weren't too happy with him because he hadn't taken the day off and gone with them.

Nevertheless, they parked themselves close enough to hear the discussion at the main table the others were gathered round.

"I thought you said there would only be two of them there, not twelve."

"I was just as surprised as you, why the hell do you think I ran out so fast."

"We all did, but Jesus got nicked anyway, and Carlos went down."

"Do you think he's dead?"

"I dunno. But if he isn't, he will be. Those Russians will chop him into hamburger."

"What should we do, call the cops?"

"Are you crazy? They'll arrest every one of us, and probably deport us all. Better not to do nothing."

"Still, I feel bad for Carlos. He didn't even want to go. We dragged him along."

"What about that fella who bailed him out, gave him the job...that sword fella?"

"No way! Ain't he suspected of something? You keep seeing him in the news."

"I bet he's in league with those Russians. That's why Carlos

232

didn't want to go."

"Carlos is on his own now. Only God can save him."

Cesar nudged Miguel. "What'ya think? Ya think he's a goner?"

"Probably. Nothin' I can do 'bout it."

"Somebody should go talk to that fella they was mentioning, that sword fella. He got Carlos out of a jam before, maybe he can do it again. Do you believe that stuff he's one of them terrorists?"

Miguel paused from sipping his beer. "He isn't."

The finality in his voice made Cesar stare. "Yeah? What makes you so sure?"

"Huh. Oh, I don't know, I just know."

"Then maybe we should go tell him."

"You go."

"What's wrong with you, Miguel? A week ago, you were all high and mighty about how we Latinos get shit on by Americans and now you act like everything's fine and we got no problem."

"I don't want to have anything to do with this. I don't want to have anything to do anymore with swords and killing and any of that shit. I just want to be left alone."

Miguel took another drink of his beer and turned away. Pissed, Cesar grabbed his beer, drained it and stood up.

Miguel looked up at him. "Where you going?"

Cesar pulled on his jacket. "Like you said, I'm going alone. See ya at work tomorrow."

He walked out the door and hailed a cab.

The cabbie leaned over the seat. "Where to?"

"I want to go to see that sword guy that's been on the TV, but I don't know where he's at."

"No problem, we'll find him. Let me radio it in."

***

An interruption at the door drew Alexander away. Robert watched a young Latino man saying something to him in his native language, then leave, allowing Alexander to return.

"I'm sorry, Mr. Grimmson. But I must pay attention to my students. The hour is late and I need to wrap up this session."

"No problem. I'll let myself out."

As he reached the entryway, he glanced back to see Alexander lining up a number of bamboo men, and taking a huge swing with his katana. He found it interesting the number of mannequins cut in half totaled six.

Chapter Thirty-Seven

David's phone rang. It was Lakshanthan, calling from the building entrance. "I'm coming up. We have to wait for Saleem."

David let him in and made drinks while they waited. "How long until he gets here?"

"He said he'd be a bit. In the meantime, turn on the late news."

"You aren't going to like what you see." He found the remote and flicked through the menu to the news stations, picked one and sat down.

After some other headlines, the reporter got to the story they were waiting for.

"Police cordoned off a piece of Little Moscow today as a shootout between two groups occurred. Involved were members of the purported Russian mafia and a Latino drug gang.

Although no one was killed, evidence at the scene showed a large number of weapons fired and at least one Russian-American was wounded."

The camera changed to a police sergeant standing outside the crime scene. An out of camera view reporter fired questions. "What do you think this was about, Sergeant?"

"Our suspicions of what caused this are the dead dealer found early this morning. Informants tell us his killer was of Russian descent."

"I've heard the dead dealer had his head cut off, is this true?"

"Yeah, you heard right, a messy business."

"So is this death tied to the earlier killings by the group calling themselves the Sword Masters?"

"Yeah, anything's possible."

The police sergeant moved off and the reporter took his place in the picture.

"It's possible the whole thing is nothing but a drug turf war with the whole terrorist thing made up as cover. When you consider the victims to date, an opium-using Asian, a Venezuelan with ties back home, a heroin addicted hooker and a Latino dealer; one can see a pattern in all of this. Back to you."

The news anchor moved on to other stories and as David hit the mute button his phone rang. Saleem was on the other end.

"Come on up."

David popped his apartment door open then went and refreshed their drinks while finding a cola for Saleem.

He returned into the living room to find a pensive looking Lakshanthan. "See? Our message is getting lost. We've been too tentative. Saleem was right."

He heard the door close behind him.

Saleem had entered. "What was I right about?"

David turned to face him. "About the terror level of our group not being high enough, did you watch the news?"

"Yeah, I saw it. So what's the plan? If it involves another beheading, I'm in."

For his part, Lakshanthan seemed lost, deep in thought. He gave his head a small shake. "I can't believe that Homeland Security would just dismiss us, they wouldn't continue to take our threats and messages as real."

David sat down. "You're probably right. They probably do. But it's not them we need to be concerned about. It's the public in general. They're the ones who have to believe we're real and our message is change or else."

Lakshanthan teepeed his hands over his nose. David nodded to Saleem who shrugged then looked back to Lakshanthan. Only then did he realize how much the group accepted the former Tamil Tiger as the leader.

Maybe it's time for a change. "Alright, no more thinking. I say we go out tonight and pick a target that won't be misconstrued for a drug war victim, and I have just the person in mind."

Saleem, who had just sat, jumped up. "Now you're talking. Let's go."

David stood as well. "Well, Lakshanthan?"

A weary sigh escaped Lakshanthan then he rose from his seat. "Okay, okay, let's go."

***

They circled the block one more time. At three in the morning, there were almost no lights save the street lights and no sign of people either. But each time they went to park, a car would appear, or a house light would flick on somewhere nearby, making them nervous.

"Enough's enough, Lakshanthan. Park the car. No one's watching."

"I'm just trying to make sure we aren't being spotted. We're going to be the only car parked on the street."

Scanning the neighborhood, David realized he was right. "Okay, let's park a few blocks away and walk."

They went back to a spot they marked in their minds earlier as a good place to leave the car and got out. As they walked along they looked at the high-end homes.

Saleem could no longer remain quiet. "Everybody in this neighborhood must be filthy rich!"

Lakshanthan shushed him then stepped close to David as they walked. "I hope this is worth it. We're taking a big chance here. I bet some of these have security cameras."

Saleem closed ranks. "Are you kidding? This is exciting, and we're going to hit them where it will matter most, affluent America. It will make them shit themselves to learn they aren't safe in their own homes."

David led them to one of the houses, and using the lush shrubbery and trees for cover, they circled around to the back. "So far, so good, we're unnoticed. Now to break in and get down to business."

Lakshanthan grabbed hold of his arm. "What if there's an alarm?"

"There is, but I already disabled it online. The only noises will be the ones we make."

"It looks like you've thought of everything."

"Let's hope so."

He pulled out a crowbar and worked it into the space between the door and the frame. With a powerful heave, he popped the door open and the three of them rushed inside. Once in the kitchen, they stopped and listened and scanned the neighborhood once more. No lights were coming on from any of the neighbors, so far luck was on their side. No sounds from inside the house either which surprised him a bit; the break-in was noisy enough.

The two empty wine bottles on the counter told him why their entry hadn't woken anyone.

They moved through the house in darkness and found the door to what they suspected was the master bedroom. David lifted his foot and took careful aim. "I've always wanted to try this." His foot hammered

238

down onto the door right beside the handle. In a shower of splinters, the door blasted open.

They jumped in and the woman woke up screaming, but just managed a short burst before Saleem ended it with a vicious slash to the throat. As she fell back into her pillow, the blood spurted out and soaked the linen red. The man sat up, still appearing in somewhat of a daze. He turned to see his wife dying beside him and while trying to stem the flow of blood looked back at David. "Why?"

David lifted his great-grandfather's saber aloft. "You know why."

In a vicious stroke he swung and cut the man's head clean off. Saleem positioned himself near the woman and swung again, finishing the severing there as well.

Lakshanthan tapped David on the shoulder. "That's it, we're done here. Let's get out now."

"Hold on, I need a picture."

David pulled out a camera and snapped off a dozen or so quick pics, then put it back in his pocket. "Okay, let's go."

The three of them retraced their steps back to the car. When they were moving and a couple of blocks passed, Saleem let out a whoop. "That'll show them we mean business!"

They merged into a traffic flow on a main street. Lakshanthan smiled for the first time that night. "No one's catching us now. That was good work, David."

"Yes, it was, and wait until you see what I've planned next."

Chapter Thirty-Eight

A fair number of people still lingered in the cafeteria late into the night. The imam had stayed the previous night, then, after visiting the mosque for prayers for the day, returned once more that evening to maintain the vigil for those who remained.

As he walked among his parishioners still at the hospital, he found his legs weary and sought a place to sit. Someone brought him a cup of tea, which he sipped.

Gazing around the room, he was able to discern, of those remaining, besides the two policemen by the door, all were immediate family members of the four boys who'd gotten into trouble. In fact, the other three, who had been released into the custody of their parents, were seated close by. Like everyone, they were waiting for word on how the fourth fared.

He gave his head a gentle shake. *I'll never understand this country. It corrupts so easily. But I would have no doubt not one of these families would go back to their homelands. Such is the lure of America.*

He had an area of the room cleared as a makeshift spot where he could hold prayers. Waiting there on their prayer mats was the family of the injured boy.

He sighed. Making his way around the group, he stood before the father. "Mohamed, you have proved your faith to God. You should prove your faith to your family as well. Take them home. Let them sleep in their own beds."

"Imam, I dare not. What if something should happen while I am gone?"

He put a hand on Mohamed's shoulder. "Then I will send for you right away. I am here and will continue the prayers for your son while you are gone."

He faced east then kneeled down beside Mohamed. Though very tired, he put on as brave a face as he could muster. "Go now. I will keep the vigil. May Allah be merciful and restore your son to you healthy and whole."

Mohamed slumped at first then rose. "Come, children, I will take you home."

His other four children joined him, along with Mohamed's wife, rubbing sleepily at their eyes. But hardly did they take two steps toward the door when two doctors came into the cafeteria, straight for Mohamed. He gathered his family as the doctors approached.

"Mohamed El-Barai?"

"You have news?"

"Yes, Mohamed. I'm afraid we must tell you the worst. Your son is gone. The swelling in his brain as a result of the bullet was too much for him to bear. We did all we could."

The imam's heart ached at the news. He rose from the mat to go and give Mohamed and his comfort. "Allah has called Khafra to him. He must have had great need of the boy. Such is the will of Allah."

Mohamed's wife started wailing and the other Muslim women in the cafeteria took up the call. The children started to cry, and the bereft father wilted to the floor.

Some of the men behind the imam began arguing about vengeance against the infidel who killed Khafra. He turned to face them. "Do nothing. Be of good Muslim faith and respect the will of Allah."

The keening of the women grew and the two police officers who still remained came over. "Imam, you need to quiet these people. This is a hospital."

"It is their way in dealing with it. You must allow them their right to deal with death in their own way."

The two officers exchanged glances, and then returned to their posts. He focused his attention on the angry men. "We must kneel and pray. It is the only proper course of action."

He sank to the floor and the others knelt around him. As he began a prayer, the doors to the cafeteria burst open and a hospital security man came in. "What is the meaning of all this noise? You people need to shut the hell up!"

The men jumped up and attacked him. The two police officers moved to intercede, one calling for backup.

The imam struggled to his feet and moved between the parishioners and the police. He tried to pull the Muslim men away. "Please, please, you must not fight. It is not the way!"

The policemen managed to extricate the security officer from under the men and stood between the man and the group. A lot of shouting and shoving continued, and then two more officers came barreling through the double doors, billy clubs in hand. One of the Muslim faithful threw a chair.

"Stop! Stop! This is madness!"

It mattered not what council he gave. His fellow Muslims charged the club-wielding policemen. As the imam milled in the middle, trying to restore calm, he walked into one of the officers taking an errant swing and it clipped him on the temple.

As he fell to the floor, he could hear men shouting about him being hit. He managed one last "Don't fight." before fading into unconsciousness.

***

His shoulder hurt. He felt real groggy. His shoulder hurt. He could not move his arms or legs. His shoulder hurt. The air in the room felt heavy and hot. His shoulder hurt. He needed a drink of water. His shoulder hurt. He could not see as there was no light. His shoulder hurt.

The cycle had repeated itself for what seemed like days when a noise from somewhere above to and to Carlos' left bought his attention and he strained to see in the dark. There were voices, talking loud, in a language he did not know, and they sounded like they were coming nearer. He heard a rattling, like someone turning a door handle and the creak of a door swinging open was accompanied by a shaft of light. Then a click followed and the room became brilliant from a single incandescent bulb overhead.

Closing his eyes at the sudden brightness, he heard the sound of many footsteps coming down the stairs.

"So how is our guest doing?"

He peeked to find a large fellow standing before him, and in the same instant the hard slap of the man's hand crossed his left cheek before he could react. The intensity of the blow should have sent him sprawling, but the ropes tying him to the chair held.

"Not so well, I see. My friend, if you think you're not so well now, just wait a little bit and we will see how not so well you really will be."

The man placed a hand on his wounded shoulder and pressed a thumb into the wound. Carlos could do no more than scream, bound as he was.

The man withdrew his thumb. "Augh, now I have blood on me.

243

You know how much dry cleaning costs nowadays?"

When he stepped away, another took his place. Carlos, his eyes wide open now, took in the room. Five men crowded the small space. One wiped his hand on a cloth then started away. "Find out what you can from him, then finish him off and dump his body elsewhere."

As he disappeared up the steps, the others grinned, one producing a knife, another, a long heavy pipe. Carlos began to pray.

They started by hitting him with the pipe, asking a question after each blow. At first he just screamed with pain but as the beating continued, he tried to answer them in hopes they would stop. He told them all he could—his name, where he lived, where he worked, and who he worked for. The names of all who'd raided the restaurant, of his friends, his family and anybody else he could think of.

He could no longer see clearly. In a moment of respite from the attack on his body, he could hear them talk among themselves. *They will kill me now.*

The door at the stairs creaked open again. He tried to look, but his blurry vision made the scene seem surreal. A dark-clad being, like a demon, came rushing down the stairs with a sword in hand and cleaved the first man in two while the others watched and shouted obscenities at the intruder. Two reached for guns while the man with the pipe tried to fend off the sword to no avail. He died just as quick as the first as the sharp blade ran him through. The fiend twirled and slashed the third man who fell to the corner just as the fourth took aim and fired. Two shots bounced off the sword now held close to the chest of the invader who then launched the blade forward, severing the shooter's head from his body.

In an instant, the bonds holding Carlos were cut and as he was lifted from his chair, feeling as if he were floating.

244

"Come, Carlos, we must leave this black hole."

The thought of being rescued from certain death allowed him to relax ever so little and with it came the darkness of unconsciousness.

Chapter Thirty-Nine

The six o'clock alarm sounded a little louder than usual. As Robert roused and rubbed at his face he put it toward being tired. Finding these terrorists continued to consume all of his energy. If he didn't make some headway, soon he would need to take a day off, regardless, or burn up.

He glanced at his cell phone next to his bed, blinking away.

Oh, great. What the hell happened now?

An urgent message insisted he call the office. He walked into the kitchen and put on some coffee first, then sat down to make his call while it brewed.

"Morning, Bob, glad you're up. It was one hell of a night. Things got pretty warm at a couple of the hospitals."

"What happened?"

"For starters, that kid who got shot died last night."

"That's not good. How did the family take it?"

"That's just it, they didn't. A near riot broke out in the cafeteria with both the imam and a couple of officers getting hurt. They arrested six men and are holding them downtown."

"Jesus! That's all we need is a police battle with the Muslim community. Is the imam okay?"

"Yeah, he'll make it. He just got a nasty lump on the head. One of the officers suffered a broken arm and the other various cuts and bruises."

"Wonderful news. Thanks for making my day at six o'clock in the morning."

"Wait. It gets even better."

"Hold on, my coffee's ready and I think I'm going to need it."

Robert poured a large cup of black coffee then sat back down. "Okay, hit me."

"You know that fellow, Carlos Jose Santiago?"

"The one working for Suten-Mdjai? He showed up?"

"Yeah, in the hospital, with a bullet wound in his shoulder and enough busted and cracked bones to make you sick."

"Who brought him in?"

"Showed up in a cab. Cabbie says he knows nothing. He was parked when the door opened, and Carlos landed in the backseat with a note on him saying *hospital* and a C-note attached. He looked around, but whoever put Carlos in the cab was gone."

"I guess we better find out what happened to him."

"I have a man parked at the hospital waiting for him to get out of surgery. He isn't going anywhere. But I'm not finished yet."

"You mean there's more?"

Gleeful chuckling followed. "Listen to this, across town they took in a Russian mob fella with a huge sword wound. He got off lucky. Three of his friends are in the morgue, all chopped up."

"Three of them? Dead?"

"Yup, and the survivor's still in surgery."

"Alright, you've had your fun. I'm on my way in. Get everybody else out of bed and we'll go over it all when I get there."

He hung up and finished his coffee then headed for the shower. *So much for thinking about a day off.*

Robert walked into his office at the same time as a couple of his agents. "Let's snap to it, guys, I'm not supposed to beat you in."

He chuckled as they jogged off. He called out to the first person he saw. "Is the coffee made?"

Once he learned the answer to be in the affirmative he headed to the commissary, poured a coffee and headed for his office. He pulled up the online reports and smiled as they were all short and sweet but with no real progress. *At least they aren't spending the whole day typing.*

Everyone gathered in his office and he began reviewing the previous night and the steps needed that day. "The media frenzy over the dead Russians should hit any minute now. You can't hide three cut up bodies, and a fourth guy sliced open but still alive. I think we should run with the angle presented by the media yesterday, a gang war. Let them think these killings are all related and it won't happen to the average guy on the street, only if you're a thug."

One of his tech guys came in the office, ashen faced. "Bob, the other guys are sending it to your comp now. You better look at what just got posted."

Robert turned his monitor for all to see and clicked the link. A slide show popped up showing a middle aged couple dead in their bed, decapitated. He recognized the computer modulated voice as the same as from the earlier tapes. "We are the Sword Masters, and we will not be ignored any longer. Rumors of a drug war behind the decapitations are false. We are still here, and we still have our demands. Capitulate or we will continue to decapitate. No one is safe. No one."

Robert sat frozen while his staff complained.

"Jesus Christ, did you see that?"

"What the hell are we going to do, Bob?" "Who'd they kill?"

"Boy, is the shit going to hit the fan now."

"Enough!"

Everyone silenced.

"What we don't need is panic. Work with the police, find these victims, pronto. Block this thing on line ASAP. Time to get serious. Have the police bring in every remaining suspect for questioning."

"But Bob, the list is still in the hundreds."

"Then we better get started right away, shouldn't we? If I have to arrest half of New York, then that's what I'm going to do. No one else is going to get their head cut off or your heads will be rolling, along with mine. Now let's go."

About ten minutes after they scattered, he got paged. "Bob, the mayor's office on line one and Chief Flaherty on two."

"Tell the chief to hold on until after I talk to the mayor."

He sat down and gathered himself, taking a deep calming breath.

"Hello, Mr. Mayor…yes I did see the video…no we have not had a chance to…no I am not stalling…no I do not believe…yes, Mr. Mayor, I understand…yes, Mr. Mayor…good-bye."

He picked up line two. "Seamus, how the hell does the mayor see these videos so quick?"

"And good morning to you, too, Bobby boy. You know, you're not the only one monitoring what's getting posted. The mayor ordered the police to notify him the instant any new videos appear."

"So you told him?"

"Not me exactly, but yeah, my staff."

"Why the hell did you do that?"

"Now, listen here, Bobby boy. Don't start tellin' me how to do my job! The mayor is still my boss, ya know!"

"Sorry, Seamus. It's just he ripped me a new one."

"Well ya better toughen up, because ya ain't seen nothin' yet. These new murders are goin' to cause some real panic. I was just tryin' to give ya a heads up."

"Yeah, I know. So is that why you called?"

"That and lunch. It's your turn to buy."

Robert turned his attention to reviewing a number of reports. The next call he received came from the deputy secretary.

He wrapped up the call almost two hours later. One of his agents was waiting at the door. "Hey, Bob, we found the victims."

"Who were they?"

"A Dr. Bellemore, the guy's a shrink. Him and his wife, right in their home. Their state of the art security system was shut off. How stupid is that?"

"Stupid only if he was the one to turn it off. Check that out with his provider. Something tells me otherwise."

"Right boss, I'm on it."

"I'm off to go meet Chief Flaherty for lunch. When I get back, I hope to find a complete profile on this psychologist and his wife."

***

He found Seamus not alone. "G'day, Bobby. I want you to meet Detective Brown. I figured I'd shorten the communication line and have you two talk directly."

Robert shook the detective's hand. "Please to see you again, Larry. I've heard good things, and your reports have been very helpful."

"Yeah, I just want to catch these sonofabitches, and I'm hoping you're going to do whatever it takes."

"That's the plan, Larry. That's the plan. So have you been to the new crime site yet?"

"Just came from there, a real mess. So far not a lot of evidence, but from the footprints in the lawn, we know there were three of them."

250

"Only three? We're positive there's five of them. Wonder what happened to the other two?"

Standing in front of the hot dog seller, Seamus interrupted. "Lost their nerve, my guess…the usual?"

Robert nodded his approval. "Yeah, that makes sense. Hot dog, Larry?"

"Sure, extra mustard. I was thinking the same thing, which means if we rattle them a little harder, maybe they'll crack and we'll get a good lead."

Robert finished a bite then took a swig of his cola to wash it down. "Let's hope you're right. I've ordered every suspect on the list to be brought in for questioning. If one of them is in there, we might get lucky."

Seamus handed Detective Brown an extra napkin. "Here, ya might need this. Bottom line, we need to make an arrest soon or we can all kiss our arses good-bye."

They chatted for a little longer then Robert headed out. "I'll touch base with both of you prior to the nightly media statement."

Seamus waved. "Let's hope it's not our last."

Chapter Forty

Power.

It was what Pallabee had always craved. And only in the halls of government was power most succinct. It was why he started in politics. It was why he stayed in politics. Starting as a simple town council member, he worked his way up through the ranks to mayor, then state representative, then state senator, finally becoming a US Senator.

But in the last few years, his rise had suffered stagnation. The next rung up the ladder seemed to elude him. When the Department of Homeland Security became a reality, he recognized a new window of opportunity. It took all his skills to wrangle the chairman's position for the oversight committee, something his many years of stagnation came in handy for. The seniority associated with it made his selection possible, which also further infuriated him as to being the factor which best qualified him.

The list of measures available to Homeland Security was impressive, but the exacting of such would put him and the whole committee under deep scrutiny. Only with the surety of a unanimous decision did he feel comfortable in his announcement.

As he strode into the media room, the sea of reporters waiting behind the countless camera flashes gave him a refreshing sense of power. Not just a local media event, the gathering featured not just a national, but an international flavor. He disliked that when he smiled, it appeared as a smirk, so he resorted to pursing his lips. It covered the appearance of smugness to one he felt gave him an image of thoughtfulness.

"Good afternoon, everyone. I have a prepared statement so please

252

hold all questions until the end."

The initial hubbub quieted as he settled himself on the podium.

"Thank you. As you are all aware, a difficult situation has arisen in New York. Since these atrocities began, it has been nearly a week without results for both local law enforcement and Homeland Security in their attempts to apprehend these culprits."

"They call themselves the Sword Masters and have begun a campaign of terror through the decapitation of our good citizens in an attempt to force us to amend our foreign policies. In the first couple of days, they beheaded three Americans and posted these grisly deeds for all the world to see."

"What ensued was the largest manhunt in history. All law enforcement personnel on leave were recalled to duty. Thousands began a systematic door-to-door search."

"Since then a fourth murder occurred along the way and so far our efforts have all been for naught. This morning, we learned of two more beheadings. Combined with the racial tension erupting into a riot at a hospital as a result of a shooting the night before, the situation is a powder keg about to go off."

"Make no mistake about it. Failure to contain this crisis will lead to a denigration of our cherished American society. As a result, the committee met today with the Deputy Secretary of Homeland Security, and has fully endorsed a course of action to bring this situation under control. We have notified the President who has signed off on this action and hopes all will cooperate in this crisis."

"Starting immediately, the National Guard will be called to full duty throughout the State of New York and will begin a complete cordoning off of the city. Checkpoints will be set at all perimeters and throughout the city in an attempt to apprehend these terrorists. We appreciate the strain this will put on the good citizens and so we apologize for these drastic but necessary measures."

"As is our policy regarding terrorism, we do not negotiate. And we will persevere. God save America."

The room broke into a furor as reporters yelled a myriad of questions at him. He resisted smiling by pursing his lips once more. He decided to let them clamor for an extra moment before answering, wallowing in the attention.

He picked out the most recognizable reporter in the crowd and began to answer questions. As he fielded them, he considered what the average voter might be thinking. *Senator Joshua Pallabee, a man of decisions. A man who protects our country and our values, a leader.*

***

As he watched the news and the announcement by Senator Pallabee, a feeling of euphoria swept through him. This was the opportunity he waited for, what he worked for.

He stepped out of his office and called for his attendant. "We have received a calling. Gather those in the flock in this list." He handed Alan a print out.

He went back into his private quarters. He started to hum a marching hymn and went to his closet. Digging through, he pulled out what he sought. Unzipping the protective bag, he pulled it free. A few years had passed since he last wore it, and the few extra pounds he'd added since then might cause a problem. The trousers worried him the most and he tried them first. Sucking in his stomach, he managed to fasten the top button. Finding it a little snug, but satisfied he could get away wearing it, he tried the jacket. It slid on a lot easier.

He pranced over to the nearest mirror to get a visual perspective. As he posed left, front, right, then peering over his shoulder to see the back, he nodded. No need for any urgent tailoring. Using the cuff of his sleeve, he polished the silver bars set on each shoulder.

Standing straight, he gave one last tug at the bottom of the jacket and looked into the mirror.

Captain Jebediah Wamsley on duty, ready to restore God's will.

***

Robert turned off the radio and killed the ignition. The news of the decision to mobilize the National Guard left a bitter taste in his mouth. Should he do what he was about to do or return to the office. After a moment he decided to continue. National Guard or no, he had a job to do. He climbed out of his car and headed into the lobby, taking the elevator to the third floor.

In the studio, he found Alexander in a training session. He made eye contact then indicated he would wait by pointing and making his way to the small kitchen area. Looking at the elaborate and unmanned coffee machine made him think of the man lying in the hospital with all the broken bones.

Unable to avail himself of a cup, he decided to wander the perimeter and peruse once more the swords on display. His knowledge of this type of weapon had grown significantly in the past week and he could now recognize a large number of styles. When he came to a new one, he paused to give it a closer look. Long and large, like a broadsword, but with just a single edge, though no curve like a saber or a katana. He could not categorize it.

"It's a Viking sword, known as a beserker."

The voice from behind him startled Robert. He turned to find Suten-Mdjai standing there smiling. "Oh, you surprised me. I thought you were still training."

I've given them a number of tasks to be followed by a break, which gives me the time to see how I can help you."

"I wanted to talk to you about Carlos. Do you know what happened?"

"He's still unconscious so no one has been able to talk to him yet."

"Too bad, because I have a theory and thought I'd run it by you, see if you could corroborate it."

"I'm listening. Tell me this theory."

"I think that somehow Carlos got mixed up with those Latinos who got into a gunfight with the Russian mob. I'm figuring they were under orders from his cousin down in Brazil, you know the one. Anyway, Carlos isn't exactly the bravest guy I ever met, and I figure when the shooting started he became a casualty, took a bullet and fell right there. His buddies vamoosed, leaving him all alone in the hands of the Russians, who worked him over for information. Then, in the middle of the night, somebody shows up and with a sword kills the Russians guarding him, makes off with him to the nearest cab, throws him in and sends him to the hospital."

"An interesting theory, Mr. Grimmson. I suspect you have been listening to too many of my tales."

"I'm also thinking the guy who killed those Russians and rescued Carlos might have been you."

"An honorable thing, I recognize that. And I can understand your suspicion I was the one who rescued him."

Robert stared hard at Alexander but nothing in his demeanor or facial expression gave any indication of his hiding something.

Alexander stepped past him to the mounted sword. "You know, Carlos, like me, is just another wishing to come to America to make a new life for himself. This sword has an interesting tale. It belonged to Gursif Suten-Mdjai.

The Tale Of Gursif Suten-Mdjai

"I am going."

"And pray tell, Gursif, what will I tell Father?"

He stopped to face his little sister, Tanika, her pose, hands on hips, shrieking. "Tell him whatever you want. I wish to visit the North Lands. I've made many friends with the Varangian guard. I'm welcome there."

Tanika gave him a hug. "Before you go, promise me, if you do not find what you are looking for, you will come home."

He bent and kissed her on the forehead. "I promise. Now, I must go. The longship sets sail soon, and the head Varangian has told me he will not wait and miss the tide."

He tossed his sack over his shoulder and strode away from his sister's tears at his leaving. He had argued with his father over the past days without resolve and decided the night before he would just go.

He took one glance back and blew Tanika a kiss, then took off on a jog to reach the city docks.

He ran up just as the longboat cast off. Throwing his bag in, he jumped from the wharf into the boat much to the amusement of those already aboard.

Gursif bounced up from his landing. "I'm here!"

More laughter, and then one of the men handed him an oar.

257

"You're here, now you can row!"

A third round of guffaws followed as he took his place. As he pulled on the oar, the spray from the water now and then caught him and he felt more alive than ever before. Adventure called to him.

Each night they put into shore to camp. Sitting near the fire, one night, he nudged the man beside him. "So who rules in Norway?"

"A good man. In fact, we call him Haakon the Good. He treats the people well and protects our borders."

"Protects your borders…from who?"

"From the Danes and the Swedes."

"But are you not all North men together?"

"At times, yes, but there are always those who seek power, like the sons of Erik the Bloodaxe."

"The Bloodaxe, is that really his name?"

"Yes, and a good thing he's dead, but his offspring are nothing to sneer at."

In the days that followed, he learned more and more from the men and managed to comprehend their native language to some degree. They arrived at their destination a full three months after their start and tied off at a quiet dock. The leader of their group scanned the pier. "Where is everybody?"

Grabbing their packs, they headed into town but once inside the palisade, they were surrounded.

A man brazened a pike before them. "Declare your loyalty!"

Gursif tensed, prepared to draw his weapon. "What's happening?"

One of his shipmates elbowed him and whispered. "Keep your tongue inside you, if you know what's best."

One of the men surrounding them overheard the remark and stepped forward, hitting the man across the cheek with the back of his hand. He then glared at Gursif and placed himself directly in front of him, eye to eye. "Your loyalty, speak!"

A few others in the surrounding troop held bows at the ready and took aim at him. "I am a stranger to these lands. I hold no preference."

The man gestured to others of his troop. "Take him away."

Gursif found himself bound and dragged off to a pen where he spent the rest of the day and night tied to a stake. Another man sat tied across from him. He nodded an acknowledgement of their joint predicament. "What's going on?"

"King Haakon the Good is dead. We have a new ruler now, Harald the Second. We await judgment."

"What of the others I came with?"

"Oh, I reckon they'll pledge to the new king and be done with it."

"Then perhaps I'll be able to pledge, too."

"You? You're a stranger here, not of the people. Only Odin's will can save you from death."

He sat back and let what he just learned sink in. "What of you then? Will they not let you pledge?"

The man chuckled. "I am Thorvald Asvaldsson. My crime is different. I stand accused of murder."

"I am Gursif Suten-Mdjai. Though the circumstances are not pleasant, nevertheless I am pleased to meet you Thorvald Asvaldsson. May Odin's wind blow in your favor."

Thorvald squinted at him. "You speak our language and know our ways well for a stranger, Gursif Suten-Mdjai. Perhaps all hope is not lost for you."

The next morning, they were brought before the new king whose chair sat atop a table. They placed Thorvald in front of the king first. "Thorvald, you have killed a man who is my cousin thrice removed.

259

What say you?"

"I defended my honor and killed him for the rogue that he was."

"Personally, I always thought he was an ass." A laugh broke out among those assembled. "But still, my relative he was. I have no choice but to banish you or there will be no peace in my house. I know you to be a family man. Take your kin and go."

They untied Thorvald and brought Gursif forward. The king studied him for a moment. "What am I to do with you, stranger?"

"If my lord would but allow, I am greatly skilled in the sword and can provide much of my art to you and your men."

"An interesting proposition, but one I cannot accept. I suspect you to be an assassin." He motioned to a man to Gursif's left. "Kill him."

The man pulled his sword and went to run Gursif through. Twisting his body, he pulled his bound hands up around the blade and wrenched it free of the man's grasp. The severed ropes fell away, and a quick movement rotated the blade into his own grip.

An outcry rose from all around as they went for their weapons, when Thorvald called out for them to hold.

All eyes turned to him. "Good King, it would be a waste to kill him outright. I will leave for Iceland on the tide with my family. Let me take the stranger with me as a mentor and guardian to my young children. He will trouble you no more."

The king raised a hand and all stayed, awaiting his decision. "It shall be as you request, Thorvald. Take him with you, but be sure to be gone with the tide as you promised or I shall put you and all of your kin to death as well as the stranger."

Gursif accompanied Thorvald to his home to collect his family and things. As soon as they loaded the boat and all were aboard, Thorvald took the helm. "Odin's wind does indeed blow in your favor, young Gursif. Let us hope it continues to blow as we cross the sea."

***

When they arrived in Iceland, they settled on the west part of the island in a town called Haukadale. Many hands were needed to raise a home and establish the farm. Gursif helped as best he could, but when time allowed, he practiced his swordsmanship and even began giving lesson's to Thorvald's ten year old son.

"Now control your blade, Erik. Swing all the way through and you lose your balance. The key is to maintain your posture."

The lad swung again and Gursif tripped the boy into the mud. Infuriated, the lad came up wildly once more only to have Gursif upend him once again.

"You are not listening. You allow your temper to lead you, not your mind. One day, it will be your downfall."

***

After several years of peaceful farming, a cold winter came and struck Thorvald down. As Gursif stood by his friend's bed, Thorvald motioned him close. "When I am gone, Gursif, what will you do?"

"My debt of life to you, dear friend, will be paid. I shall return to my own family."

"This is your family now. I need you to stay, watch over Erik."

"Erik is a man, and will be chieftain upon your death. What need will he have of me?"

"Clan chief, yes, but his temper and brashness will be his undoing. You must protect him from himself."

Gursif paused in thought. How he wished to see his own sister again. "I will stay, but only for a while."

Thorvald smiled and fell asleep. During the night, he passed away and Gursif wept.

***

"Come, Gursif, bring your sword. I'm in need of your help."

"What is it, Erik?"

"Eyjolf and his family have attacked my thralls, I will have my vengeance."

Before Gursif could reply, Erik ran out. He grabbed his sword as quick as he could. A group of ten armed men were coming toward the house. Without pause, Erik charged and Gursif found himself with no choice but to follow.

His years of tutoring young Erik were visible as the fight began. Gursif tried to limit his strokes to just wounding his combatants so they would leave the field alive, but Erik struck to kill. When it was over, seven men fled with wounds to mend and Eyjolf and his two sons lay dead.

"Did you have to kill them, Erik? What will happen now?"

"I am chieftain here, nothing will happen."

But when the time came for the annual meeting of the thing, a group of chieftains ruled against Erik and he was banished for three years.

With a sad heart, Gursif helped him with preparations to leave his home. "Where will you go? You are forever banished from Norway as Thorvald's son."

"Then I will go west. There is rumor of a new land that will

262

provide me safe harbor until I can return."

The calling of his own home pulled at him once more, but so did the promise to Thorvald. "Then I shall go with you."

They sailed west and found the new lands. Erik believed they would make a better home and called the new land Greenland. When the three years were over, he returned to Iceland with a promise of a new life for those who followed him. Hundreds came and a new community grew up on the eastern shores, with Erik as their jarl.

The years passed, and Gursif grew older. His time was now spent tutoring Erik's four children, the son Thorvald becoming his favorite. His memories of home were all but forgotten.

One day Erik summoned him.

"Gursif, my children wish to explore further west, and I fear for them. I ask for the task you have provided all these years in protecting me be the same for my children. I wish for you to accompany them and see them from no harm."

In Gursif's mind, his own family was just the faintest of memories. "I will see them safely home."

***

They set sail and made landfall several times, each landing more bounteous than the time before. Erik's children wanted to make a permanent camp and call it Vinland.

"Is it wise for us to stay here, Thorvald?"

"Gursif, I know my father puts great trust in you. You have been a mentor to me and my family over my life, but look about you. This is a land of plenty. The rivers teem with fish, the land with fruit and the woods with game."

"It is the woods that most trouble me."

"Come now. If they bother you so, we will turn them into lumber for our houses."

"It is not the trees themselves that concern me, but what may lurk inside them."

Thorvald would hear none of it, and they set up a permanent camp to stay the winter. At times, he would espy almost naked men moving in the distance, carrying bows. None approached the camp, but it was obvious they were watching.

On a bright morning, Gursif stood near the palisade gate, staring out into the woods. The last vestiges of the morning fog still clung in the dark places. He stretched out to relieve a few aching muscles. *Damn, I'm getting old.*

In mid-stretch, he froze. Deep in the woods, he recognized movement. And it was many. *They're coming.*

He dashed to the iron shield hung at the edge of camp and rapped it with the hammer hung nearby. "To arms! Rise and defend, we are set upon!"

Arrows whistled at him, which he blocked easily with a hoisted shield. Manning the entry, he held off the charge until his comrades arrived. The Norse men rallied and attacked the tribesmen. Gursif lay about with his sword, slashing through the enemy with ease. What little clothing they wore consisted of nothing more than leather jerkins. It wasn't a battle. It was a slaughter.

Despite their greater numbers, the natives broke and ran. When it appeared the last of them was gone, Gursif and the others relaxed and laughed over their easy victory. He did not see the straggler who stopped and let loose an arrow until it was too late. Struck in the midriff, Thorvald fell to the ground.

264

Gursif leapt the palisade and raced after the man, who fired another arrow at him, which he knocked aside. In two more strides, he reached the native, and in one blow cleaved the man's head and right arm from his body.

He returned to the camp to find Thorvald being tended by the others. Thorvald, who must have been in great pain, smiled. "This is a rich country we have found. There is plenty of fat around my belly. We've found a land of fine resources, though we'll hardly enjoy most of them."

He died that night and they buried him there. Gursif found himself weeping once again for a Thorvald. In his duty to protect him, he had failed.

In time they packed camp and returned to Greenland. Upon arriving, he paid his respects to Erik then found passage on the first boat heading east. It was time to go home.

Chapter Forty-One

"So you see, Mr. Grimmson, I am not the first Suten-Mdjai to come to America."

Alexander looked behind him. "And now, I must return to my students."

Robert watched him go, and then returned to his car. He needed to get back to headquarters right away. More than likely, the deputy secretary would have instructions as to how the National Guard were to be incorporated into this manhunt.

As he turned the key, his cell rang. "Hey, Bobby boy. Why don't ya come on by? I got the plan on this National Guard stuff. Let's go over it together."

"Seamus, you must have been reading my mind. I'm on my way."

He called the office and instructed his own team to come down and meet as well. The logistics were going to be a nightmare.

***

A large throng of people were protesting outside the police station. As Robert walked through the crowd, it didn't take long to recognize them as Muslim Americans. Seamus met him on the steps.

"Ya'd think we was the United Nations or something."

"What are they protesting about?"

"The guys we arrested last night at the hospital."

"You still holding them?"

"It's not like it's intentional. There's been no time to process them. Things have been a bit crazy about here lately."

"Let them go, Seamus. You can always collect them later if you need to."

"But what about charges? I got two injured cops."

"You don't need that trouble right now. Let them go. If you get grief from the police association, tell them the mayor told you to."

Seamus shook his head in disagreement. "But the mayor didn't—"

"He will, after you call him. You don't need a riot down here."

They went into the chief's office and closed the door.

Seamus sat down and put his feet up on his desk. "So have you talked yet to the D.S.?"

Robert plopped into a chair across from Seamus. "No, not yet. He sent over the directive, but I think he's still pissed at me, so no face to face."

"Well, I got the basics. All guardsmen are to report to the football stadium for briefing. We'll have their patrol districts lined up by then. I got a bunch of guys working on that now. I just hope we can control these guys."

"I hear you. Let's hope none of them think they're too empowered. Last thing we need is a bunch of vigilantes running around."

***

Ivan slumped into a chair. "Somebody bring me a drink."

Nikita motioned a stop to the waitress. "Bring him only coffee."

"Aw, Nicky. What's the matter? You know I like to have a vodka or two this time of day."

"With you, Ivan, it's a vodka or two any time of day. Now, tell

267

me, why did you cut that guy's head off?"

"I didn't."

"What do you mean you didn't? You shot him. Everyone knows that greaseball is missing his head."

"Yeah, but I didn't do it."

Nikita slapped the table and leaned back. "You didn't do it? Who did then?"

"Saleem."

"You mean that vermin you hang around with?"

"Yeah, he's the one."

A waitress arrived bringing Ivan a plate of food. He grabbed a fork but before he could put a bite in his mouth, Nikita slapped the fork from his hand. "You idiot! I lost three good men last night, maybe four, all because you let your pet cockroach play. They cut up my guys real bad."

The door opened and another one of Nikita's men came in. "Hey, Nicky. I just came from the hospital. Stan's going to make it. They finished his surgery, and he's resting right now."

"We need to find out who did this. Can he talk?"

"No, not yet, and the police are with him so I don't think we'll find out anything real soon."

"What about this guy who that spic worked for, what's his name? Alexander something. Supposed to be some kinda sword trainer. Saw him on the news. Maybe he gave those guys the swords and a few tips on how to use them."

One of the guys piped up. "Yeah, I saw that as well, fellah got caught at the airport, bringing a whole shitload of those things."

Nikita pointed at one of his men sitting near him. "Go with him and find out what you can about this swordsman. I think we're going to need to pay him a visit."

"Ya serious, boss? I hear they're going to shut the whole town down this weekend. They got the National Guard coming in."

"A bunch of nerds playing soldier. It's not a problem, now go."

Ivan retrieved his fork and began to eat. "What about me, Nicky? You want I go with you?"

"You sit there and eat. Just stay out of our way. I don't need you messing things up any worse than they already are."

"Okay, Nicky. Whatever you say."

Nikita stood up and waved to the rest of his men to follow. "Come on. Let's go to the hospital. See what Stan can tell us. We'll tell them we're family."

Ivan waited until Nikita left then chased down the waitress. "Get me a vodka and Coke and make it a double!"

***

Jim dropped the box on the floor next to his desk.

Tim peeked inside. "So they really making you pack up?"

"Yeah, at least until my trial, but at least its paid leave."

"If it's paid leave, then why are they making you clean out your desk?"

He scratched at his head. "Huh, I never thought of that."

"My guess is, they don't want you coming back."

He sat down and picked up his favorite coffee mug. WORLD'S GREATEST DAD. His oldest child had given it to him for Father's Day ten years ago. He reached across and picked up his name plate— James Munroe, Senior Inspector. He could not remember how long it had sat there, but the grime and dust on it gave a good indication of it being a long time. "Do you really think so?"

Tim pulled the name plate from his hand, found a towelette in his own desk, cleaned it off and handed it back to him. "It must be. Their lawyers will make sure of it, even if they have to pay them big bucks."

He banged the desk top. "But I've been here almost twenty-five goddamned years, I got a pension coming!"

"I hope I'm wrong, but guys like you and me, we're just replaceable parts."

He started to empty his desk drawers, but paused holding each item and trying and think back to when he got it. When the drawers were empty, he began on the last things on the desk top, including the picture of his wife and family. He stopped and leaned back in the chair to stare at the photograph.

This has to be at least ten years old. The kids are just babies.

He wiped away the moisture pooling in his eyelids.

"Jim…you okay?"

He blinked quickly to try and stop the tears. "Yeah, yeah, I'm fine. It's just, ya know, I never wanted to kill anyone, just scare them, chase them away, that's all. It was my house after all, goddammit. My house, my family."

Sniffing hard, he placed the picture in the box. He folded over the flaps and stood up. Then, bending down, he lifted the box and extended a hand to Tim. "Well, see ya. If I don't make it back, then I suppose they'll put you in charge."

Tim took his hand and held it a little extra longer than usual. "You'll be back. I just know it."

"Yeah, I hope you're right. I gotta go."

He breathed in, exhaled, and then began walking slowly. Never before in his career had the walk seem to take so long.

270

Mohamed El-Barai returned from the graveyard. He kissed his wife and put his other children to bed.

Climbing into his own, he took the framed picture of his son from on top of bureau and held it close to his chest and cried himself to sleep.

Chapter Forty-Two

"So tell me, Doc, what's the story on these dead Russkies?"

"Steven, you shouldn't even be in here. Now give me a break."

He followed the coroner down the hall, determined not to let him get away. "Look, everyone knows these guys were butchered, cut up. You're going to confirm that at the afternoon press release. I've been following this story from the start. Hell, I broke it. Don't leave me out of this one. This is my baby. All I'm looking for is an angle."

The coroner stopped to face him. "Yeah, I know. Okay, I'll give you one thing only, then stop bugging me."

"That's a deal, Doc. Lay it on me."

"They were all killed by the same weapon. A sword, I suppose, but one like I've never seen before. The cuts are incredibly clean, even right through the bones, meaning this blade has one hell of a sharp hard edge, like from out of this world."

Something clicked in Steven's mind. He needed to get back to his computer to confirm it. "Thanks, I'll get out of your hair."

"Please."

He made for the exit and grabbed a cab. When he got to the paper, the receptionist stopped him on the way in. "Hank's looking for you."

Waltzing into Hank's office, he found a couple of other reporters sitting with him. "Hey, Hank, I'm here."

"Steve, are you going to go cover the story on the National Guard?"

"No, send one of these guys. I just got a tip I want to follow."

"Am I going to be able to go to press with it today?"

"I hope so. Let me get to work on it."

"Okay, we'll cover this end. I hope what you're working on is good."

"I think it will be."

Steven retreated to his office and pulled up his files saved so far on the story. He'd discounted the media reports he'd read earlier, as they didn't feature decapitations. But now, as he scanned over them again, he found some recognizable similarities in a few of the stories. And not just in America, but around the world.

He time-lined them as best as he could and put together his theory.

What he needed now involved a little more research. A quoted authority would help the story, someone who specialized in the facts of sword prowess.

He dialed the number and after a few connections found who he was searching for.

"Bartholomew Higginbottom, at your service."

"Good afternoon, Mr. Higginbottom. This is Steven Bishop, I'm a freelance reporter covering the terrorists calling themselves the Sword Masters. I was curious if you might help me with a little bit of your knowledge."

"Call me Bartholomew. Anything I can do to help, Mr. Bishop. I aim to please."

"Then if you wouldn't mind...Bartholomew, what type of sword offers the hardest, sharpest edge? One that can make the cleanest cut through flesh and bone."

"Oh dear, this is a nasty question. Well, if I had to say, it would be a Japanese sword known as a katana. The methodology of making the blade is unique in the world as it features two parts, the back part where it is thickest to withstand breakage and provide some flexibility and the

273

front part where the edge is being extra hard and sharp. Normally, an overly hard blade will break, but the other part of the weapon saves it from this mishap. Further, the curve of the blade allows it to slice through without the tip snagging and causing the weapon to get lodged in its victim."

"Uh huh. So a weapon such as this one could cut through, say, four men, one after another, and leave a clean cut every time."

"I dare say, Mr. Bishop, this is a ghastly conversation. But I think such an occurrence would be unlikely, as even though very hard, the weapon will receive some nicks from the bones as it passes through."

"Then you're telling me it's impossible to have a blade going un-scarred when used."

"Not quite so, Mr. Bishop. I merely stated unlikely. But you can see for yourself, if you like. I have a number of swords here at the museum, though not on display at this time. They all bear the marks of damage from use. In ancient times, the swordsman would constantly need to maintain his sword. As in Othello, keep up your bright swords, for the dew will rust them. Surely you have read some Shakespeare in your time?"

"Actually, yes. I read Othello and a few others as well."

"Then you can appreciate his reference to sword maintenance. For example, I have had the pleasure of seeing the finest collection of old swords ever. Those of Alexander Suten-Mdjai are outstanding, simply outstanding!"

"Yes, I've been to his studio. Many of them line the walls."

"When Mr. Suten-Mdjai first came to this country last week, Homeland Security required me to catalogue each and every one of them. I dare say it took me all day, there were so many. Then you have seen his katana, one of the most amazing blades I have ever witnessed.

When he told me of its making and the metal used, I was astounded."

"Oh, how so?"

"Why, my good man, he used the ore from a meteorite. Very rare indeed! The metal is incredibly dense. Now there might be a blade to do what you want."

"Yes, an out of this world blade."

"Unworldly indeed, Mr. Bishop. Unworldly indeed."

He thanked Bartholomew for his time then over the next several hours finished putting the final touches to the piece on his screen. Satisfied, he hit send and fired it over.

In less than five minutes, Hank appeared at his door. "Are you out of your mind?"

"All the details are there, Hank."

"I don't know. I mean, will people really believe this stuff? It's like one of those *B* movies down at the cinema."

"What's so hard to believe? It's a fact that here, in New York City, we have an international assassin in our midst."

Chapter Forty-Three

The afternoon wore on as Robert and Seamus reviewed the new procedures. Detective Brown stopped by to find out where he fit in all of it. A ping on Robert's phone told him a new file just got imported.

He leaned back to scan through it, then stopped. He called his staff. "Listen, send the entire thing to Seamus' comp, I want to see this in full."

The chief looked up from the stack of team assignments. "What is it, Bobby boy?"

Robert moved to sit behind the screen and pull up the report. "A new lead."

He finished reading then grabbed the phone. "Get me that guy I talked to before at the State Department, right away, no ifs, ands or buts."

A couple of minutes passed then his cell rang. "You called again, Director Grimmson?"

"Alright then, I think we need to talk a little more frankly, and don't give me any crap this time."

"We told you before. We are not at liberty to divulge any details about Mr. Suten-Mdjai."

"I'm not asking about Mr. Suten-Mdjai. I'm asking about David Crombie."

"Let's see, I suppose I can discuss what I know about him. He was one of the six captured, you know, down there in Bolivia. Him and his fiancée, Jennifer, and four others. Unfortunately, Jennifer was killed in the action. Apparently, Mr. Crombie went into some kind of shock. The State Department arranged for a psychiatrist to assess and assist

Mr. Crombie in his recovery. As a matter of a fact, I have Dr. Bellemore's most recent assessment right here, Not very promising, I'm afraid."

"Why should I not be surprised? In case you didn't know, Dr. Bellemore and his wife were executed in their beds last night."

"He was? That's terrible!"

"Don't you read the news? My God man, it's on all the headlines."

"Oh my, and you think Mr. Crombie did it?"

"I think he's involved, yeah. I need you to forward me those files ASAP."

"Gee, I don't know, doctor client privilege—"

"Screw that! The doctor's dead, I want those files now. You got one minute before I get in my car and drive down to wherever you are and strangle them out of you."

"Alright, alright. Sending now. Anything else, Mr. Grimmson?"

"If there is, I'll let you know."

Listening in, Detective Brown went for his notebook. "David Crombie, that name rings a bell."

Seamus moved around to join the two men. "Watcha got, Larry?"

"A hunch that's paid off. I pulled the phone records of an organization called Feed The People. I was looking for matches in my short list of candidates as members of the Sword Masters. There weren't any, at the time, but by chance, I kept in mind there were a number of calls between one of my favorite suspects, Lakshanthan Vairaviyar, and your David Crombie."

Robert smiled. "Seems like we got us a match! Let's pull David's calls and find the mutual ones between him and your Lakshanthan character. I bet we find the other three members of the Sword Masters in there."

As he called his office to get the search done, Seamus sat down, leaned back, and put up his feet. "Now we're cookin' with gas!"

"Seamus, just how old *are* you?"

"Don't be sassin' me now, Bobby boy. I aim to catch these killers by nightfall. Just make your call and let's get this show on the road."

He couldn't help but snicker then completed his call to his office and gave the instructions.

When he hung up, he glanced at the time. "Seamus, we have to be at the football field. All those National Guardsmen will be waiting as it is. Let's leave this with Larry to follow up. If you and I aren't there, both the mayor and the deputy director will tell us to hit the road."

Seamus got up and put on his jacket. "Larry, get arrest warrants for these two. In the meantime, chase them down right away. I don't want them disappearing. Once you figure out the rest, get warrants for them as well. Tell the judge to call me if he's got a problem issuing them.

"Right on it, Chief."

Let's go, Bobby boy. We don't wanna keep them waitin'."

***

He scanned about him. On the field and in the stands were an awful lot of men and women, all National Guardsmen. To his left, a contingent from his parish waited for his command.

The entryway cleared, allowing a group of men to enter the stadium. They made their way to the podium where he and all the other officers were waiting. As they neared, he identified out the two men in the middle of the group as Police Chief Seamus Flaherty and Homeland

278

Security Director Robert Grimmson.

The smile left his face. Grimmson was the man who defended that sword fellow and caused his protest group to go home, and he'd just heard how Flaherty released those Muslim non-believers.

Where is Senator Pallabee?

He watched as they each took turns addressing the crowd. A police officer handed him a packet indicating the intersections where his team was to set up checkpoints and the instructions on how they were to be manned. At the end, when Chief Flaherty concluded with "God be with ya," he felt revulsion.

As it began to wrap up he got down from the podium and joined up with his men.

"What's the plan, Pastor?"

He pulled out the orders. "Here are the locations we have to set up checkpoints. You men get this started. Once set up, I want you six to meet me at this spot here."

He showed his special team a spot on the map.

"We're to arrest anyone under the guidelines they gave, using force if necessary. God has given us a mission. We are going to do it."

***

David walked into the bar. Lakshanthan and Saleem were already there. He sat down and ordered a Manhattan. In a few moments, the news came on.

The anchorman looked grim. "Pandemonium in New York tonight as everyone is trying to get out of town. All roadways from the city are packed with vehicles as people try to beat the National Guard-imposed curfew set to begin at ten p.m. tonight."

279

The image changed to a number of scenes of traffic backed up as far as the eye could see, accompanied by the sound of blaring horns blaring from impatient drivers.

"No one knows for how long this lockdown will be in place, and no one's offering any clues."

The image changed to Chief Flaherty. "I ain't sayin' when's it to be over. The sooner we catch these terrorists, the sooner we can all get back to a normal life."

The screen returned to the reporter. "These are dark days for this city, and darker still for citizens. Terror has truly struck home, here in America."

The story changed to coverage of the death of Dr. Bellemore and his wife, featuring an interview with a middle-aged couple who lived next door. "It's simply horrible. We can't even be safe in our own homes. What are we paying the police for? They should be protecting us."

The anchorman once again appeared on the screen. "And yet our politicians remain stalwart in their position."

The image now changed to Senator Joshua Pallabee. "America will not wilt. We will not bend. We will not submit to the will of terrorism."

The scene returned once more to the reporter. "I, for one, wonder. For how long will America act in such a way as to put ourselves into terrorism's path?"

David nodded to Lakshanthan and Saleem. "It's starting to sound like they're ready to buckle. One more push, and they should go over the edge."

At a noise by the door, they all watched Ivan coming in, dragging Miguel with him. "Hey guys, we're here. Sorry it took so long. Miguel needed a little convincing."

Miguel plopped down into a seat, folded his arms and stared away.

David smiled. "Evening, Miguel. How have you been? We haven't seen you lately."

Miguel said nothing, looking left and right, everywhere but meeting David's gaze.

He's thinking on making a dash for it.

Ivan thumped down next to Miguel. Miguel looked at Ivan then finally at David. "I…I haven't been feeling well."

"What you need is a vacation. We all do. This whole business is starting to wear on everyone."

Miguel lit up. "Really?"

David nodded and winked at Saleem. "Really. That's why tonight is our last caper. After that you can go on your merry way as if nothing happened."

"Ah, um, I don't know…"

"What's to know, Miguel? You're coming with us, plain and simple. We started this thing together. We're going to finish it together."

Before he could respond again, Lakshanthan leaned in. "So, David, you haven't told us yet. What is the target?"

David leaned back and smiled. They were all listening to him now; he was in charge. He looked from the eager eyes of Saleem to the cold calculating ones of Lakshanthan, from the distrustful flitting eyes of Miguel to the devil may care ones of Ivan.

"We're going to make it clear who the real Sword Masters are. We're going to kill the imposter Alexander Suten-Mdjai."

Lakshanthan's eyes went wide. "I don't know, David. That's a tall order. The guy is skilled in sword play. I don't think we could take him that way."

Saleem leaped in. "Lakshanthan, don't be such a coward. There are five of us. He's only one man. Personally, I like the plan."

Miguel rubbed at his neck. "I don't know, if this guy's really good—"

Ivan slapped him on the back. "Don't worry, Miguel. I've always got backup on me." He pulled his gun from the holster under his arm, waved it for everybody to see and then put it back.

Ivan's drink arrived and he slammed it back. "Besides, hitting that guy will do me some good with the boys. Nicky thinks Suten...whatever his name is, is behind that hit last night."

Miguel looked horrified. "You...you mean those four Russians who got cut up last night?"

"The same. They got it bad, they did. Me, I think it was the spics. Not you, of course, but the Latino drug gangs pissed 'cause we killed one of their dogs."

Lakshanthan steepled his hands in front of him. "But what about the National Guard? They begin checkpoints tonight."

David pointed the newspaper on the table. "Not until ten o'clock. We have time before then. His classes end at nine, which gives us a full hour to catch him alone, do the job and get back before they start checking."

They turned back to the television and a couple of analysts were on discussing the current situation and whether the Deputy Director of Homeland Security was overplaying his hand. They were debating the finer points of the anti-terrorism laws and just exactly how much power it wielded.

"Don't forget the Oversight Committee has endorsed this action and the President himself has given his assent."

"Exactly my point. Yes, he is the commander in chief, but we are not in a state of war. I would like to think it would take an act of Congress to instigate such draconian measures."

The analysts continued to argue back and forth and David returned his attention to his four confederates at the table. They were engaged in their own various discussions when David interrupted. "This is history in the making, gentlemen. I can sense it. We will be able to achieve what governments have been unable to do. I suggest a toast."

The others paused, and then lifted their glasses.

"To success."

They echoed the toast and drank. They ordered dinner and more drinks. It would be a while before they should go.

Chapter Forty-Four

Nikita sat next to the bed. "Stan, who did this? Who cut you up?"

Stan, still groggy from the medication, looked bleary. "I don't know, Nicky. It happened so fast. One person, dressed all in black and wearing a mask. I couldn't make out much. All I know is, I pulled my gun and the next thing I knew my belly gets sliced open and I'm on the floor. I think I blacked out then."

"Okay, Stan, okay, you take it easy. I'll come see you tomorrow."

"Thanks, Nicky."

He got up and left the room, receiving a curt nod from the police officer stationed outside the door. The others who were with him sat waiting down the hall. "Let's go, boys. Stan's tired. He's going back to sleep. We'll come visit tomorrow."

They got up and joined him as he rang for the elevator. Once the doors closed and he pushed the button for the garage, his cell rang.

"Nicky, the cops are here."

"What do they want?"

"They're looking for Ivan."

"Ivan? What did that overgrown sack of shit do now?"

"They won't say, but they got a warrant for his arrest."

"Where is he?"

"Said he was off to hook up with some friends."

Nikita thought of the crowd he had seen Ivan with. "Must be those cockroaches he hangs with."

"What do you want me to do?"

"Nothing. Let them look. I got something to do. I'll be there in a while."

What possible kind of shit could Ivan be into now? He'd worry about it later. The issue at hand was the fact Stan and the boys got bumped off by one person, not a gang. There was only one person it could be.

Time to pay Mr. Suten-Mdjai a visit.

***

Detective Brown stood outside the door with four other officers. Tenants up and down the halls were peeking out to watch. He knocked. "Lakshanthan Vairaviyar, open the door. This is the police."

Nothing.

He knocked again, but much harder. "Mr. Vairaviyar, open up or I will be forced to break in."

Nothing again.

He motioned to the officers holding the ram. "Open it up, boys."

The two men swung the ram into the door. The steel frame held on the first hit, as the metal door buckled, but the second one worked, and they were through. A quick run through the apartment proved it to be empty.

"Search the place."

While the men combed the rooms, his phone rang. "Brown here."

"Hey Larry, we're over here at the Crombie place. He's not here. We're going through it now. You sure about this guy? This place is amazing. Must be worth a lot of bucks. Why would somebody so well off want to mess with it? It doesn't make sense."

"Just do the search, seize any computers, and bring the stuff down to the station."

"Will do."

Two more calls came in from officers making successful arrests, both people claiming innocence. Two other calls came of no one home.

He walked out into the hallway. One of the neighbors waved him over. "A young fellow came by about an hour ago, and the two of them left together."

"What's this fellow look like?"

"Oh, slender, olive complexion. I think he was Arabic or something."

"Thank you. We'll take things from here."

The description could possibly fit Saleem Al-Nijjar. *They're together now, all of them. I know it.*

***

Robert got to his car and left Chief Flaherty to catch a ride with one of his men. His phone blinked like mad with the number of messages he needed to answer. Rather than read through, he called his office.

"Hi Bob. A lot's been happening tonight. We did the cross reference as you suggested and came up with seven possibles. So far, they've nabbed two and have them down at police headquarters."

"Are either Crombie or Vairaviyar among the two?"

"No, it looks like the two grabbed so far might just be a couple of coincidental acquaintances. Detective Brown thinks the five are together. He's worried they might try another decapitation tonight. In other news, Carlos Jose Santiago is awake. When questioned about what happened the previous night, he says an avenging angel in black rescued him."

"Did he say who this angel was? Alexander Suten-Mdjai,

286

perhaps?"

"No, just 'a beautiful avenging angel,' over and over."

"Okay, thanks for the update, keep me informed."

He drove over to the building to see Alexander. He glanced at his watch, eight o'clock. He would still have a class running.

This can't wait. I'm going to have to pull him from his class.

Robert got out and headed for the front door. The parking lot was empty. The thought occurred to him that perhaps there were no classes tonight.

He walked in and could hear the sounds of swords clashing. Half expecting to find the same group of men he encountered the night before, instead he found Alexander alone with a single woman among the sea of mannequins. In her hands, the woman held the identical sword as Alexander, a katana. And it showed the same darkness in the metal as his.

"Good evening, Alexander. Sorry to disturb you, but I need a moment of your time."

"Good evening, Director Grimmson. What can I do for you?"

He approached them and glanced over at the woman beside him, both breathing heavy from exertion. It was the receptionist, Jasmine. "I didn't know you were a master of the sword as well."

"I'm just a student of the art. Only Alexander is the true master."

"Nevertheless, it's clear to me you know how to handle the weapon well. And an exquisite one, I see. Is this the twin blade you referred to earlier, Alexander?"

"Why yes, it is."

"After what you told me these cost, you must be paying your receptionist a pretty penny. Or did you give it to her? I thought you closely guarded your swords as family heirlooms."

"Jasmine *is* family."

Robert studied her face. Yes, after some consideration, there was a faint resemblance. "My apologies, I meant no offense. But back to matters at hand, I need to speak with Alexander. You'll excuse us, would you please, Jasmine?"

"It's okay; I'll go take a shower while you two chat. All this perspiration just won't do. You guys like to think it makes you manly. For me, it's just stink, and I need to wash it off if I wish to maintain my femininity."

They laughed as she walked away. Seeing an actual pot of coffee on the warmer of the coffee machine became irresistible for Robert. "May I?"

"Help yourself."

After pouring himself a cup, he faced his host again. "Alexander, what happened in Bolivia with David Crombie?"

Alexander looked to the floor, then composed himself and faced Robert straight on.

"They were kidnapped by a drug cartel and used as bargaining chips with the Bolivian government. Trouble is, the Bolivians didn't care about a group of Americans. Your government came for my father, but he had passed away from a virus. I now ran the school. I agreed to go in and rescue them on the condition I could migrate to the United States with my background kept secret. They agreed.

"I went into the jungle and tracked the men to their main camp in the hills. In the middle of the night, I tried to extricate them without notice, but things went wrong. The girl, Jennifer, wasn't in the makeshift prison with them. She had been kept in the main building. Her beauty was her downfall. They had repeatedly raped her, and when they were finished, killed her, although I did not know this. I got the others out then went back for Jennifer."

Alexander paced a bit then faced Robert once more.

"Understand, what happened next was not to my liking. The kidnappers were awake, though far from alert, and I was forced to kill many if I wanted to win through to the room I was told she was in. When I got there, she was already dead. I picked her body up and carried it out.

When I caught up with the others, David broke down. He howled with grief and I needed to slap him in an attempt to quiet him down in case there were any others nearby. He went into a rage and attacked me, claiming it was my fault she was dead. I needed him to be quiet, so with the butt of my sword, I knocked him unconscious with the butt of my sword.

The others helped me carry him and Jennifer out. When he came to the next day, he seemed to be in some kind of mental dilemma. Apparently his condition stayed that way for some time. Word got to me that he finally came out of it but seemed to have a blockage of any memory relating to things down there and to Jennifer in particular.

When I saw him here the other day, I was surprised but happy to see him looking well. He seemed to recognize me and yet not, so I didn't push it. He had suffered a terrible tragedy. I feel for him."

Robert weighed how much he should tell Alexander but decided to hold off for the moment. A quick glance at the psych profile had already told him all he needed to know.

Chapter Forty-Five

Noise from the entry, as the elevator doors opened, caused them to turn their heads. Coming in the double doors was a contingent of National Guardsmen, armed and ready. Robert reached for his wallet to pull out his identification. "What is the meaning of this? You men are supposed to be patrolling the street, nothing more. I am Director Grimmson of Homeland Security. Who is the commanding officer here? I want to speak to him."

A man in a captain's uniform strode in last. "We know who you are, Director Grimmson. But understand this; your authority cannot supersede the higher authority that is God. This man and all he represents is a blasphemy to America. Now stand aside. We are going to take him."

Several of the men raised weapons and pointed them at Robert, who raised his hands and backed up a few steps.

Alexander stepped in front of him. "I recognize you, Pastor Wamsley, from the day you staged the protest outside this building. And I also recognize these four thugs as the ones who attempted to come in here and smash up the place. Shall I have to teach them a lesson again?"

Alexander picked up one of his wooden swords and one of the Guardsmen took aim and stepped closer. "No bats this time, sword guy. So unless you want me put a bullet through your head right now, put down the stick. You ain't going to whack me with one of those again."

Robert stepped between. "Wamsley, are you off your rocker? You'll go to jail for this, all of you."

Wamsley smiled and pulled out a document. "Item seven,

paragraph three reads...*In the face of an absolute threat, the use of necessary force may be your only option.*" He folded it up and put it back in his pocket. "The rules of engagement for the National Guard as set down by the deputy director and endorsed by Senator Pallabee and the Oversight Committee and consented to by the President of the United States and distributed to me by none other than you."

He walked forward and pointed a finger at Alexander. "Standing before me is the absolute threat, and I intend to take action."

Robert chuckled. "And I thought the Sword Masters were crazy."

Pastor Wamsley purpled and charged up to him. "God has brought us this crisis to see who will turn to him and embrace him and who will turn from him and embrace the heathens and their ways!"

Robert stepped back for no other reason than to avoid the spittle from Wamsley's outburst, when the sound of the elevator once again made all eyes turn to the entry. In walked David Crombie and four others who he guessed could only be the other members of the Sword Masters. David and two others carried swords.

A couple of the guardsmen pointed their guns at the new entries, unsure of what to do.

One of Sword Masters, an East Indian fellow who was probably Lakshanthan Vairaviyar, leaned into David. "I told you this might be a bad idea." Robert figured out the rest of the troop—the small, olive-skinned one as Saleem, the big man as Ivan and the Latino as Miguel.

Pastor Wamsley confronted David. "Class is cancelled tonight, gentlemen. But I can see that you have embraced the heathen ways as well. You shall all be consumed by the apocalypse."

David jumped Wamsley, grabbed him and spun him to hold as a shield and held the sword to Wamsley's throat. "Okay, Lieutenant, you're going to tell your playmates to drop their guns."

"I am not a lieutenant. I am a captain!"

"Lieutenant, captain, what's the diff. You're in charge, so tell them to drop those guns."

From the doorway, a new voice broke in. "Well, well, well, Ivan and his cockroach friends playing with some toy soldiers."

Ivan stepped toward the new arrivals. "Nicky, you're just in time. We come to get that guy for ya who killed the boys, when these other guys got in the way."

Nicky held a gun, as did the other eleven guys with him. He looked from face to face, and when his eyes found Alexander, he stopped. "Are you the one they call the Sword Master?"

Before Alexander could reply, David threw Pastor Wamsley to the ground. "We are the Sword Masters! We are! He's the master of nothing! Nothing. Do you hear me? Nothing! He couldn't even save one single girl, just one. It's all he had to do, but he couldn't do it, he's nothing!"

"Is this true, Ivan? You and these cockroaches, you guys are the Sword Masters? The ones who've been going around cutting off people's heads?"

"Yeah Nicky, you know, just going out having some fun."

"And because you were out…having fun, I lost three guys."

Nicky turned to the men who had arrived with him. "Kill them all."

A hard shove threw Robert to the floor under the coffee table. From his position, he could see the Russians opening fire. The National Guard guys all dropped their guns and ran for cover and the four Sword Masters bolted as well. All except for Miguel who froze where he was until the gunfire from Nicky and his men cut him down.

That's one less Sword Master to worry about.

In the next instant, from what seemed like out of nowhere, a black-clad body rushed between the Russians, cut the head from one, and was gone.

Nicky and the rest of the Russians tried to shoot at whoever it was, but the figure ducked behind a number of the mannequins and disappeared. Jasmine. And then what struck him were the words of Carlos...the avenging angel.

Nicky and a few others chased into the labyrinth of mannequins after her, shooting away, leaving two others by the door.

In a flash, Alexander appeared among them, and in two lightning stokes, they were both down, then he, too disappeared into the mannequins.

Pastor Wamsley got up from where he lay sprawled on the floor. "Get up, you fools, go after them!" The guardsmen got up, picked up their guns, and crouched their way into the sea of bamboo men.

Wamsley pulled out a pistol and stayed near the entry. Behind him, Saleem crept out from behind one of the workout machines and tried to make a dash for the door. The pastor turned and fired, catching Saleem in the back. "Judgment has come!" Saleem fell to the floor, blood drenching him, and moved no more.

Two down, three to go.

At this moment, Robert cursed his decision not to carry a gun. He always felt his executive position put him above that sort of stuff. He promised himself, should he get out of there alive, he'd go down to the range and get some practice in.

From amid the mannequins, gunfire continued to erupt, accompanied by what could only be sword strokes and the screams of dying men.

Someone nearby shouted "Screw this! I'm outta here!" In the next moment four of the guardsmen raced out the door. During their exodus, Pastor Wamsley continued to rant. "Stay and fight, God commands you!"

Nicky and two of his cohorts emerged next. Ivan popped up from behind some equipment. "Nicky, you're okay, did you get them?"

Nicky took a look at Ivan that seethed venom. "This is all your fault!" Then, in quick succession, he fired two bullets into Ivan's chest.

Three down, just Crombie and Vairaviyar left.

In the next moment he felt the hairs on the back of his neck prickle. Someone was behind him!

"Alright, Mr. Fancy Pants Director, get up, you're my ticket out."

Robert crawled out from under the table. He dared not move too fast, as the sword David held at his throat felt awfully sharp and a small cut already dripped onto the back of his hand as he moved.

One of Nicky's men was bleeding badly from a gash that had taken his left ear, the other bled from his thigh. Neither were able to do more than hold the wounds in an attempt to stem the flow.

As Robert stood, he saw Lakshanthan with a sword to Wamsley as well. "What should I do with this one?"

Nicky chuckled. "Let me make it easy for you." And he emptied his gun into both Wamsley and Lakshanthan.

Only David remains, of the five.

As Wamsley fell to the floor, he lamented, "God...why?" then he rolled over and died.

Before Robert's eyes, things started to slow down. Nicky grabbed a machine gun from one of his men, swung around and aimed at David and him. As Nicky leveled his weapon, Alexander appeared in front of him and whispered. "I'm sorry, David, good-bye." In a blinding flash, Alexander's sword slid by his head in a lighting stroke and David's sword slipped away from his throat. From the corner of his eye, he saw David's head rollover his shoulder and to the floor, followed by the collapse of the man's body.

Gunfire from Nicky sent Alexander into Robert, and the two of them tumbled to the floor. As he fell, he once again saw the black clad Jasmine appear and decapitate Nicky in one smooth stroke then finish off Nicky's two bleeding comrades.

Robert sat up, and then bent to help Alexander, who held him off with one hand. "Don't."

Jasmine came over and crouched down next to the two of them. Alexander gazed up at her. "Cousin, I was too slow."

Though a tear marked her face, she smiled. "No cousin, as usual, you were too fast. I am the one who was too slow."

Alexander sank down a little more. "No matter. If I was any slower, the good Director Grimmson would now be dead."

Alexander tried to lift his head, and then slumped back. "Where is Lucia? Is she here?"

"She'll be here soon, cousin. I promise."

"Good. Lucia will know what to do. She always does."

And then Robert watched as the true Sword Master died.

The Tale Of Alexander Suten-Mdjai

Robert found his phone in his pocket and called Seamus. He babbled out as quickly as possible all that just transpired then returned to sit with Alexander and Jasmine.

He picked up the sword lying beside Alexander. It wasn't the one he had seen Alexander practicing with on his arrival–the katana—it was something different. One he hadn't seen before.

"So this is the sword of Alexander Suten-Mdjai." He held it in his hands. The blade was short, perhaps sixteen inches or so long, wide, and edged on both sides.

"It is a xiphos, the weapon of Ancient Greece. He always would say it was his heritage. Though we carry the name Suten-Mdjai, given to his line by the Egyptian pharaohs, our ancestry dates back to Greece, in particular, to Sparta. The discipline of lifelong training is inherited from them."

"His line? I thought you were of the same."

"No, my last name is different. Only the Suten-Mdjais ran true from father to son throughout the ages. He...was the last...the Suten-Mdjais are no more."

"So what next?"

"I will take over the school. There are still others who will come to train, others like me, like him. I cannot match his skill, but I shall try."

"Others?"

"Ours is a heritage of killers for the state. We must continue to train."

"Wait, you mean you...Alexander are...were...assassins?"

"Yes, and now the state we work for is yours, the United States."

Robert sat back. "I don't know about this. I mean, once I tell the story, once it gets out that there are assassins here, what will happen? And that they are in the employ of our government. I can't not report what you've told me."

"You can...and you will. You will be required to. Those men you saw yesterday are all American Special Forces. It's part of his deal with your government, to provide training to your people."

People began arriving—police officers, ambulance attendants,

Chief Flaherty himself and many more.

Lucia Suten-Mdjai arrived. She was given a few private moments with the body of her husband, with Jasmine to console her.

When they took Alexander out, she left with him, and Jasmine came over to stand with Robert once more. Though her face was streaked with tears, a smile shone on her lips.

He found a napkin by the coffee machine for her to wipe her face. "You need not smile for appearances. It's alright to be sad. No one will fault you."

She smiled at him and gave him a kiss on the cheek. "I'm not sad. These are tears of joy. The reason Lucia was so late is she was at the doctors. She's pregnant!"

***

Steven got up and grabbed the morning paper. The headlines of the Sword Masters all dead and the lockdown by the National Guard being terminated dominated the front pages. More surprising was finding his name on the byline as author. But he could find no trace of the story he wrote elucidating Alexander Suten-Mdjai as an assassin.

He got dressed and raced down to the paper.

"Hank! What the heck happened? Where's my story?"

"Come on in Steve, and I'll tell you the whole story as it was explained to me last night by this guy from Washington."

A half hour later, he emerged from Hank's office with a new perspective. He went into his office and decided there was one more story to write.

I wish to tell the story of a man I met only recently, one who died last night. You can go your whole lifetime and never meet one, but I

was lucky enough to do so, to meet a true hero...
This is the Tale of Alexander-Suten Mdjai...

OTHER NOVELS by MICHAEL DRAKICH

GRAVE IS THE DAY

In October of 1957, more than Sputnik fell to Earth...

Set against the back drop of the Space Race and the Cold War, both the United States and the Soviet Union have a new issue to deal with, aliens from outer space. Both the Braannoo and the Muurgu are at war with each other and Earth becomes the newest battleground in their struggle. Spanning time from the launch of Sputnik to the near future, the interplay of historical events from a new light make you ask the question, could this all be true? The capture of aliens near small town USA unites three players from different quarters, Commander Kraanox of the Braannoo, First Lieutenant Wayne Bucknell as his captor and seven year old Justin Spencer, the first to make alien contact.

Grave Is The Day is a superb read! This story is a must read for all the science fiction, extraterrestrial lovers on Earth. Grave Is The Day has earned my rating of 5 stars! --Ramsey's Reviews

I have read books that meld fantasy with historical events before, but never one that takes such minute details and blends them so thoroughly. This is a great read and an exceptional rewrite of history for all ages. – Bitten By Books

He created each character with amazing attention to detail and development. I thoroughly enjoyed this book and found myself identifying with more than one of the delightful characters. --Paranormal Romance Guild - Beth Price

THE BROTHERHOOD OF PIAXIA

Years have passed since the overthrow of the monarchy by the Brotherhood of Warlocks and they rule Piaxia in peaceful accord. But now forces are at work to disrupt this rule from outside the Brotherhood as well as within! In the border town of Rok, a young warlock acolyte, Tarlok and his older brother, Savan, captain of the guard, become embroiled in the machinations of dominance. While in the capital city, Tessia, the daughter of Piaxia's most influential merchant, begins a journey of survival. Follow the three as their paths intertwine, with members of the Brotherhood in pursuit and the powerful merchant's guild manipulating the populace for their own ends.

Great, well-rounded characters? Magic running rampant? A lost princess? Yes, this book has it all. – tHe crooked WorD

If you love fantasy that mixes magic, lost royalty, sacrifices, heroes, and strong characters, I would suggest The Brotherhood of Piaxia. – Captivated Reading

The Brotherhood of Piaxia is what it wants to be - a real entertaining fantasy story. It comes along with more characters than you normally get but a lot less then you meet in a famous series you can watch at HBO. It has definitely more magic than a famous fantasy trilogy you could see in cinemas. There is less blood and gore than in a book with a title how to serve a drink. It is also a book which does not drown in romance. For me is a book which you like to read when you want to have a well dosed mix of well-known books. Or in simple words The Brotherhood of Piaxia is like the espresso you enjoy after a good meal. – Edi's Book Lighthouse

THE INFINITE WITHIN

Going into outer space calls to Astronaut Brooke Jones like the sirens of old, and when the chance to be part of the first manned mission to Mars arises, she is ecstatic. But little does she know the fate that awaits her on the surface of the red planet or the results of her encounter when she gets back to Earth.

This book is very entertaining. It will grab hold of you, and keep poking at you to finish it. I would recommend this story to science fiction readers that enjoy something a little different. This will not give you the highs of the shoot-em-up in outer space. It takes place place on earth, for the most part. It could be a real story and has enough elements be good fiction. I look forward to reading more by this author. – Charles Kravetz – Keeping Dreams

I loved the uniqueness of the story and the high-caliber action scenes. The adventure and the sense of awe kept me reading late into wee hours. – Laurie Jenkins – Laurie's Thoughts and Reviews

Wow. First off I'll start by saying the book was amazing. In the beginning I was a little iffy about the whole deal then the book got better, and better, and obviously better. I was surprised at the level of detail in the storytelling – Ezekiel Carsella – Books N Tech

DEMON STONES

It's been almost a hundred years since warlock meddling freed the demons from their underground domain. Their eventual capture has encased them in large stones across all the lands. They became known as the *demon stones*.

Over time, the truth of their imprisonment devolved into legend and tales to frighten children.

Now, the seven kingdoms are in upheaval. The demon stones are being opened and the vile creatures once more roam the land. War has broken open between realms as the fingers of accusation are pointed.

Caught in the middle is Gar Murdach, a farm boy who recently passed the age of ascension of sixteen marking him as a man, and his younger sister, Darlee, as they both struggle in their separate ways to escape the horrors wrought by the demons and the war that swarms round them.

Sometimes a trip into a fantasy world, filled with the magic of the mind is a good place to go, add the intense story line, the detailed world and a young hero who clearly started out WAY out of his league and it becomes clear that sometimes fantasy characters mirror reality. – Diane at Tome Tender (Amazon Top 500 Reviewer)

Die-hard fantasy fans, particularly those who like a bit of high fantasy, will adore this book just as I did. – Kyra – The Review List

I would recommend this book to those who enjoy a good fantasy which is well-written and easy to follow. Well done, Mr. Drakich! – S. A. Molteni – And So It Begins...

Made in the USA
Charleston, SC
14 November 2014